A CASE OF SERENDIPITY

A NOVEL

K.J. FARNHAM

MORE BOOKS BY K. J.

Click Date Repeat

Click Date Repeat Again

Don't Call Me Kit Kat

Visit kjfarnham.com for more information.

DEDICATION

This book is for my husband and children.
Thank you for putting up with me! xo

CHAPTER 1

Friday, April 15
Ruth

"Oh, Lance, you weren't kidding," I say to myself as I scan the expansive flower garden that borders the front and sides of my house. The bright greens of freshly emerging perennials are muted by an early morning haze, supporting my favorite weatherman's prediction of a rainy day.

"Good morning, Ruth!" Like clockwork, my elderly neighbor, Joan, is out watering her freshly potted annual arrangements. When the watering is finished, she'll pull weeds and use blue-handled scissors to trim the grass bordering her walkway. Then she'll take her feisty Bichon, Winston, for no less than a three-mile walk. Other neighbors are put off by Joan's straightforwardness, like when she suggests people might want to mow their lawn or when she hollers out the window for dog walkers to remember to clean up after their pets. But personally, I like her spunk and hope to be as active and independent as she is when I'm her age.

"Hi, Joan," I say cheerily as I make my way down my front steps and over to the cedar picket fence that separates our yards. Winston yips at me until I reach down and poke a few fingers through the fence to say hello. "You might be able to hold off on watering everything today. The forecast calls for rain."

"Bleh. Those weathermen don't know what they're talking about. These clouds will clear out of here by mid-morning." With a wave, she goes back to watering her fiery red begonias. "Have a good one, Ruth!"

"You, too, Joan." I give Winston's ear one last scratch before standing and heading off to work.

I walk at a slow pace for the first few blocks, taking the time to turn on my phone. A couple of text notifications pop up, and for a split second, I hope to find a message from Mitchell reiterating that he'd had a good time last night or asking if I'd like to have dinner this weekend, or even just saying hi. That hope vanishes with a click of my text message app. I recover quickly, though, and smile at the messages staring back at me. Correction. I smile at the first two messages from my friend, Sue, and my mom, but I wrinkle my nose at the third.

BUCKY'S PERKS: BUY A BEV & CHECK-IN THIS SAT OR SUN AND EARN TWO FOR $6 MEDIUM BEVERAGES ON 4/18! PARTICIPATING LOCATIONS. TXTSTOPTOEND MSG&DATARATESMAYAPPLY

Perplexed as to why I keep receiving texts from Bucky's Beans Coffee Roasters, despite my attempts to unsubscribe, I delete this message just like I've been doing with the others.

My mom's message is to remind me that she's going to Door County with her boyfriend this weekend, and that she'll call on Sunday to tell me all about it. I text back telling her to have fun and that I love her.

Sue wants to know all about my blind date with her neighbor, aka Mitchell. This requires more than a text response, so I pop in my ear buds and call her instead. While I wait for her to pick up, I tighten the strap of my Timbuk2 sling bag so that it's snug across my chest and pick up my pace.

"Hello." I can barely make out Sue's whispered greeting.

"Hi. Why are we whispering?"

I hear padded footsteps and then a door closes.

"Okay, now I can talk. My kids are still sleeping! Do you believe it? Must be this dreary weather. So, how are you? How was your date with Mitchell? Did you like him?"

"Breathe, Sue! Breeeathe," I laugh.

"Sorry. It's been a long week with these kids, and the only adult interactions I've had were with the GE repairman and a telemarketer." She takes a deep breath. "Thank God Stuart is on his way home."

"Plus, it's Friday," I offer. I know moms don't get weekends off, but who isn't happy when it's Friday? "And you'll be back to work before you know it. What do you have? Three weeks left of maternity leave?"

She emits a sigh. I can't tell if it's one of relief or remorse.

Sue has always wanted to be a mom. Back in middle school she made a list of baby names, which she saved and referred to when naming her two children. But nowadays she's torn between her role as a mother and her career. "I really need to enjoy the time I get to spend with them. They'll be dating and driving and trying to sneak out of the house before we know it." It was definitely a remorseful sigh. "Anyway, back to Mitchell. Tell me everything."

"He's great, a really nice guy. Easy on the eyes, too. But . . ."

"But nothing. You've been divorced for two years, so it's about time you put yourself out there. And Mitchell is—wait, was he boring? Did he talk your ear off about bikes? He's been known to do that at neighborhood functions."

I laugh because Mitchell did indeed spend a big chunk of time talking about his bike shop, as well as the bikes he personally owns, proper bike maintenance, the varied terrain of bike trails across the state, and which tires work best on which trails. "We definitely talked about bikes . . . and about his favorite places to go biking. But his enthusiasm kept things interesting, so I wasn't bored at all."

"So, you had a good time then?"

"Yeees . . ." I say as I press the pedestrian button at the final crosswalk before arriving at work. I march in place to keep my heart rate up as I wait for the light to change.

"Buuuut?"

"But when he walked me to my car at the end of our date, he shook my hand instead of giving me the farewell hug I'd imagined."

"Oh . . . could it be that he didn't get the impression you wanted a hug?"

"I have no idea, Sue. You know how rusty I am when it comes to dating."

"Wait . . . you wore something other than workout clothes and did your hair, right?" She asks, her tone dubious.

"Not that either of those things should really matter, but yes, I did. I wore my black maxi with a jean jacket and spent nearly thirty minutes straightening my hair. That'll never happen again, by the way."

"Hmmmm . . ." Sue's introspective sigh is accompanied by the sound of a toddler's voice and a baby crying in the background. "Well, maybe he was just trying to be a gentleman. You know, saving a hug for the second date?"

"Maybe," I say, smiling because I did have a good time and wouldn't mind a second date. But something tells me Mitchell probably won't ask me out again. "Hey, sounds like Eva and Brenton are ready for you, and I just arrived at work. Talk later?"

"Sounds good. Have a good day!"

"You too, momma. Give those goobers a hug from me," I say as I make my way around to the back entrance of Wixley Chiropractic.

I let myself in with the key the Wixleys gave to me back when they hired me as their office manager. Before I enter, I wave and smile up at the motion camera. They probably aren't watching, but just in case . . .

CHAPTER 2

I'm awake, but my alarm hasn't gone off yet. Instead of getting up like most people probably would, I lay perfectly still, hands folded across my chest, trying to guess how long I'll be waiting. The amount of light penetrating my eyelids is off for this time of year, probably because the weather forecast called for dreary skies today, but my internal clock is never wrong, so I'm guessing it won't be more than a couple of minutes. To pass the time, I visualize my work agenda for the day. The Bucky's Beans case has been at the top of my to-do list for two weeks now, so I tell myself today's the day I'll find a lead plaintiff.

My alarm buzzes for a split second before I press the on/off button, causing a crisp *click*. I immediately hop out of bed and straighten my clock before stretching my arms high above my head, leaning slowly from side to side a few times. Constance has already made her side of the bed, so I only need to smooth out my side of the sheet and comforter before tossing the throw pillows from the mahogany chest at the foot of the bed against the headboard.

I'm about to enter the bathroom when I hear Constance's voice coming from the kitchen. She sounds upset, so I change course and head to see what's wrong. Instead of finding her on her phone, she's bent over with her torso lying flat against the counter, and she's craning her neck to look up into the Keurig's dispenser. Her position causes the oversized t-shirt she wore to bed to creep up high enough to reveal the curves of her apple bottom. I raise both hands, about to cup her hips but think again when she angrily grumbles, "Why? Why would you do this to me right now?"

"Constance. What's going on?" I ask with a sigh, my hands (and something else) relaxing back to their default positions.

She jolts upright, throwing her arms in the air. "I don't know. Each brew cycle is only yielding about *this* much coffee." She holds her pointer finger and thumb about an inch apart. "And that's on the mug-sized setting." She huffs and spins back toward the counter to continue berating my Keurig.

I run my fingers through my hair before approaching the problem with an immediate solution. "Hey, Constance?" She ignores me and continues opening and closing the K-Cup holder. "Constance," I say, gently placing my hands on her shoulders and turning her to face me. "I'll take care of this later. It probably just needs to be descaled."

"But I need coffee now," she groans.

"Well," I say, dropping my arms from her shoulders and straightening my posture, "If we hurry, we can grab coffee from Coffee Cave on our way to the office." There. Problem solved. I ignore Constance's forlorn expression and begin preparing my breakfast. "Would you like some oatmeal with strawberries?"

"No, thanks. You know I'm on a diet, silly." Constance is always on some type of diet, but I refrain from pointing this out to her. Instead, I nod and proceed to make myself some oatmeal.

She moves past me to collect the items I hadn't noticed on the island: a QuickForm Shake-N-Go tumbler, a packet of QuickForm Nutrition breakfast powder, and a handful of vitamins. "I need coffee first, so I guess I'll have to eat at the office," she says as she makes her way out of the kitchen. Seconds after she disappears into the hallway, she hollers, "Let's go to Bucky's instead."

I stop quartering strawberries for a moment and sigh at the mention of Bucky's. The case I'm trying to build against everyone's favorite coffeehouse is probably the last thing on her mind.

"I'd much rather go to Coffee Cave, even if it is a couple miles out of the way," I holler back. "You know? Because of the case?"

Constance peeks her head around the hallway corner. I can tell from her bare shoulders, she's naked. "Henry, my morning routine has already been thrown off enough. Can we please just go to Bucky's?

Besides, you don't even have a case yet. Not without a lead plaintiff, anyway." She tilts her head and shrugs before disappearing.

After I finish my oatmeal and load the dishes into the dishwasher, I find something unexpected when I open the cabinet next to the fridge to retrieve my own multivitamins. All my vitamins and supplements have been shoved to one side to make room for Constance's QuickForm Nutrition powder packets and snacks. Sighing, I take a step back and survey her stash. Apparently, her idea of keeping things casual has evolved. I glance over at the shoe rack in the entryway of my condo. She'd said it was a gift, but both tiers are now lined with her shoes.

It's not that I don't adore Constance. Sure, she can be stubborn and a bit particular, but she's also an intelligent, independent woman with a lot to offer. Not to mention, she's gorgeous. I'm just not ready to take our relationship to the next level, and I'm not sure why. On one hand her penchant for organization is appealing. After all, I'm the same way— maybe even a little more so. In fact, she even pokes fun at the way I iron my jeans and organize them by color on hangers. But on the other hand, our similarities annoy me at times, which confuses me. Shouldn't I be happy I've found someone who's just as regimented as I am? These thoughts are what prompted the talk we had a few weeks ago. To my surprise, instead of her agreeing she shouldn't have to wait for me to figure out what I want, she insisted that she isn't ready for anything too serious either.

Maybe she brought the nutrition items and shoes strictly for convenience's sake.

"Henry? I'm done showering," Constance calls from the bedroom, snapping me out of my introspection.

I retrieve my daily vitamins and close the cabinet. Time to focus on getting Constance her coffee and getting to work.

CHAPTER 3

Friday, April 15
Ruth

"Good morning," I call out before inhaling the exhilarating spa-like scent of the office. When I get to the front desk, I immediately take a seat and give my ankle a good rub.

"Tell me you didn't walk." Beverly peeks her head around the corner before coming into full view. "Never mind. Of course, you did."

I look up, ready to defend my preference for walking or biking places when I can. Instead, I remain silent and grin appreciatively because she's focused on my ankle. Her concern reminds me how lucky I am to have her as a boss and friend. She glances up at the clock above my head. The message above the bone-shaped hands reads: *Make time for your spine!*

"Why don't you hop on a table and let me adjust you before we open? It might help. Or I could call Jackson from our office. He's just going over some X-rays."

"Thanks, but I'm not due for an adjustment until Wednesday. Besides, it's just this damp weather that has my ankle acting up. It'll be fine in no time."

"You sure?" She raises her perfectly sculpted eyebrows at me, temporarily eliminating the eleven o'clock lines in her forehead.

"Positive," I say, as I stand to remove my bag and jacket.

Beverly nods. "How was your date?" She asks, eyeing me as she makes her way over to unlock the front door.

"It was fun. I had a good time," I chirp as I turn on my computer. Beverly's silence prompts me to question her gentle, probing stare. "What?"

"Did you really though? Because it's okay if you didn't, hon." She turns on the speaker system, filling the office with sounds of ocean waves. "I'm just really pulling for you to meet that special someone, Ruth. Love is on the horizon for you. I can feel it." She holds up go-get-em fists and shakes them in an enthusiastic display of support, causing the emerald aventurine beads dangling from her left wrist to rattle. I grin because it's exactly the way my mom used to cheer during my high school track meets.

"Morning, Ruth!" Dr. Jackson Wixley breezes by and into the warm-up area where clients do stretches prior to being adjusted. "Bevie, please tell me you're not harassing Ruth about her love life again." He eyes her as he weaves back and forth through the rows of chairs, straightening the wobble cushions atop them. "Go ahead and meddle in our children's affairs until you're blue in the face, but let Ruth be. She'll let us know when she meets someone worthy. Won't you, Ruth?" He gives me one of his distinctive chuckle-grins, then glances out the window. "And here's our first customer," he says as he makes his way to the front door and greets one of our long-term patients as she enters.

As soon as Dr. Jackson is engrossed in conversation with his patient, Beverly pauses the filing she's pretending to do and probes me a little further for information about my date. I know her curiosity is out of concern. She was there for me after my divorce and witnessed my slow recovery from depressed hermit back to who I was before my ex-husband's affair, the pain pills, the weight gain, the accident, and all the QuickForm Fitness madness. If it weren't for Beverly and Dr. Jackson, who knows where I'd be. So, I fill her in on what I would describe as a perfect first date, up until the end when he walked me to my car, anyway.

"Oh, Ruth, don't psych yourself out over some guy not giving you a hug. I have a hard time believing any straight, single man would pass up a second date with you."

"I suppose I could have imagined the sudden awkwardness between us when he walked me to my car," I say with a shrug. "But if he doesn't call, he doesn't call. Honestly, I'll be fine. It was one date."

My phone vibrates, and Beverly's eyes widen. "Oh! Maybe that's him!" She waggles her fingers toward my phone. "Go on and check."

I can't help but laugh at how excited she is, and suddenly I'm excited too. Perhaps due to osmosis. But the excitement oozes out of me as I read the text, not necessarily because it isn't from Mitchell, but rather because of who it is from.

BUCKY'S PERKS: CONGRATULATIONS. YOU HAVE EARNED A COMPLIMENTARY SIZE UPGRADE! VIEW YOUR CURRENT REWARDS AT BIT.LY/BUCKYSPERKS TXTSTOPTOEND

I emit an exaggerated sigh.

"Wasn't him?" Beverly asks.

"No," I groan as I reply *STOP* like I've already done at least a dozen times. "It's a text from Bucky's Beans."

"You get texts from them, too?" A newer client asks as he scans his ID. I smile and check his name on the computer. Stan Boyd.

"Hi Stan," I say. Beverly greets him as well and then relocates to her position at the file cabinets, leaving me to converse with him. "I do, but I never signed up for them. In fact, I haven't been to a Bucky's Beans in ages."

My phone vibrates again, but I politely maintain eye contact with Stan. I have an inkling who the text is from.

"No? Well, maybe the texts are a sign that you need to give their coffee another try. I get some pretty good discount codes from them. You can't beat a BOGO." With that, Stan heads into the warm-up room, leaving me to check my phone.

BUCKY'S PERKS: YOU ARE NOT OPTED IN.

"Argh."

"What's that, hon?" Beverly asks.

"Oh nothing. It's just . . . I can't seem to opt out of these texts I've been getting from Bucky's Beans. The messages usually say *text stop to end*, but when I text *stop*, I get this weird message. See?" I show her the response from Bucky's.

She shakes her head and says, "I don't know much about how this text business works. Whatever happened to paper coupons?"

I shrug, and Beverly goes back to filing. Then I try to unsubscribe from the Bucky's texts several more times by responding with various words, phrases, and case combinations. Sometimes I use punctuation and sometimes I don't.

STOP

STOP.

STOP TO END.

STOPtoEnd

STOPtoEnd.

STOP TO END

STOP!

I repeatedly receive the exact same response: *You are not opted in.* Finally, I give up and silence my phone.

CHAPTER 4

Saturday, April 16
Henry

"So? What do you think?" Constance asks, her tone expectant. She glances over at me as she tightens her sleek, black ponytail.

"It's a pretty good workout so far . . . but I'd still rather go for a run," I respond, as we enter the next room of the circuit. A large QuickForm sign on the wall says *Station 3: CHEST*.

Her face falls. "Really? But it's so efficient and . . . quick."

Hence the name of the fitness franchise.

She hands me a weight bar and then grabs one for herself. "Maybe you'll change your mind after we complete the entire circuit."

"Maybe." I give her an appreciative grin before following her lead, adding free weights to both sides of my bar, nearly double what she adds. Then we find a couple of empty spots and follow the instructional video that's playing on a loop on a large screen at the front of the room. As we begin our chest workout, others finish and move on to the triceps room. The screen is identical to all the others that are displayed in the various rooms—one for the warm up routine, one for cool down, and one for each of the large muscle groups. While the QuickForm strength training circuit model has removed the need for instructors and showing up for your workout at a specific time, it's still a group workout setting, of which I've never been fond.

"Well?" Constance asks after we've completed the entire circuit nearly an hour later. She's sitting on a bench looking up at me as she changes out of her indoor sneakers and into her outdoor ones. I swear the woman has a pair of shoes for every activity, occasion, and season.

"It was fine. They have a good concept here," I say as I use my towel to dry a few beads of sweat from my forehead, "but I'd still rather go for a jog."

She stands and playfully throws her towel at me.

"Is everything okay here, Constance?"

"Oh, hi Dax. What are you doing here? I didn't know you worked on Saturdays." Constance briefly places her hand on the arm of the muscular man who just approached us. She's a touchy-feely kind of person, so I don't think anything of it. But I wouldn't be surprised if this Dax character doesn't have a thing for Constance, judging by the way he's looking at her.

"Hi," I extend my hand to him. "I'm Henry."

"Oh, how rude of me," Constance croons as the Dwayne Johnson look-alike shakes my hand. "Dax, this is my boyfriend Henry."

"Boyfriend?" Dax and I ask simultaneously as we both look at Constance whose cheeks pinken.

"What I mean is . . ." Constance is talking to Dax, but she's looking at me. "Henry and I are dating." She smiles sweetly, glancing over at Dax and then back at me.

"Yeah, yeah, yeah. That's right," Dax says as he palms his forehead. A smile that screams genuinely nice guy spreads across his face, and he talks directly to me this time. "She mentioned you'd probably enjoy our setup here at QuickForm. Glad you finally made it in. What do you think?"

"It's a good workout," I say, nodding. "Can't say it's one hundred percent for me, but I can see the appeal."

Dax returns the nod with the same nice-guy smile plastered to his face, but I swear he puffs out his chest. He may have even popped a peck or two. I suppose even a nice guy can have an inflated ego when you factor in pheromones and a pretty woman. I glance down at my own chest muscles, which are barely visible through the t-shirt I'm wearing. Maybe I need to start buying mediums.

"Henry is more of a runner," Constance blurts, causing me to eye her.

I hope she doesn't think I need her to defend my physique here. I grew up with two oversized, all-around athletes for brothers. I don't have a problem with the fact that my muscles are on the lean side.

"Well, good to meet you, Henry." Dax grips my shoulder for only a second, but it's long enough to make me wonder how much he can bench. "Constance," he says with a parting nod, his voice oozing with charm. I wave even though Dax has his eyes on Constance until he turns to greet another QuickForm member. Constance is already busy putting her towel and water bottle into her bag. She seems oblivious to his obvious interest in her.

"I think someone has a crush on you," I whisper as we walk to the nutrition counter.

"Oh, Henry, please. Dax does not have a thing for me. He's just a friendly guy."

"Uh huh, okay," I say, smiling. "Trust me. I can tell."

"Oh really? How?"

"Just trust me. I'm a guy."

She sighs and steps up to the counter. "Two shots of wheatgrass infused with QuickDrops, please."

The nutrition counter employee nods and disappears to retrieve our shots.

"QuickDrops?" I ask.

"Yeah. It's their proprietary blend of essential vitamins, minerals, and antioxidants." She removes a small glass bottle from her bag. "I have a couple drops of it a few times a day."

I take the bottle from her and am not surprised to find that the liquid is basically a mixture of things you'd find in any over-the-counter multivitamin. At ten dollars a pop for a two-ounce bottle, QuickForm has quite a moneymaker here.

After we down our shots and head out the door, Constance brings up Dax again.

"You know, you don't have to be jealous of Dax. I'm not interested in him." Her hand grazes mine, but I happen to sneeze just when I think she's about to take hold of it. "Bless you."

"Thanks," I say, eyeing her sideways. My condo is five blocks away, which leaves plenty of time for her to make another play for my hand. This makes me nervous since I'm not a fan of public displays of affection. So, I insert both hands in my pockets, and we walk in silence for about a block.

"I mean, I do consider Dax a friend, but that's all. Nothing more."

I feel her eyes on me as we walk, making me feel even more uncomfortable than I did when she attempted to hold my hand. I like her. A lot. But we've both agreed several times that we're just a casual thing, for the time being anyway. However, her actions this morning, along with her meal packets and shoes at my apartment, have me wondering if she's being completely honest with me about what she really wants.

"Constance," I say with a nervous chuckle, "you don't have to tell me any details about your relationship with Dax. Honestly, he seems like a nice guy, and if you are interested in him—"

"But I'm not." She stops walking, causing me to stop too. I'm a few feet ahead of her at this point, so I turn to face her. "I agree, he is a nice guy, but . . ."

My heart rate increases, and I feel terrible for the thoughts that are running through my head. But I'm a firm believer that honesty is the best policy, so I know I need to nip this in the bud. "Look, Constance—"

"He works at a gym." She raises both hands only to let them come slapping down against her thighs. "I know it sounds horrible, but can you honestly see me dating someone who lifts weights for a living?" She starts walking again, and I stare after her for a beat, mouth ajar, before I jog to catch up.

I guess I don't have to worry about honesty, or beating around the bush, when it comes to Constance.

CHAPTER 5

Saturday, April 16
Ruth

I've just finished washing my dinner dishes and am about to turn off the music streaming from my phone when I hear the first few chords of "You Say" by Lisa Loeb. This is one song I can't resist singing along to, so I pluck a wire whisk from the jar of cooking utensils on the counter. I pause for a second to admire the lopsided turquoise jar, which I made a year ago in a pottery class. I always kind of loved that it wasn't perfect. It was my own little reminder that perfection is overrated.

I dance around from the kitchen through the dining room to the living room and back as I sing into the whisk. On my second pass-through, I stop to pick up a puzzle piece peeking out from under the area rug below my dining room table. It's the piece I'd been searching for earlier. I pop it into its rightful position as the center of a sunflower, completing the puzzle. Then I take a step back to admire the five-thousand-piece beast that consumed most of my free time for the past few weeks. Tomorrow I'll apply a coat of puzzle glue to the field of sunflowers, then I'll frame it as a gift to the White Pines Nursing Home where my mom and I have been attending Parkinson's caregiver support group meetings since before my dad passed away.

The song ends, prompting me to check the oversized clock hanging above the natural stone fireplace in the living room. I still have about an hour before my shift at Posh begins, so I take a few minutes to add some fresh water to the vase, another pottery class creation, sitting on the fireplace mantle. Then I crouch down to pick up several wilted tulip petals that have fallen from the week-old bunch in the vase. They'll be replaced with daisies from the farmers' market soon enough.

When I return to the kitchen to toss the petals and put the watering can away, my phone vibrates, interrupting the next tune on my playlist. I pick it up and unplug it, so I can walk as I read.

BUCKY'S PERKS: CONGRATULATIONS, YOU HAVE EARNED A COMPLIMENTARY SIZE UPGRADE! VIEW YOUR CURRENT REWARDS AT BIT.LY/BUCKYSPERKS TextSTOPtoEnd

"You have got to be kidding me," I say with a laugh. I was confused when I first started receiving the texts a few weeks ago, and I figured they'd eventually stop since I never signed up for them. But now, the never-ending messages have me teetering on the brink of madness. So, I laugh because it's better than allowing myself to be upset about it. Since texting STOP never works, I try clicking the link instead, but nothing happens. "Grrr," I grumble as I delete the message.

I toss my phone on the bed and change into black jeans and a fitted black t-shirt that says POSH in white letters across the front. As I use my fingers to rake my thick, curly hair into a messy bun, it occurs to me that my brother might have something to do with all these unwanted texts from Bucky's. After all, he has been known to pull a prank or two. A loose honey blonde curl falls over my right eye, so I blow a huge breath upward, causing it to float for a moment before falling back across my temple. Thoughts of what a royal pain in the ass my brother can be are suddenly swimming through my mind, and I make a mental note to give him a call.

"Hey, Ruth. How're you doing today?" My boss, Marty, glances up when I enter Posh. He's behind the bar taking inventory of the liquor.

I wave to Colin, the bartender, who's stocking supplies at the opposite end of the bar. "Couldn't be better. How about you? Did you get any sleep last night?" I scrutinize the bags under his eyes. Marty and his wife have a one-month-old and a toddler who refuses to sleep in his own bed.

"Not a lick. But I snuck in a couple hours early and took a nap in my office, so I'm good to go."

"You know, my offer still stands to watch your kiddos for an evening, so you and Liz can have some time to yourselves. Heck, I'll even keep them overnight if you want me to."

He pauses what he's doing long enough to make me think he might finally accept my offer. I admit this thought scares me since I don't have much experience with kids, but I'd soldier through for Marty. He's been a friend since high school, and he hired me back when I desperately needed a distraction from my divorce. He claims I saved him when I replaced a waitress who quit without notice, right before Posh's opening weekend. But in my opinion, he's really the one who saved me.

"No way." He shakes his head and goes back to prepping the bar and continues, "We have access to plenty of sitters. What you need to be doing with your free time is meeting new people . . . going on dates, not playing peekaboo with a toddler and getting spit up on by an infant."

"Well, the offer stands. Just say the word," I say as I head off to the employee lounge to hang up my jacket and bag.

On my way back to the front, I greet a couple other waitresses who've just arrived. That makes three of us working the floor, which probably isn't enough to handle a typical Saturday night crowd at Posh. The place hasn't slowed down one bit since Marty opened its doors. In fact, business seems to have picked up since it was voted one of Milwaukee's best night-spots a few months back.

"Do you need any help, Marty?" I ask, smoothing out my apron.

He sets his clipboard down on the bar between us and motions for me to move closer. He doesn't say anything until I do.

"Ruth, you know how much I appreciate everything you've done for me. But this gig? It was supposed to be temporary for you, yet here you still are years later. How long do you plan to work here?"

"Marty, I like working here. It keeps me busy."

"Well, that's kind of my point. You work your day job five days a week, sometimes six, and on top of that, you're always picking up hours here. When do you ever have free time to put yourself out there?"

I hold my arms out wide with my palms up. "I work at one of the most popular clubs in the city. How much more out there can I be?

Besides, you only have three waitresses on tonight, so you must need me," I say with a shrug.

"Sonia will be here around nine, and Beth is always open to taking on extra hours, especially during the summer months. So, while I love having you here, you're wrong; I don't really need you."

"Marty," I gasp theatrically. "How could you say such a thing? After all we've been through."

We smile at each other for a few seconds before he continues campaigning for me to give up my job at Posh. "You and I both know how slim the odds are of you meeting someone you're interested in here." He leans in a tad closer and whispers, "No offense to the customers."

I roll my eyes, but he's right. I grew out of the bar scene over a decade ago, when I was the same age as most of the clientele here. And therein lies one of my biggest problems when it comes to dating: Where am I supposed to meet people? I'm pretty sure Mitchell is probably the only single guy over thirty in Sue's neighborhood, so she won't be setting me up again anytime soon. I've heard horror stories about online dating, so that option is out for me. And as Marty has pointed out, my social life consists mainly of working here. I guess I'm holding out hope that if I just keep living my life and doing the things I do, the right person will find me.

Who am I kidding? That only happens in the movies.

"I know you told Sonia you'd cover her shift tomorrow night, but I'm putting the kibosh on that."

It takes me a moment to register what Marty has just said, so he's already cutting me off by the time I begin to protest. "Wait a sec—"

"Nope. Sorry, you don't have a say. I'm going to force you out of this nest sooner or later, Ruth." He gives me an endearing look and walks off, leaving me to wonder what I'll do with myself when I don't have Posh to keep me busy.

~

Three sets of eyes watch as I approach booth number four, but they aren't on me. Instead they're scanning the other guests. The Saturday night crowd has only been trickling in for an hour now, so the lighting is still bright enough for me to make out a certain youthful expression on their faces, the one that oozes a mixture of curiosity, desire, and anticipation for what the night might have to offer. I usually recognize it right away now that I've been cocktail waitressing for a few years. I imagine my own face with the same expression over a decade ago on the night I met my ex-husband. He and I were looking for the same thing, so I suppose we were in the right place at the right time—both so young and ready to fall in love. What I never took into consideration was that it can be just as easy to fall out of love as it can be to fall into it, for some people anyway. The romantic in me hopes none of these young women ever have to experience this unfortunate life lesson firsthand.

"Here you go, ladies," I say cheerfully as I place a cocktail in front of each of them. Two of the pretty young women thank me, but the third simply picks up her Bahama Mama and continues to scan the room while sipping. This prompts me to smile directly at her when I make my next statement. "Flag me down if you need anything else. Otherwise I'll be back to check on you a little later. Enjoy your drinks."

This tactic seems to pick away at her ice princess demeanor a tad because she stops sipping and meets my smile with a look of confusion. "Okay . . . thanks." Perhaps she's shocked to have someone smile in the face of her snobbery.

Smother 'em with kindness. That's what my mom always used to say when she worked as a secretary at my high school and had to deal with disgruntled parents and teachers.

I scoot over to booth three right away and am greeted by four handsome, smiling faces.

"Good evening, guys. What can I get for you?"

"Hi there . . ." The one with the crew cut says in a smooth, suggestive tone that doesn't quite seem to suit him since he looks more like the *Leave It to Beaver* type than the Patrick Swayze in *Dirty Dancing* type. He rises out of his seat enough to lean across the table and peer at my nametag. ". . . Ruth." He then lowers himself back into his seat, maintaining eye contact with me the whole time. But he misjudges how far his tush is from the bench and falls more abruptly than intended. It's the cheesiest come-on I've been subjected to in weeks. I can't help but breathe out a teensy chuckle, and his friends follow suit with bursts of laughter.

"Guys," Crewcut raises his palms and looks around the table, "come on. A little support here?"

The friend to Crewcut's right speaks up. "Sorry about that, Ruth. Wes here is still taking notes on how to talk to the ladies." He twerks an eyebrow, revealing a bit of an ego.

Wes sighs heavily, a sheepish grin on his face, and his friends continue to laugh.

"And I suppose you think you're qualified to provide the material for his notes?" I quip. Clearly, he knows he's an attractive guy, so he could use a bit of razzing, in my opinion.

"Oh yeah. You're looking at Shorewood High's Class of 2007 Most Likely to Succeed . . ." placing a hand on his chest, he pauses theatrically, "With the Ladies."

"Well, well, well. That's quite an accomplishment. But I happen to think your friend is extremely charming," I say, smiling at Wes. He smiles back, and the friend to his left elbows him. "Sorry to change the subject, but what can I get for you gentlemen? Oh, and I'll need to see some IDs."

The four men take turns handing me their IDs and placing their orders, and Mr. Most Likely to Succeed asks for a water with his beer. When his friends are done giving him shit, I punch in their order on my electronic pad.

"Thanks, guys. I'll be back in a jiff," I say as I turn to leave. I can feel their eyes on me, and one of them says something about my ass. I have no interest in guys who are a decade younger than me, but it's still flattering.

By the time I return with their drinks, four more guys have joined the group. The repeated process of checking IDs and taking the new orders reveals they're all gathered for a bachelor party and are expecting at least five more people before they head on to the next bar.

"New drinks for our friends here, too, please," one of the new bachelor party goers calls out after I've already rushed off to take orders for two new groups that have just arrived. I acknowledge with a smile and a thumbs-up, and punch in the delayed order as I'm on my way back to the bar.

Marty is already assisting with drink orders. He typically doesn't need to step in until much later, but tonight is shaping up to be busier than usual.

As my serving tray fills with drinks, I place my order tablet into the center pocket of my apron and add extra cocktail napkins and straws as well. Realizing my smaller orders are good to go, I grab another tray and transfer them over.

"Hey, Marty, I'm waiting on four more to complete booth three's order so I'm delivering these now. By the way, can you please add a glass of ice water to the tray?"

"Will do, Ruthie," he calls out over the music playing through the speakers and the increasing hum of the crowd.

I quickly deliver the tray of drinks, and then stop to greet new arrivals and let them know I'll be back to take their orders in a moment. While I'm doing so, the noise coming from the bachelor party multiplies as more participants arrive. I survey how many new customers I have, and notice some of the group has spread over to booth number four where the three women I served earlier are sitting. The ladies seem pleased with the sudden swarm of testosterone, even the standoffish one, who's giggling at something Mr. Most Likely to Succeed has said to her. I grin as I hightail it back to retrieve the group's drinks.

"Hello, hello! Welcome to Posh," I say, announcing my arrival. Then I begin matching drinks to faces, taking care not to spill anything or bump into anyone.

Several delayed thank yous are murmured as I shift over to table three.

I place Mr. Most Likely to Succeed's beer and a glass of ice water in front of him and attempt a quick retreat to take orders from the newcomers, but I'm called back.

"Uh, Ruth, did someone else order this?" He's pointing at the ice water.

"Nope. You tried to order one earlier, so I figured you might want to mix in a sip here and there." I turn to leave again.

"Ruth?"

I turn back. "Yes? Uh . . . sorry, I don't remember if I got your name earlier."

"No, you didn't. But since you asked, it's Anthony . . . friends call me Tony." He brings the glass of water to his lips and takes a sip, his eyes on me until he lowers the sweaty glass. The standoffish one glares at me.

"Okay then," I say with a shrug. "Do you need anything else, Tony?"

"Nothing right now, but I sure could use your number for later."

"Sorry, I don't date customers," I say with a smirk.

He hangs his head dramatically for a second and then looks back up, matching my grin. "I had to try."

Perhaps when I was younger, I would have been attracted to this guy's suave demeanor. But now I'm simply amused. I nod and turn to head back to booth four to take orders from the newest members of the group. That's when the standoffish woman calls me back.

"Excuse me, waitress?" Her tone is a bit mocking.

I turn, smiling. "Yes?"

"I'd expect the waitstaff in a place like this to be more observant," she says, holding up her cocktail, which is still half full.

"Um, Katrina . . ." One of her friends says with obvious discomfort.

"What? She didn't even bother to ask if I need a refill." She turns her attention back to me. Everyone except for the woman's friend and Tony pretend to not be paying attention to our interaction, even though I sense they all are.

"Sorry about that. Would you like another Bahama Mama or something different?"

"The same," she says, dismissing me as she brings the straw in her glass to her lips.

I nod and proceed to booth four, an amused smile plastered across my face. Miss Standoffish certainly isn't the first customer to cop an attitude, but quite frankly, I don't care. When I finish taking the newcomers' orders and turn to head back to the bar, I glance over at booth three just in time to see the catty one frown at Tony, who's shaking his head and sliding out of the booth.

"Those guys aren't giving you trouble, are they?" Marty says when I get to the bar.

I nod my head toward booths three and four. "Those guys? The ones who probably bear an uncanny resemblance to you and your frat brothers back in the day?"

"Zip your lips, Ruth!" He slowly moves his head back and forth, scowling at me playfully. "My frat brothers and I were much better looking than those guys. Still are."

"You have aged nicely. I'll give you that. Now get moving on the new orders I just entered, would ya?"

"Sonia's here now," he says, filling a tilted pint glass with beer. "Why don't you let her take care of delivering your orders, so you can hop back here and help out? I'd like to circulate a bit."

"*See*, what would you do without me?" I ask before maneuvering through the growing crowd to the end of the bar. I begin taking orders the second I get back there.

On his way out, Marty informs me that Sonia is already on her way with the order for booths three and four. I pause and glance up just in time to see her hand the final drink from her tray to Mr. Most Likely to Succeed. He thanks her and then eyes her tush when she turns to leave. This makes me chuckle and reinforces my stance that I'll never meet someone in a bar.

"Excuse me? Miss?" A voice calls out over the music, pulling my attention back to where it should be.

"Sorry, about that," I say as I step in front of the source. When we lock eyes, I'm rendered speechless, and Mitchell is too. I have no clue how long we stare at each other, but it's long enough for his date to give him an odd look before breaking the silence between us.

"Um, do you two know each other?"

And just like that, Mitchell is all smiles and nods. "We sure do. Lily, this is Ruth. I met her through a neighbor of mine, and we had dinner together last week."

Well, I certainly wasn't expecting him to disclose that last bit.

"Ruth, this is Lily."

Lily gives me a brilliant white smile, and her head bobs as we shake hands. "It's a pleasure to meet you. Do you believe Mitchell and I met through that new dating app, Swipe4Love? This is actually the first time we're meeting in person." She smiles sheepishly.

"Wow, that's—"

Mitchell clears his throat. "Ruth, I uh . . . had no idea you work here." He laughs nervously.

"I didn't mention it to you because it's only part time and . . ." I'm about to remind him that he'd said the nightclub scene isn't really his thing, but suddenly I realize it's not worth mentioning. Maybe they're here because Lily enjoys nightclubs, and Mitchell simply wants to try something that's out of his comfort zone. ". . . well, I'm actually planning to put in my notice." They both nod and then sneak a glance at each other. I see longing in Lily's eyes and can sense a certain chemistry between them that wasn't there between Mitchell and me. "But I better take your drink orders before I do," I say, smiling and secretly rooting for Mitchell and this woman I hardly know.

CHAPTER 6

Sunday, April 17
Henry

Bzzzzzzzzzz.

I moan and attempt to open my eyes, but all I can manage is a few flutters before they clamp back into place. Was that the buzzer? Or was I dreaming?

Bzzzzzzzzzz . . . Bzzzzzzzzzz . . . Bzzzzzzzzzz.

This time I force my eyes open and inch my way out of bed and into the flannel pajama bottoms on the floor. It's a good thing I passed on Constance's invitation to go out to a comedy club with her friends. My legs are killing me from the QuickForm workout we did this morning. Yesterday morning, rather, since it's now two-thirty a.m.

The buzzer continues to sound as I hobble to the intercom. I lean my forehead against the wall and clear my throat. "Hello?" I say, depressing the talk button.

"Hey lover." Constance's seductive tone usually makes me horny, but not tonight. Probably because my groin is punishing me for all the squats I did. "Can I come up?"

I buzz her in and unlock the door. Then I flick on the hall light and limp over to the sofa. Shortly after, I hear the door open and close, followed by the clank of her weekend heels falling onto the bamboo floor as she removes one after the other. I open one eye a slit and watch as she pulls her form-fitting top over her head and saunters over. She tosses the top at my feet before straddling me.

"Pfsssss," I wince.

"Oh, you poor thing," she purrs, ignoring my pain and smothering my face in her cleavage.

"Constance," I plead, "please get off my lap."

She sighs, abruptly hops off, and plops down on the sofa next to me. "Henry, I'm horny." She reaches her hand over and tries to entice me. I let her for a few seconds, wondering if anything will happen.

"I'm sorry," I say, gently removing her hand from my pants. "But I can barely walk, so the thought of moving my hips just . . . well, it's not going to happen."

Constance groans and resituates herself so that her head is in my lap. Suddenly, I'm catapulted back to college when this scenario was my dream come true. The reverie only lasts for a moment, though, because my door buzzes again.

"Ignore it," she mumbles, not the least bit concerned who could be at my door this time of night.

Bzzzzzzzzzz . . . Bzzzzzzzzz.

"Constance, I need to see who that is."

Bzzzzzzzz . . . Bzzzzzzzzz.

I cringe as she presses her palms into my thighs so she can sit up. "Fine." She sighs as she folds her arms and leans her head against the back of the sofa.

I slide off the couch and gingerly rise to my feet, the obnoxious sound of the buzzer driving me forward. "Okay, okay," I hiss as I walk. "Who's there?" I grumble into the intercom, convinced it's probably someone pressing the wrong button.

"Heeenryyyyy . . ."

Well this is a surprise. I quickly press the button to unlock the lobby door.

I glance over my shoulder at Constance, who's now leaning forward, elbows on her knees. "Who's that?" She asks curiously, the poutiness in her tone still detectable.

"It's . . . my brother. I'm going to talk to him in the hallway," I say, pointing to the door. "Maybe you should put your shirt back on." I open the door and close it behind me as I step into the hall. Moments later, my little brother, who has two inches and about twenty pounds on me, appears. He staggers toward me, a huge glassy-eyed smile plastered across his face.

"You're wasted," I say, shaking my head.

"Ding ding ding," he sings, causing me to crack a lopsided grin.

We lean in for a bro hug, slapping each other on the back. As we separate, I ask, "What's going on? What brings you by so late?"

He pulls his phone out of his pocket and shows me the blank screen. "My phone died so I couldn't call for an Uber. Mind if I crash here tonight?"

I hesitate, unsure if I want my little brother to meet Constance. But then I realize there's no way I can let him drive home in the state he's in, so I don't really have a choice in the matter. "Yeah, of course you can stay here. But, uh . . . I have a guest."

His eyes widen, and he smiles so big a dimple forms in his left cheek. "Yeah? Who is she? Wait, it is a she, right?"

"Yes, Anthony," I say, rolling my eyes, "it's a woman. Her name is Constance, and she just got here about ten minutes before you showed up."

He grips my shoulders and stares into my eyes. "Are you telling me I interrupted a booty call? Because I'm feeling wide awake now, and my car is right down the—"

"No, no, no. It's not like that," I lie. My brother is full of unsolicited relationship advice, and one of his favorite pastimes is discussing my love life (or supposed lack thereof) when my mom is around. I'm sure he means well, but my mom is desperate for me to find the one, so I don't need him telling her about Constance and getting her hopes up.

"Yeah right, Henry." He waves me off and begins turning to leave. "I'm not cock blocking you, dude."

"Hey," I grab his shoulder and steer him back around, leading him to my condo. "Come on. You're not driving home."

I'm about to reach for the knob when the door and my brother's eyes open wide. "Wowza," he whispers.

"Henry? Is everything okay?" Constance asks. Her lips are extra shiny, indicating that she took the time to apply a fresh coat of gloss, and her silky smooth, jet black hair is freshly brushed.

"Yeah, everything's fine," I say looking from Constance to Anthony, who pokes me in the ribs. "Constance, this is my brother, Anthony . . . Anthony, Constance."

Constance's eyes light up as she reaches out a hand to him. "It's so nice to meet you." He kisses it instead of shaking it, but it's not your typical two-second hand kiss. Instead, my brother's lips linger. Constance probably thinks the prolonged kiss is due to the alcohol we can smell emanating from him, but it's actually due to my brother's self-proclaimed ladies' man status.

Constance grins at me, and I roll my eyes. "Okay, Anthony, that's good," I say, giving him a firm pat on the back. He rises and releases his grip on Constance's hand. "Why don't you go inside? I'm going to walk Constance to her car."

"What do you mean? She doesn't have to leave because of me. Why don't we all go inside?" He smiles broadly, his eyes drooping again. Then he pushes past me, puts an arm around Constance, and they head into the living room. "It's nice to meet you too, Constance. Oh, and call me Tony. Henry is the only person who calls me Anthony."

"Well, it *is* your name," I mumble to myself as I close the door. Then I follow them to the living room.

Anthony releases Constance and takes a seat on the sofa. She sits too but chooses the chaise lounge instead. "So, who's older, Tony? You or Henry?"

Still standing, I cross my arms and wait for my little brother's response.

"That would be your boyfriend here . . ."

"Um, I told you, we're not—" I try to clarify my relationship with Constance, but Anthony talks over me.

"He's seven years older than me, and Rob is three years older."

"Rob? You have another brother?" Constance addresses me.

I nod, but before I can get a word out, Anthony asks, "Wait, how long have you two been together? Does Rob know? Mom and Dad?"

"I told you," I say shaking my head. "We're not together." I look at Constance and she's poking around on her phone, appearing unaffected by what I just said.

Good. Maybe the shoe rack and her QuickForm nutrition stash is no big deal.

"Well, why not? Constance here is gorgeous." He flashes a drunken grin in her direction.

Never one to shy away from a compliment, she grins back. "Why thank you, Tony. That's so sweet of you to say." Her gaze migrates over to me. "Henry, I'm going to head home."

Finally.

"Can I walk you out?"

"That's not necessary, especially with how sore you are," she says, standing.

Anthony rises too. Constance reaches her hand out to him just like when they met, and the same scenario plays out. Only this time, Anthony gives her hand a standard-length kiss. "Again, nice meeting you Constance. You'll have to come for dinner at our parents' house sometime."

"I would love that!" She smiles at me.

"Ooookay," I say, smiling back and taking hold of her hand. "I'll walk you to the door at least."

I give Constance a quick peck and watch as she disappears down the hallway. By the time I close and lock the door, Anthony is lying on the sofa and breathing heavily. Nodding off has always come easy to him. Even when we were kids. He was always the first one to fall asleep and the first one to wake up in the morning. I grab the blanket off the back of the chaise and cover him with it. Then I turn off the hall light and walk back through the living room, careful not to bump into anything as my eyes adjust to the darkness. As I walk into my bedroom, I hear Anthony's now groggy voice.

"Henry?"

"Yeah?"

"I hope your beauty queen is as nice on the inside as she is on the outside."

I sigh. "Go to sleep, Anthony. It's late." I'm just inside my bedroom when I hear him again.

"I'm serious, Henry. Because hotties can be real bitches sometimes, you know?"

I smile. Leave it to Anthony to have a poignant drunken moment that includes the words hotties and bitches. "Good night, Anthony."

"Night, bro."

Finally, I crawl back into bed and pass out almost instantly.

CHAPTER 7

Sunday, April 17
Ruth

I enter my apartment, a bouquet of daisies in one arm and a bag of fresh fruits and vegetables in the other. My heart is still pounding at an accelerated rate. Few things are as exhilarating to me as early morning bike rides to the farmers' market on Sunday mornings. And thanks to Marty, I have the rest of the day to relax.

I arrange the fruits and veggies in bowls on the kitchen counter and replace the wilted tulips in the vase on the mantelpiece with the fresh daisies. Then I plug in my phone and stream acoustic tunes before igniting the burner under the teakettle. Eighties music is my favorite, but a lazy Sunday afternoon of tea and puzzles calls for something more mellow. I glance over at the dining room table where the completed sunflower puzzle is waiting to be glazed and framed. Next to it is a brand-new one that depicts wildflowers in bloom atop Mount Rainier.

After I splash some water on my face and change out of my sweaty clothes, I readjust the muddle of curly locks pulled into a bun at the crown of my head. Whatever the weather, my mane is difficult to manage, so most days I don't bother much with it. Last month, when I told Sue I was ready to start dating, she immediately made a spa appointment for us. I went, against my will, knowing that anything they did to my hair, eyebrows, and nails would revert, just like the temporary tweaks Cinderella's fairy godmother made to her appearance. Honestly, if I straighten my hair for a couple of days, will I really be more successful with dating? If so, what happens when my hair goes back to normal? Sue, who has the red carpet rolled out for her once a month at her salon, views things differently. She says false pretenses work, often referencing the story of Cinderella and her lovestruck prince as an example. She hates when I play devil's advocate and theorize that things between the fairytale couple probably would have gone to shit in real life when he found out she thought she could talk to mice.

I've just finished glazing the sunflower puzzle with glue and am opening the new Mount Rainier puzzle when my phone vibrates. Recalling that my mom said she'd give me a buzz when she got back from Door County, I rush into the kitchen and swipe up to accept her call.

"Hi, Mom. How was your trip with Mr. Walter?"

"Ruthie, when are you going to stop calling him Mr. Walter? It sounds so . . . impersonal. And it makes Walter worry that you don't approve of our relationship."

"You know that's not true," I say apologetically, because I really do like Mr. Walter. "It just isn't that easy to retrain myself to call my old high school janitor by his first name, minus the mister. Old habits die hard, you know?"

"He wasn't a janitor. He was head of facilities and maintenance. And we've been dating for more than a year now. So, can you please try harder to stop calling him Mr. Walter? It would really mean a lot to me . . . and Walter."

"Yeah, of course. Now, how was your weekend?" I ask, eager to change the subject.

"It was absolutely fabulous! We stayed in the *cutest* little private cottage, just off the shores of Sturgeon Bay. We went fishing and attended a fish boil. We enjoyed early morning walks as the sun came up, and last night we watched the sunset from a rowboat . . . Walter surprised me with mini bottles of that Riesling I enjoy." She sighs. "Oh, Ruthie, it's been a long time since I felt this way."

"Wow, Mom, sounds like—"

"Oh! And the shops! They have the cutest little gift shops," she interrupts. "I got you a puzzle. Sorry, what were you saying?"

"Just that it sounds like spending time with Walter makes you very happy," I say, smiling broadly because my mom's happiness makes me happy.

"It does, Ruthie. It really does. And I'm praying you meet someone who makes you just as happy someday. Speaking of. . ." Her voice returns to its usual chipper tone. "How was your date with Sue's neighbor? Do you have a second date lined up?"

"Uhh . . . no."

"What do you mean no? What happened? Did he get handsy with you, Ruthie?"

"No, Mom," I say, chuckling over her instantaneous momma-bear reaction. "He was a perfect gentleman, and we had a very nice time."

"Well, what was the problem then?"

"I'm not sure, but he hasn't tried to contact me since, so I'm guessing there just wasn't the right kind of chemistry between us." She begins grumbling, but I stop her. "Mom, every guy I meet isn't going be interested in me, and vice versa."

The teakettle starts to whistle, so I make my way into the kitchen to prepare a cup of chamomile tea.

"That's preposterous. Any single guy who isn't interested in you isn't right in the head. So, you better warn Sue to keep an eye on this fella she set you up with."

I'm pretty sure she's joking, so I laugh. After she tries to pretend she was being serious for a few more seconds, she laughs too. My dad was always quick to make a joke, and my mom was always just as quick to dismiss him. But now it's as if she has adopted a bit of his subtle sarcasm. Sometimes I wonder if it helps her to continue coping with his passing, or maybe it's a way for her to keep his memory alive.

"Seriously, Ruthie, you'll meet that special someone someday. Take me for example. Who would have thought when I was working in the school office and Walter was sweeping the halls that he and I would reconnect and become a couple over a decade later? You'll see. You'll meet someone when you least expect it. I know you will. After everything you went through with Adam, the accident and . . . then the divorce. . ." Her voice trails off and the line goes quiet. I wonder if she's thinking about the rough patch I went through with the pain pills.

"Mom?"

"What? Oh, sorry. I lost my train of thought for a second. Anyway, I have some exciting news."

"Well . . . lay it on me," I say, taking a seat and setting my cup of tea on the dining room table in front of me.

"You know how I've been planning to start searching for an apartment or condo now that I've decided to sell the house?"

"Mm-hm."

"Well, it looks like I've already found a place."

"Really? That was fast," I say, wondering why she didn't ask me to look at options with her. "When? And where?"

"Walter's place. He asked me to move in with him!"

"Oh . . . wow, Mom. That's great!" I do my best to feign excitement. Mr. Walter truly is a good man. He was always respectful of me and my fellow classmates, even the ones who threw trash on the floor and behaved like assholes, and I appreciate the way he treats my mom. But, for a moment, the thought of her living with someone other than my dad has me feeling queasy.

"Isn't it? Of course, it won't be for a month or so, until I sort through everything at the house and meet with a realtor to get it on the market. Oh, and I'd also like to throw a coat or two of primer on the basement walls to cover up those stains from when we had those heavy rains last summer. Maybe you can help me with that?"

"Of course! You know I will," I say in as chipper a tone as possible.

"You and your brother will also have to go through your things. Although, I don't know if Tyler will be able to make it up here anytime soon, now that he and Molli are so busy with their new clinic. Did you look at the photos he posted on Facebook? It's so fancy and high-tech. He must be happier than a pig in mud the way he likes shiny new things so much." My phone buzzes as she takes a much-needed breath, and then continues. "I suppose I can take his bins with me to Walter's if I have to. Or perhaps you have room in your basement?"

I sneak a peek at my phone screen just as she finishes her thought and sigh because it's the second text I've received from Bucky's in the last twenty-four hours.

BUCKY'S PERKS: CHECK IN & BUY A DRINK MON & EARN $3 MED HANDCRAFTED/$1.50 MED BREWED COFFEE WED/THURS. PARTICIPATING LOCATIONS. TxTSTOPtoEnd Msg&DataRatesMayApply

"Oh, Ruthie," my mom sympathizes, "I know it's a lot to process—selling the house and me moving in with Walter . . ."

"No, mom, I was just—" I try to clarify the reason for my sigh, but she continues, cutting me off.

". . . but the most important thing I learned through grief counseling is that moving on helps foster acceptance. My feelings for your father will never diminish, sweetie, but I have to move on."

"I completely agree with you, mom. As much as I miss Dad, and as hard as it is to imagine some other family living in my childhood home, I'm ready to move on too. I only sighed a moment ago because I keep getting promotional texts from Bucky's Beans."

"Well, why in the world would you sign up for that? You hardly ever drink coffee," she snickers.

"That's the thing. I didn't sign up. The texts all of a sudden started a few weeks ago, and I have no idea why."

"Can't you call someone and tell them to take you off the list? That's what I do with telemarketers, you know? Although some seem to have trouble following through . . ."

I think about explaining to my mom that you can usually unsubscribe to these types of texts right from your phone, but I'm certain that would only confuse her, so I take an easier approach. "Yeah, that's a good idea. I'll just give Bucky's a call."

"You know what I just realized?" she says between chuckles. "Tyler probably gave them your number as a prank! He knows how much you dislike large chains like Bucky's. Remember when he signed you up to receive daily catcalls on your cell phone?"

"Yes, I remember," I say, unamused. But her laughter intensifies, which causes me to crack a smile. "And yes, I've considered that Tyler might be behind the texts."

"Your brother sure did inherit your father's mischievous nature." She sighs, and we sit in silence for a moment. "Well, I have laundry to take care of and I have to pick up some groceries, so I better let you go. What are you up to today?"

"Nothing much. I just got home from the farmers' market and now I'm getting ready to start a new puzzle. I finished the sunflower one yesterday. Just got done gluing it. We can take it with us when we go to the support group meeting next week."

"That's nice, Ruthie. The residents will love it, I'm sure. Enjoy the rest of your day and I'll talk to you in a few days."

"Sounds good, mom. I'll probably stop by some night within the next couple weeks to start going through my things."

"Okay! Love you . . ."

"Love you, too . . . Bye."

When I swipe away the call screen, the text thread from Bucky's appears. I take a few screenshots, just in case I ever need to prove the number of times I've tried to unsubscribe. Then I delete the entire thread, Google Bucky's Beans, and press the call link to connect with the nearest location.

"It's a great day for a Bucky's pick-me-up! This is Lola. How may I help you?" She sounds like she's all hopped up on caffeine.

"Hi, Lola. I'm calling because I've been receiving Bucky's Perks text messages, and I can't figure out how to unsubscribe."

"No problem. I can help you with that. All you need to do is respond with the word *stop*," she says matter-of-factly.

"Thank you for the tip, but I've already tried that. Several times."

Actually dozens.

"Did you try using all uppercase?" She asks sweetly.

"Uh, yeah. I've tried uppercase, lowercase, stop, stop to end . . . But nothing seems to work. I receive the same response every time. You are not opted in."

"Hmm, okay. Can you please hold?"

"I can. Thank you."

Moments later, she returns.

"Ma'am?"

"Yes, I'm here."

"You'll need to log in to your Bucky's Perks account online and adjust your text preferences from there."

"But I don't have a Bucky's Perks account. I don't even buy coffee there."

"Oh," she says, her tone suddenly curt, "well, I'm very sorry to hear that, but as far as I know, customers need to create an account online to receive Perks texts."

"So, you're saying someone signed me up for this?" I think of my brother again.

"No, ma'am. What I'm saying is if you didn't create an account yourself, someone may have inadvertently transposed a number causing you to receive the texts."

"Oh, okay. So, what do you suggest I do since there's no way for me to access the account associated with my number?"

"You could stop in and use one of your Perk codes," she says cheerily.

"Uh, no, that's not what I meant. Is there anyone else I can contact for help? Maybe someone can manually remove my number from the list?"

"You'll have to contact our corporate office in Madison for something like that. Would you like the number?"

I sigh. "No, that's okay. I can look it up."

"Is there anything else I can help you with?"

"No, thank you for your time."

"Have a great day then. Bye!"

Within a few clicks, I locate a customer service number for the Bucky's Beans corporate office in Madison. After two rings, a recording alerts me that the company is currently closed . . . *We appreciate your call and will do our best to respond in a timely manner. Please leave your name, phone number, and a brief* . . . Frustrated, I hang up without leaving a message. Then I pull up Bucky's Facebook page and message the company about my text message woes. I suspect most companies have someone monitoring their Facebook pages at all hours of the day, so surely, I'll receive a response faster than if I leave a message at their corporate headquarters.

Hi there. For weeks I've been receiving daily texts from Bucky's. The problem is I never signed up for them, and for some reason, I can't unsubscribe. Texting STOP doesn't work. I just got off the phone with someone at a Bucky's in my area, and she advised me to contact your corporate office to see if someone there can remove my number from the list. But as you probably know, the corporate office is closed on Sundays, so I'm hoping you might be able to help with this matter. Thank you!

Ruth Bateman

I send the message, close Messenger, and get back to my new puzzle, optimistic that Bucky's Beans Coffee Roasters will stop spamming my phone with texts.

CHAPTER 8

Sunday, April 17
Henry

"Hellooo . . . Where is everyone?" I call out as I step into my parents' home, which looks completely different than it did when I was growing up. The floral-patterned linoleum in the entryway has been switched out in favor of solid bamboo flooring, and the old pinkish ceiling globe that used to remind me of a giant jawbreaker has been replaced with a more stylish lantern-shaped fixture. Similar modern updates have been made to all the common areas.

"In here, Henry!" My mom responds from the kitchen.

I place my shoes neatly along the edge of the earth-toned entryway rug, right next to those of my brother Robert and his family. I only get a few feet down the hall before compulsively turning back to straighten Anthony's scuffed up Nikes, which are lying on their sides several inches apart.

"Henry? What are you doing?" My mom steps out of the kitchen and looks down the hall at me. "Oh. Thank you, sweetie."

"And you wonder why Anthony doesn't have a girlfriend," I say with a smirk. My mom laughs and waves for me to follow her back into the kitchen when a timer begins beeping. "Is everyone in the basement?"

"Everyone but Lori. She ran to the grocery store because I'm running low on Parmesan and forgot to buy a new block. Would you please put the colander in the sink and turn on the water?" she asks as she turns off the stove and silences the timer.

I nod and do as she asks.

Gripping the handles of a steaming pot with Ove Gloves, she meets me at the sink and pours pasta into the colander. "I hear Anthony slept at your place last night?"

Please don't tell me he mentioned Constance. I turn my head, mostly to avoid the cloud of steam rising from the sink, but also to hide my paranoia.

"Yeah, that wasn't any fun getting woken up at two in the morning." I purse my lips before popping a couple of fresh basil leaves in my mouth. "But he was pretty drunk, so . . ."

"Well, thank you for not letting him drive. You're a good big brother." She puts an arm around me and gives me a squeeze. Then she returns to the stove to stir her homemade spinach basil marinara.

Still leery, I wait a few seconds before speaking again. If Anthony did mention Constance, I'd much rather my mom ask about her when we're alone as opposed to later in front of the entire family. But by some miracle, she doesn't appear to be gearing up to ask any questions. Maybe Anthony kept his big mouth shut for once.

"Do you need any more help in here, Mom? Otherwise I'm going to head downstairs to say hi to everyone."

"Nope, you go ahead. Your nephews are excited to see you. Dinner will be ready in about ten minutes."

"Okay, I'll let them know. Holler if you need anything."

When I open the door to the basement, my ears are met with a plethora of sounds—a baseball game on TV, a ping pong ball, the pop and hiss of a beverage being opened, and laughter. As soon as I get to the bottom of the stairs, my nephew, Alex, drops his ping pong paddle on the table and rushes over to hug my legs. Right behind him is his little brother, Wyatt, who had to slide off my dad's lap before toddling over with his hand up for a high five.

"Hey, bro." My brother Robert waves with the ping pong paddle he's holding. Then he turns his attention to Alex. "Get back here, squirt. We need to finish this game. Maybe Uncle Henry can play the winner."

I rustle Alex's hair as he bolts back to the ping pong table. Then I give Wyatt a few high fives before picking him up and carrying him over to the family room where my dad and Anthony are watching the Brewers game.

"Hey, Dad." I take a seat on the mammoth leather sectional, and Wyatt wiggles out of my arms to chase after a stray ping pong ball.

As I settle in, I can't help but scan the walls, which are adorned with medals, plaques, and photos from when my brothers were both all-star athletes in high school. Robert played football and soccer, and Anthony was a natural at football, basketball, and baseball. He even played Division I basketball for UW-Milwaukee. My only athletic stint in high school was when I joined the cross-country team my freshman year. Unfortunately, a bad case of patellar tendonitis prevented me from finishing out the season, and I never tried out again. My mom, always a proponent of the phrase 'fair not equal' among my brothers and I, made up for my lack of athleticism by decorating the wall behind the bar with my academic excellence awards and framed degrees and honors certificates spanning from high school through law school.

"Hey there, counselor." My dad leans over and gives my knee a couple of pats. "What's new with my favorite oldest son?"

"Yeah, Henry, what's new?" Anthony asks. Paranoid that he's messing with me, I snap my head to look at him, but his eyes are peeled to the TV. He takes a sip of Diet Dr. Pepper, then glances back and forth from me to the TV a few times as I eye him suspiciously. Is it possible he was so drunk last night he doesn't even remember Constance? "What?"

"Nothing. Just . . ." I point haphazardly at his shirt. "You have Cheeto crumbs all over you."

"Oh." He looks down and brushes the orange dust onto the floor and the chair he's sitting on.

"Anthony! Your mother would have a cow if she saw you doing that," my dad scolds. But if there's one thing we know about our dad, it's that his bark is way worse than his bite. Actually, he doesn't even have a bite, so Anthony simply shrugs and goes back to watching the game.

I sigh and wonder for the millionth time how it's possible that Anthony and I are related.

"Now tell me what's going on in your life, Henry. You still working on that patent lawsuit? What was it about again?"

"Wasn't it over some photo organizing app?" Anthony chimes in. "As if there aren't dozens of those already . . ."

I nod, about to fill them in on the progression of the case, when my sister-in-law calls us up to eat.

"Boys! Dinner's ready!"

We all scurry for the stairs, knowing that my mom is a stickler for eating while the food is still hot. Within five minutes everyone is seated around the dining room table and the salad, garlic rolls, and pasta are being passed around. As I wait for the main dish, I shake out my napkin and place it on my lap. Then I straighten my knife, dinner fork, and water glass before taking a bite of my salad.

"Mommy, can I put my napkin on my lap like Uncle Henry?" Alex asks my sister-in-law.

"Of course you can, bud." Lori helps my other nephew place a napkin over his lap before placing one on her own as well. The stare she gives Robert prompts him to follow suit.

"You know what? That's a great idea, Alex. We should all use our napkins and refrain from putting our elbows on the table." My mom gives Anthony a hard stare, as she and my dad shake their napkins out and place them on their laps.

Anthony rolls his eyes as he heeds our mom's suggestions. Then he kicks me in the calf under the table.

"Ow," I say under my breath, first glaring at Anthony and then sneaking a peek at Robert. He's hunched over, trying not to laugh.

"Can we just have a nice dinner without all this nonsense?" Again, my mom looks directly at Anthony, who has just shoveled a ridiculously large bite of pasta into his mouth. Wide-eyed, he pauses, a stray noodle hanging from the corner of his mouth. "Well?" Mom persists, prompting my mischievous baby brother to slurp the rest of the food into his mouth.

"Sure, Mom. Sorry about that."

"So, Henry," my dad says, topping his meal with an extra spoonful of freshly grated parmesan, "you were going to fill us in on what's new in your life."

I nod as I finish chewing the bite I just took. Then I use my napkin to wipe the corners of my mouth. "Other than work, nothing much is new since the last time we talked. But I'm not sure anyone here is interested in mundane details about litigation and lawsuits though. So how's business going? Robert told me you snagged two dozen lots over in that new development in Franklin. Any plans to build a model?" When my paternal grandfather started his own landscape/contractor business fifty years ago, I'm certain he never imagined Mancuso Construction's portfolio would grow to include luxury custom-built homes.

"Oh, poo," my mom says. "You know how conversations around here always revolve around the business or overpaid athletes. Wouldn't everyone be more than happy to discuss something different for a change?"

"Okay," I say with a shrug, certain that my parents will be the only ones who listen anyway. "But I want to hear about your plans for the Franklin development later."

Mom pats Dad's hand, and he nods. "Yeah, of course. After dinner."

"The patent case I'm working on for Memory Hub is coming along, but not as smoothly as we'd hoped. We're in the middle of discovery, and the other side is digging in their heels about producing some documents and claiming they are proprietary. So, we may have to file a motion to compel because we think they may be hiding information. I've also been assigned a couple of class action suits."

"Who are you trying to sue now?" Robert asks.

"DigiScan and Bucky's Beans Coffee Roasters."

"Don't tell me. Some PTO mom burned her tongue on a latte and now she thinks she's entitled to millions of dollars because of a few swollen taste buds?" Robert shakes his head in disgust.

"Stahhhhp," Lori coaxes my highly-opinionated brother. Then she warns Alex to stop playing with his food and goes back to picking up the silverware that Wyatt keeps dropping.

"Not even close. They've been blatantly breaking TCPA laws for over a year, according to all the complaints I've seen online. So, they could be on the hook for five hundred dollars *per* text they've sent in violation of the TCPA."

"What does that have to do with coffee?" Anthony asks.

"Well, it has nothing to do with the coffee itself, Anthony. It's about the way they're trying to market their products to customers. You see, they have this program people can subscribe to called Bucky's Perks."

"Oh! I've thought about signing up for that," Lori chimes in.

"Better hurry up so you can get a piece of this class action pie Henry is cooking up," Anthony says, picking up his plate and scraping the remains of his food into his mouth.

"Okay, okay. Let your brother continue. I want to hear more." My mom smiles at me and squeezes my hand. It's reminiscent of the way she used to shush my little brothers when we were kids and I would try to talk about things I was interested in, like debate team topics, chess club, or possible Jeopardy categories.

"Go on, Henry."

"You see, a lot of people claim to be receiving texts from Bucky's even though they never enrolled in the program."

"Bullshit."

"Anthony!" My mom silently looks to my dad for backup, and he obliges.

"That's enough, Anthony. Quit interrupting your brother."

"Hang on now. I call bullshit, too." Robert jumps to Anthony's defense. "Sounds like a ploy some professional gold digger dreamed up. I'm no tech genius, but I highly doubt people would be getting texts from a company as big as Bucky's if they didn't sign up for it."

"No, no, no," I disagree, calmly shaking my head. "It's actually highly possible, *especially* with larger companies that hire outside marketing firms to handle loyalty programs such as Bucky's Perks. And as far as this gold digger theory of yours is concerned, I've already explained this to you guys dozens of times—my firm does not pursue frivolous class action suits."

"So how serious is this case against Bucky's? I haven't seen anything in the paper." My dad is probably the last person in my parents' neighborhood who still gets the Milwaukee Journal Sentinel delivered to his doorstep each morning.

"No, Dad, there wouldn't be anything in the paper about this, not yet anyway. You'd have to look at online law websites to keep up with something like this. Although, there wouldn't be anything online yet either because I still haven't been able to file a complaint."

"Well, I'm sure you'll get that complaint filed soon enough, Son, workhorse that you are."

"Not likely," I grumble, standing to reach across the table for the bowl of garlic bread. I take a piece and pass the bowl to my mom.

"No? How come?" My mom asks as she accepts the bowl and passes it to my dad.

At this point, my parents are the only family members still participating in the conversation. Robert and Lori are busy with my nephews, and Anthony is focused on his phone.

"It's just an awful lot of work to try to find someone willing to be the lead plaintiff in a large class action suit like this. People don't want to spend the time because they assume it won't be worth it in the end. Or they're afraid of what the public might think." I glance at Robert when I say this. "So, it involves hours and hours of searching for people who've made any sort of public complaint regarding Bucky's Beans. Of course, most of the complaints we've come across have nothing to do with the unsolicited text messages, so that's a whole other issue."

"You've said *we* a few times. Do you have someone else helping you with this?" My dad asks.

I nod. "My colleague, Constance, has helped with some of the online leg work."

"Did you say Constance?" Anthony looks up from his phone in his lap.

Oh no. I nod nonchalantly, certain that the Cheshire grin on his face means he remembers her and is about to start running his mouth. Attempting to dash his next attention-seeking move, I say, "That's right. Constance. You met her last night. Although, I'm sure you barely remember showing up while we were going over the case. She left shortly after you arrived." I look from my dad to my mom as I eat my garlic bread. Neither reacts to the fact that I had a female coworker over that late on a Saturday night for supposed work purposes. After all, out of my brothers and I, I'm the only one who ever had dates that were truly meant for studying.

"Oh yeahhhh," Anthony snickers. "I remember. How could I forget? Except, it didn't seem like the two of you were meeting over *business* . . . more like about to get down to business." He guffaws.

Robert's disbelieving laugh is cut short by an elbow to the ribs from my sister-in-law who then asks him to take Alex to the bathroom. She goes back to showing Wyatt how to twist noodles around his Spiderman fork.

"Tell us more about this Constance, Henry." My mom briefly widens her eyes at me before taking a sip of her wine.

"Oh boy," my dad mumbles as he stands to refill his plate.

"There isn't much to tell, Mom." I remove my napkin from my lap, fold it neatly, and place it next to my empty plate. "Like I said, we work together, and she's assisting with the Bucky's case. Sorry, to disappoint you, Anthony," I say, raising an eyebrow at him and then looking back at my mom who takes another sip of her wine.

"Whatever you say. But if that really is the case, what reason could you possibly have for ignoring an opportunity with a woman like that? You're not still pining over Tracey Mullins, are you?" He shakes his head and scoffs. "Time to get over that one, bro. She's long gone."

Anthony goes back to his phone, and the table goes silent for a moment. As I glance from face to face, everyone goes back to what they were doing before my ex from college—the only woman who ever broke my heart—was mentioned. For a moment I consider countering Anthony's insinuation that I'm still not over Tracey, but the fear that I might prove myself wrong if I engage in even a brief discussion about her holds me back.

"Well," my mom stands, picking up her plate, "friend or colleague or . . . whatever she is to you, we'd love to have her over for dinner sometime." She smiles and picks up my plate too.

Shaking my head, I shrug and take a sip of water, dismissing her assumption about Constance and me.

Before she heads to the kitchen, she leans in close and whispers, "Going over a case at your apartment late on a Saturday night? As your father always used to tell your brothers, I wasn't born last week, you know."

My eyes sweep the table, but no one besides my dad heard what my mom just said. As soon as he swallows the food in his mouth, he says, "Your mother has a point, Henry. I know you don't like her pressuring you to date, but few things would make us happier than a little reassurance that you have a social life."

I'm about to tell my dad that there's really nothing between

Constance and I worth mentioning when Anthony rejoins the conversation right where he exited. "Seriously, Henry, if there's really nothing going on between you and Constance, any chance I could get her number?"

I throw my napkin at him.

CHAPTER 9

Monday, April 18
Ruth

When I'm ready to go somewhere, I go. There's no sense in sitting around waiting. As a result, I arrive at work extra early this morning. The first thing I do before prepping the office for customers is turn on some music. I'm not in the mood for the usual sounds of nature Beverly prefers, so I opt for eighties music. While "Girls Just Want To Have Fun" blares through the speakers, I dance around opening the blinds, straightening the chairs and wobble cushions, turning on the computers, resetting all the weighting timers, straightening up the kids' play area, and replenishing the paper cups next to the water cooler.

The bone clock on the wall says it's six-forty—twenty minutes before the door needs to be unlocked and at least ten before the Wixleys arrive, so I head behind the counter and roll my chair off to the side. As I lean forward into a left hamstring stretch and log into Facebook, Wang Chung reminds me that the music is far too loud for Beverly's liking, so I use the remote to turn the volume down low enough that it might be midmorning before she realizes I changed the station. Then I switch to my right hamstring and begin scrolling through my newsfeed.

A couple years ago, I almost missed a good friend's wedding because she sent out invitations via Facebook Messenger. Shortly after the paperwork for my divorce had been filed, I'd deleted the Messenger app from my phone because QuickForm clients kept messaging me. Some wanted to know if I was ill and when I'd be returning, some had questions about membership, autopayments, or the nutrition regimen, some were inquiring about becoming a franchisee, and some had heard rumors about the divorce and wanted to know if I was okay. I kept telling my then business partner of ten years and soon-to-be ex, Adam, that he had to remove my name and contact information from everything, but he still held out hope that I'd stick with QuickForm even though he wasn't willing to change a thing to stick with our marriage. Like I told him, I was done living his out-of-control dream of being a fitness industry mogul. It had been my dream too when we first met and bonded over our passions for health and wellness. But as our small business expanded into a franchise and grew to include a nutrition program, Adam's modest dream of helping people achieve their fitness goals became a daily nightmare for me. It was just too much, too fast, and too constant. And all the success, left little room for us. He still doesn't believe me, but my willful exit from the life we'd built together had nothing to do with my on-the-job accident or the affair he'd had with our receptionist. Instead, it had everything to do with the fact that I just wasn't happy. If he'd agreed to give it all up and move to a remote island in the Pacific, I would have done so in a heartbeat. I would have even forgiven him for the affair, mostly because I honestly don't blame him for that indiscretion since I'm the one who ultimately stopped trying, personally and professionally. But to this day, he remains the King of QuickForm, which I have no doubt makes him happier than any relationship ever could.

So after nearly a year of some much-needed time to refocus and reacquaint myself with the simple things in life, such as waking up happy and doing things because I wanted to do them not because I had to, I received a call from my old high-school friend and cross-country teammate Maggie. My initial reaction when she called to see if I'd gotten the wedding "invitation" she'd sent via Facebook Messenger was to wonder if she truly wanted me at her wedding. Who invites people to a wedding through Facebook? But as I read her message further, it dawned on me that she didn't know about my divorce or about the fact that I'd relinquished my portions of QuickForm Fitness and QuickForm Nutrition. It was a wonder she'd thought to invite me at all since I hadn't reached out to her in years. In fact, the last time I'd seen her was at the grand opening of the original QuickForm Fitness Center right down the road from the farmers' market. The last time before that had been at my father's funeral.

I hardly ever post anything on Facebook myself, but ever since I received Maggie's call, I make it a point to check in at least once a week to keep up with friends and family. The goal is to make sure I don't miss anything important or life-altering, but in the big scheme of things, people's posts are usually anything but. Sure, there's the occasional pregnancy, birth, or death announcement, but then there are also the everyday things like pictures of what people had for lunch or the shoes they wore to work, or a cat sitting in a bathroom sink. Sometimes people even post things they'd never dream of sharing with someone face-to-face, like the fact that they walked in on an unfaithful spouse. I don't judge, though, because a picture of a cat drinking water from a faucet might brighten someone's day, and a post about a cheating spouse might force someone to open her eyes.

I scroll through, reacting with a thumbs-up to post after post—something funny a five-year-old said, my neighbor Joan's flower pots, a Door County sunset posted by my mom, a golden retriever jumping for a Frisbee, a sponsored ad for Posh. As Howard Jones fills the brief silence that follows Wang Chung, I come across a post that makes me click the little red heart. It's about the pending birth of a QuickForm Fitness trainer's first child. Elisha was always one of my favorites, and she's the only former colleague I'm friends with on Facebook. I begin typing a comment, then quickly delete it, and instead make a mental note to check Elisha's wall for news about the baby the next time I log on.

As I scroll to the next post, my phone vibrates. I swipe the screen to reveal another unwanted text from Bucky's.

BUCKY'S PERKS: STOP IN WED-FRI BETWEEN NOON AND CLOSE AND GET A $3.50 MED HANDCRAFTED BEVERAGE! PARTICIPATING LOCATIONS. TEXTSTOPTOEND. MSG&DATARATESMAYAPPLY

My frustrated guffaw is halted when I suddenly remember the message I'd sent via Bucky's Facebook page the day before. I delete the text and in one swift movement pull the chair back in front of my computer and take a seat. Then I open Messenger to find that no one from Bucky's Beans Coffee Roasters has responded to my message.

How can this be? They're able to text me on a daily basis, sometimes twice per day, yet no one is available to respond to my message? Surely the company has someone monitoring their Facebook page.

That's it. I've had it.

I click on Bucky's logo and am taken to their page where I compose a public post in which I refrain from saying exactly what's on my mind.

Hello. For some reason, I've been receiving Bucky's Perks text messages for about a month now, even though I never signed up for the program. After dozens of unsuccessful attempts to unsubscribe, I finally contacted a local Bucky's and was told I would have to log in to my Perks account and change my preferences. However, since I never signed up for the program, I don't have an account. So, the employee I spoke with suggested I contact your corporate office in Madison. They were closed when I called, so instead I sent a message to this page, but no one has responded. Can someone please help me?

I read the message a few times before posting it. Then instead of logging out of Facebook, I close the browser, intent on checking for a response during my lunch break.

CHAPTER 10

Monday, April 18
Henry

"Damn it," I say as I cross another name off the list of potential lead plaintiffs for the Bucky's case. Six had commented on the post on our firm's page about our investigation into the Bucky's Perks program, and two had responded to the Facebook ad we're running.

I tap the tip of my pen rapidly against a half-used pad of Post-it notes while I reread Julia Simon's response. *Sorry, but I just don't have time for something like this . . .* Of the eight people, this woman was the last to confirm she isn't interested in getting involved beyond signing a petition or being a silent member of the class.

Sighing, I toss the fountain pen onto my desk, causing it to slide over the edge and land on the ground with a thud. Wondering why I even use something so expensive and heavy, I open the top right-hand drawer of my desk and grab a plastic Bic with a black cap. I only tap it a few times before compulsively bending to retrieve the pen on the floor, which I return to its monogrammed granite holder on my desk.

"Okay, Henry, back at it," I say as I move on to new inquires of our post and ad. The first is from a man named Sergio Medina. I click the link he provided to view the negative Google review he left for Bucky's several weeks ago, then I send him a personalized private message to see if he's willing to chat about the unsolicited texts he's been receiving. I repeat the process three more times, personalizing each message, then I place the list into the Bucky's file folder.

Before I switch gears to the DigiScan case, I take a peek at Bucky's Facebook page, just to see if any customers have posted publicly about issues with the Perk's Program. Lo and behold, there's a brand-new comment from a woman named Ruth Bateman. It seems this is her second attempt to message Bucky's via Facebook.

The excitement of putting a case together, even if there are roadblocks and pitfalls, never gets old. So, despite my lack of luck with the Bucky's case thus far, my heart rate increases. All we need is a name, just one person to let us use his or her name. Giddy with anticipation, I click to view Ms. Bateman's profile.

Her profile photo is of a woman, who I assume to be her, standing in front of a body of water. Perhaps Lake Michigan? She's wearing a Yankees baseball cap with the rim pulled down low so that the upper portion of her face is obscured. It looks like her arm is around someone, but the person is cropped out of the photo. She's wearing a loose-fitting tank top and has a medal around her neck. Perhaps the photo was taken after a running event? Her arms are slim and defined, so I assume she's into fitness, and I'd guess her to be in her early thirties. But who knows? It could be an old photo, or maybe it isn't even her. Either way, the woman in the photo has a nice smile.

I glance down to find out more about Ms. Bateman, but the only thing she's made public is that she attended Pius High School and UW-La Crosse, and she works for Wixley Health and Wellness Chiropractors. The only thing visible on her feed is her profile picture. Even her friends list is hidden. It's the Facebook profile equivalent to Fort Knox.

"Wait a second. . ." I whisper as I begin typing in my old frat brother's name. I get as far as Mar- before Martin Meyer's profile appears in the search results. Sure enough, Marty went to Pius, too, and as luck would have it, Ruth Bateman is on his list of friends. "Looks like we might need to catch up soon, Marty."

I contemplate messaging my old friend but hate to do so under these circumstances. He's made several attempts to get together with me over the years, but I've never taken him up on any of his invitations, mostly because I'm a workaholic, but also because I'm not a huge fan of social gatherings where I tend to end up off in a corner checking my email. So, I Google Ruth Bateman instead, but the only relevant result is an obituary for her father who passed away a few years ago. It says he died peacefully at White Pines Nursing Home in Wauwatosa, but no cause of death is listed.

I click back to Ms. Bateman's profile and then on the Messenger icon at the top of the screen. My fingers hover over the keyboard, anxious thoughts of what could be swirling around in my brain. According to Wisconsin Supreme Court Rule 20:7.3, which basically states a lawyer should not solicit business in person or via live telephone or real-time electronic correspondence unless the potential client made initial contact, this move could get me into serious trouble *. . . Screw it. She's a friend of Marty's, and she probably won't respond anyway.*

Good morning, Ms. Bateman. I hope this message finds you well. As you can see . . .

A knock on my office door, startles me. "Hey, handsome." Constance breezes in and stands before me, QuickForm tumbler in hand. "What are you working on?"

"Oh, I was just about to respond to another potential plaintiff for the Bucky's case," I say, trying to sound nonchalant. I lower my hands from their poised positions above the keyboard and do my best to relax the cat-who-swallowed-the-canary expression that's plastered on my face.

"Well, finish up. Then we can make a quick lap around the building." She swirls her free pointer finger in a circular motion then takes a sip of whatever QuickForm concoction is in her tumbler.

"Ahhh, why don't you go ahead without me? I really need to get this done and then I have a lot of things to go over for the DigiScan case. So . . ."

"Henry, it isn't good for you or anyone to sit at a desk for hours at a time. Come on. My uncle wants everyone to take regular breaks. Remember? We talked about it at the last office meeting. It'll be good for your body and your brain."

I'm not too keen on being reminded that Mr. Whitmore is Constance's uncle because sometimes it makes me feel as though she's my boss by default. But in this case, her mention of him is purely benign. Plus, we *have* been instructed to take regular breaks due to the company's new wellness in the workplace initiative, so I agree to join her.

"Yes, fine. I remember. Just . . ." I raise a finger and then return my hands to the keyboard and my attention to the screen. ". . . one . . . moment."

Constance stays put and sips her drink for a minute or two as I type. Her presence causes me to make several errors, so I end up rereading the message several times to be sure there are no typos.

"I'm sure it's fine, Henry. Are you going to send it already?"

In lieu of a verbal response, I press the enter key and meet Constance's imploring blue gaze. She smiles her unnaturally white smile, and I marvel at her manufactured beauty. As a regular witness to the amount of time it takes for her to apply her makeup every morning, I'm privy to all her hidden imperfections, but to other people, she's flawless. I personally think she—like most women—looks more beautiful without makeup. Of course, since Tracey, I've only dated primpers like Constance because they are nothing like Tracey. It started when she moved clear across the country to attend law school. Somewhere she knew I'd never follow. I still wonder if she transferred to Stanford because it was easier than just telling me she didn't want to be with me anymore. That's the only way I could ever make heads or tails of the fact that she started dating other guys just a few months after she moved, just when I was beginning to think the long-distance thing was going well. Hurt by the way everything shook out in the end, when Tracey's unspoken truth was made apparent by her actions, I began dating girls who were polar-opposite to her. But what started as a coping mechanism gradually became a habit.

As I stare at Constance, my heart wonders if her perfect persona is what's preventing my feelings for her from progressing, but habits can be hard to break. Or perhaps it's the fact that she's nothing like Tracey, whom I haven't decided yet if I still have feelings for. Goodness knows I've been thinking about her ever since my brother brought her up.

Damn it, Anthony.

"What? Why are you staring at me?" She sets her tumbler down on my desk and uses a finger on each hand to swipe the delicate skin beneath her eyes. "Do I have smoothie on my face?"

"No, you look great," I say as I roll my chair away from my desk and stand. "Shall we take a break?"

She nods as she smoothes her hair, grabs her tumbler, and then walks elegantly to the door, her high heels clicking as she sways.

I follow her but wonder if I might need more than just a break from the office.

CHAPTER 11

Monday, April 18
Ruth

"Bye-bye, Mr. Hoveland," I say, waving after the Wixleys' most consistent patient as he shuffles through the door with his cane. He has been getting adjusted by Dr. Jackson for nearly ten years, shows up religiously every Monday between ten thirty and ten forty-five, and is always the last patient out the door before we close shop from eleven to one. When I see that he's safely in his car, I close and lock the door.

"Hey, Ruthie," Beverly calls from the stretching room.

"Yeah?" I bypass the front counter and peek my head around the corner to find her rocking side to side on a wobble cushion.

"After Jackson adjusts me, we're going to walk over to Lulu Café for lunch. Are you interested in joining us?"

"Thanks for the offer, but I brought a lunch."

"Save it for tomorrow." She stops rocking from side to side and begins leaning forward and backward with her hands on her hips.

"But it's hummus with fresh veggies and pita chips. I've been thinking about the chips all morning." I enter the room and begin straightening the rows of chairs surrounding her.

"Are they the homemade ones with the olive oil and parmesan cheese?"

I grin and nod. "I added some basil this time, and I brought an extra bag for you."

"Well aren't you the bee's knees?" She switches to torso twists. "You sure you don't want to join us?"

"Really I can't. I have to put together a few dozen home care kits and make a couple of phone calls to insurance companies." I lean to the left to check the wall clock above my desk. Then I start backing out of the room. "In fact, it's just about the best time to reach Sally at Cigna . . . If I'm on the phone when you leave, have a good lunch."

She smiles and nods, then wrinkles her brow and says to no one, "Is this Boy George?"

I turn to head back to my desk and crack a knowing grin. I guess we'll be back to listening to ocean waves or crickets chirping this afternoon.

I get comfortable in my chair and then wiggle the mouse to wake up my computer. When I drag the little arrow up to the top of the screen to click the bookmarked Cigna Contact Us page, my attention is diverted to the red notification circle above the Facebook icon. I click it, curious to see if Bucky's Beans has responded.

Still nothing. In fact, it appears no one has even read my message. However, I do have a message request from someone named Henry Mancuso. Not recognizing the name, I allow the arrow to hover over the thumbnail of his profile photo, and trusty Facebook clues me in to the fact that he's a lawyer and works for Benson Tillman & Whitmore. I recognize this firm from billboards. Even so, this could still be a fake profile. Why would a lawyer message me? QuickForm Fitness is represented by a different law firm, and the attorney Adam hired to handle our divorce works somewhere else too. Besides, my legal ties to Adam and the business were officially severed years ago.

Henry Mancuso. . . Henry Mancuso. . . I wrack my brain trying to recall if I've ever met this person before. Nothing comes to me, so I click to view his full profile. His enlarged profile photo is a bit blurry but still causes me to take pause. Henry is an attractive guy.

Shocked to realize that I'm nibbling my lower lip, I look up to make sure Beverly and Jackson are still preoccupied in the next room. Wouldn't want them wondering why I'm drooling over my computer screen. *Come on, Ruth. Where is this coming from? Just like women, men are not pieces of meat.* I sigh over my stagnant sex life and return to Mr. Mancuso's profile. Former Shareholder/Attorney at Gallegos Timmerman & Rondell, PC. Went to Shorewood High School. Studied Law at Marquette University. Attended Marquette University Law School. Lives in Milwaukee, Wisconsin. *Impressive.* But is this a real person? I scroll to view the public posts on Mr. Mancuso's wall. It's mostly legal news, but there are also a handful of lawyerish memes shared to his wall by others.

Lawyer: Stressed, Depressed, Well-dressed.

Teacher asked what comes after a sentence . . . I told her an appeal!

A good lawyer knows the law . . . A great lawyer knows the judge!

Mr. Mancuso hasn't interacted with any of the meme posts, but there is one he shared himself that got a lot of reactions. It says: *It's going to happen because I'm going to make it happen.* I like this sentiment, so I navigate back to view his message.

Good morning, Ms. Bateman. I hope this message finds you well. As you can see from my profile, my name is Henry Mancuso, and I'm an attorney with Benson Tillman & Whitmore LLP. I just came across your message to Bucky's Beans Coffee Roasters regarding the unsolicited text messages you've been receiving via the company's Perks program. For quite some time now, my firm has been aware of an issue with the Bucky's Perks program. Please let me know if you're interested in discussing how we might be of assistance with this matter.

Thank you for your time.
Henry J. Mancuso

I sigh, thinking this inquiry must be some sort of scam to try to obtain personal information from people.

"Everything okay, Ruth?"

I look up and quickly minimize the Facebook window on my screen. Dr. Jackson and Beverly are standing before me, all smiles. The placement of his hand on her back reminds me of the affection my mom and dad always used to display toward one another.

"Yes, everything's fine. I'm just . . . about to get to work on these insurance claims," I say, pointing at my computer.

"Are you sure you don't want to join us?" Dr. Jackson asks. "Our treat?"

"Oh, no, of course not, but thank you for the offer. Some other time, okay?"

He nods, and Beverly shrugs, giving him an I-told-you-so sort of look.

"Okay, then. We'll be back soon," he says as they head past the counter.

Beverly smiles and says, "I'll have those pita chips as a snack later this afternoon." Then they disappear down the hallway toward the back door.

"You got it!" I call after her. "Enjoy your lunch!"

I wait until I hear the door close before maximizing the Facebook window. I contemplate accepting Mr. Mancuso's request, so I can politely decline his offer, but all the what ifs associated with being contacted by an unfamiliar attorney have me leaning toward simply deleting it.

Then I think, *what if Bucky's never responds and I continue to receive texts from them?* It certainly wouldn't be the end of the world, but it sure would be annoying. So, I go back to Mr. Mancuso's profile for one last look, curious to see if we have any friends in common.

After a quick scroll through his friends list, which he has surprisingly made public, I see a familiar name. Martin Meyer.

"Well isn't that a coincidence?" I say to myself, grinning.

Then it hits me. Marty attended Marquette University too.

"Fine, I'll accept your request, Mr. Mancuso. But only because you know Marty."

Mr. Mancuso,

I appreciate you taking the time to contact me, but I believe the texts from Bucky's won't be an issue much longer. I'm sure they will remove my number from their system as soon as someone sees my message. Besides, I'm not really the suing type. Thank you, anyway.

Sincerely,

Ruth Bateman

Before I close out of Facebook for the day, I go back to my post on Bucky's page and consider deleting it, concerned that it might encourage even more weirdos to contact me. But then my phone vibrates.

BUCKY'S PERKS: CHECK IN & BUY A DRINK MON AFTER 2PM TO RECEIVE A $3 MED HANDCRAFTED BEVERAGE TUE/WED! PARTICIPATING LOCATIONS. TEXTSTOPTOEND MSG&DATARATESMAYAPPLY

Maybe I'll wait a day or two to ensure someone from Bucky's has a chance to see it. After all, it could be my only hope of putting an end to these texts!

CHAPTER 12

Monday, April 18
Henry

"... So, I explained to him that he would need to know exactly what was said to determine if any lies were told, and even then, he would need to be able to prove that these statements were lies. And that's what upset him, the fact that no lawyer can do anything about the things his ex has reported to his employer, not solely based on his word that it's all lies, anyway . . . Henry?" Constance waves a hand in front of my face, causing me to nearly trip as we enter the building that houses our office. "Are you even listening to me?"

"Yeah, yeah. That's a pretty typical response, though, don't you think? Sure, he could be lying, but you can't assume he is just because he got defensive." My phone vibrates so I pull it out of my pocket.

"I understand that, Henry, but . . ."

Constance's voice fades into the background noises of our office as I open Ruth Bateman's response to my message. My chest falls, and I stop dead in my tracks when I read her last sentence. "*. . . Thank you anyway . . .*"

"Henry?"

"Yes?" Lowering my phone, I look up at Constance.

"What sandwich should I order for you?

"Sandwich?"

"From Potbelly? Or would you rather have a salad? That's what I'm getting. Here's the menu." She hands me her phone.

"Oh, uhhhh . . . I'd like an Uptown salad. Thank you," I say, handing her phone back. I actually don't want anything, but my disappointment over Ms. Bateman's message has me eager to get back to work. Giving Constance my order should speed up our parting.

"Okay . . . are you sure? You barely glanced at the screen." She cocks her head. "Are you okay? What were you just looking at?" She eyes my phone.

Sighing, I unlock the device and let her read Ms. Bateman's message for herself. She purses her lips as she reads, and then gives my arm a supportive rub as she hands back my phone.

"It's fine, Henry. You'll find someone else in due time . . . See you in the lounge in a couple hours for lunch?"

"I've got a lot of work to do, so I'm going to eat in my office today. But I'll leave some cash for the deliveryman up front with Janice. Okay?"

"Henry," Constance leads me into my office and closes the door, "I wish you wouldn't be so tough on yourself. You work harder than anyone at this firm, myself included. There is no deadline on this Bucky's case or the DigiScan case, so I don't understand why you feel the need to continue using them to fill every moment of free time you might have between the cases that do have deadlines. Your standing at this firm is *solid*." She wraps her arms around my waist and presses her body against mine. "My uncle loves you, and so do Mr. Benson and Mr. Tillman. Trust me."

"Constance," I pull back from her, "my work ethic won't change based on whether or not my bosses like me." And I really wish she'd stop bringing up the fact that she's related to one of the men who pays my salary, but I don't say it because I knew the situation when we started seeing each other.

"Relax, Henry. I didn't mean it that way. All I'm saying is I wish you would lighten up a little. Obviously, work is important, but other things are important too." With that, she exits my office, closing the door decisively behind her.

I suspect she's upset that I snubbed her for lunch, so I grip the doorknob, poised to go after her and tell her I changed my mind about eating alone in my office. But something holds me back. Is it my frustration over being at a standstill with the Bucky's case? Is it the fact that Tracey has been lingering in the back of my mind ever since

Anthony brought her up during dinner at our parents' house? Or could it be that Constance simply isn't the one for me?

Flustered with myself because I can't make heads or tails of why I feel the way I do about anything right now, my hand falls to my side. I decide to take the easy route, the one that doesn't require analysis of what my heart wants, and I go back to work.

CHAPTER 13

Thursday, April 21
Ruth

"Promise you won't stay too late, Ruth," Beverly says as she puts her jacket on. "If you can't get all these done within the next hour or so, just go. I can always come in a little early tomorrow morning or stay late to help finish up."

Dr. Jackson and Beverly host a wellness workshop four times a year at the Marriott in downtown Milwaukee where a long-term patient gets them a deal on the largest ballroom. This quarter's presentation is on cancer prevention and holistic treatment for which I'm busy assembling handouts. A last-minute issue with our office printer has me behind schedule by a couple of days.

"Oh, no worries, Beverly. I don't have to work at Posh tonight, so I'm fully prepared to stay until I get this done. Then I can help you and Dr. Jackson load all of this up in your car tomorrow, and I'll help you unload it at the hotel on Saturday morning."

"Thank you, Ruth. You are one in a million." Dr. Jackson appears, his booming voice overpowering Beverly's protests. He flashes an adoring smile at her and swings his keys around his index finger. "Are you ready, dear? We're supposed to meet the kids at six."

She nods at him, then looks back at me. "One hour, Ruth. Then skedaddle."

"Yes, ma'am," I say with playful sternness, causing Dr. Jackson to chuckle. He takes ahold of Beverly's hand and leads her toward the back door.

"See you tomorrow morning, Ruth," he says.

"One hour! Then go home and enjoy your night off!" Beverly calls over her shoulder.

"Have fun! Tell your kids I say hello!" I respond.

As the door closes, my phone pings, but packet assembly has already commenced, so I commit to completing ten handouts before checking to see what the notification is for.

Finally, a response from Bucky's! All the frustration I've been feeling since posting to the company's Facebook page on Monday and continuing to receive daily Bucky's Perks texts melts away. Surely, this message is to confirm they've removed my number.

Bucky's Beans - *Thank you for letting us know, Ruth. Please PM us your email so we can take a look at our email system and solve this.*

So they can take a look at their email system? I've been receiving texts, not emails, so how is giving them my email address going to help? Confused, I reread my post from four days ago.

Hello. For some reason, I've been receiving Bucky's Perks text messages for about a month now, even though I never signed up for the program. After dozens of unsuccessful attempts to unsubscribe, I finally contacted a local Bucky's and was told I would have to log in to my Perks account and change my preferences. However, since I never signed up for the program, I don't have an account. So, the employee I spoke with suggested I contact your corporate office in Madison. They were closed when I called, so instead I sent a message to this page, but no one has responded. Can someone please help me?

Sighing, I send a private message to the page as the Bucky's representative requested.

Hello. I'm sending my info per your response to my concern over the constant TEXT messages I've been receiving over the past month or so. I just want to clarify, though, that I never signed up for the Bucky's Perks program, so it's doubtful you'll find my email address in your system. Email: ruthieb@gmail.com Text/Cell #: 414-555-2122 Thank you for your assistance with this matter!

I set my phone down faceup among the stacks of papers on the table in front of me and resume assembly. Packet number thirty-five . . . forty-two . . . fifty-three.

My phone vibrates and slides a few centimeters across the table. I set down the half-assembled packet in my hands, stretch my arms high above my head, and do a few torso twists before picking it up.

Bucky's Perks: Take a late break after 2PM 4/22-4/23 and get a BOGO! Mention offer to redeem. Participating locations. TextSTOPtoEND Msg&DataRatesMayApply

I close my eyes and take a deep cleansing breath. It isn't often that I feel as frustrated as I do with Bucky's. How hard could it be to remove a stinking number from a list?

After one more deep breath, I open my eyes and screenshot the message before deleting it. Then I get back to work and resolve to give my brother a call if I receive one more message from Bucky's. If he's the prankster who signed me up for the Perks program, then putting an end to the texts could be as simple as finding out what email he used.

~

Friday, April 22
Ruth

On a typical Friday, Wixley Chiropractic closes as six, but since we all need to be at the Marriott bright and early for the cancer seminar tomorrow morning, the Wixleys closed shop at four. Which means I have an extra two hours to get ready for my shift at Posh.

I pop in my earbuds and wave to the Wixleys as they pull out of the parking lot. Then I scroll through my playlists before selecting the one called Misheard Lyrics. I'm already speed-walking toward the alley when "Bohemian Rhapsody" comes on, causing me to laugh out loud as

I imagine my brother botching the lyrics to it. *Got a moose! Got a moose! Will you do the fandango?*

I've already covered half the distance to my house by the time the iconic Queen song ends and "Wake Me Up Before You Go-Go" begins. This one makes me want to dance, so I do, but not well. Over the lyrical genius of George Michael, I hear a few honks from drivers who either appreciate my moves, think I look like an idiot, or hope to give me a few pointers. Whatever their reasons, I wave and proceed to shimmy my way home.

A few blocks from my house, my music is interrupted by the ding of a message notification. The brief pause allows me to hear an obnoxious whistle, which I ignore as I remove my phone from my pocket. I let out a growl when I see it's a text from good old Bucky's, but I keep dancing. Earlier today someone from Bucky's followed up to let me know my information had been sent along to their IT team. The person also echoed the same suggestion made by the Bucky's employee I spoke with last week—that maybe another customer made a typo when he signed up for the Perks program—but they assured me that my number would be removed by the end of the day. That was early this morning, so perhaps the Bucky's employee meant my number would be removed by midnight, or perhaps the text I just received was already programmed to go out before my number was removed. How long can it possibly take the IT department to remove my number? Could it really be that complicated?

I screenshot and delete the text. Then I set a reminder to call my brother before I leave for Posh tonight just in case Bucky's is having trouble removing my number without knowing the corresponding email address that was provided for enrollment in the Perks program.

The sidewalk in front of Joan's house is the final stretch before I reach my house. She waves from her front porch and says something to me as she descends the steps and makes her way over to the fence that divides our yards. Winston follows her. I remove my earbuds and join her.

"What were you saying, Joan? I couldn't hear you."

"Yeah, I figured that based on the way you were flailing and gyrating. What exactly are you listening to, young lady?"

Laughing, I say, "A song I'm guessing you might not have heard of before. It's called "Uptown Funk"."

Her eyes widen as she shakes her head and sighs. "If you ever want to learn some real dance moves, stop over and I'll give you a lesson. My record collection is filled with all the classics. I've got Elvis, the Four Tops, Buddy Holly, Tony Bennett . . . all the good ones. Oh, and Ol' Blue Eyes, of course. You know who that is, right?" She narrows her eyes at me as if our relationship depends on my answer.

"Frank Sinatra?"

"Yes, Ruth! Yes!" Excited by Joan's reaction, Winston starts whining and jumping up on her leg.

I let out a slow relieved breath, glad to have pleased her. "My mom and dad loved to dance to "The Way You Look Tonight" back before . . . well, back when I was a kid."

"Well, if your parents have such good taste in music, then what are you doing bopping around to that hippity-hop garbage?" I open my mouth to answer, but she continues before I get a word out. "It's settled then, you'll come over sometime and I'll teach you some real dance moves." She nods, confirming our future social engagement, and turns to leave. Winston follows.

"Have a good night, Joan," I call after her, suppressing the laugh that's welling up deep within my belly. Joan's curmudgeonly personality may be off-putting to some, but I think she's delightful.

She waves without looking back.

～

It's Friday night, and I'm sitting in the break room at Posh icing my good ankle because I twisted it when someone bumped into me. Since I'm alone, I power on my phone and dial my brother. He and Molli tend to stay in and watch movies on Friday nights, so now is probably the perfect time to catch him.

"Hey, Ruthie," my brother answers the phone in a pleasant, hushed voice. "What's going on?"

"Sorry to call so late. Is Molli sleeping or something?"

69

"Yeah, we had a long week. Sorry I missed your call earlier. We were out to dinner. Our first proper meal in days."

"Oh, no biggie. Congrats on the newly renovated office, by the way. The pics on Facebook look fabulous."

"Thanks, but that was all Molli. I'll let her know you like how everything looks. So, what's up? You're not calling for Mom, are you?"

"No. Why?"

"Eh, she's all gung ho about me making a trip up there to go through my stuff. I told her I don't want any of it. It's just stuff, you know? But you know her. She insists there are things I will want to give to my future children."

"Then just ask her to hold everything for you until you and Molli can visit. It's your practice, so I'm sure you can take a few days off whenever you want to, right?"

"Yeah, the same way you could take a few days off whenever you wanted to back when you owned QuickForm."

Ouch. He must be stressed with how busy they are lately. For him to bring up QuickForm, the dream my ex-husband and I saw through to become reality and the very thing that tore us apart, is a low blow. It reminds me that I've been meaning to have a discussion with Tyler about the stress the new practice could put on his relationship with Molli, but now's obviously not the time.

"Sorry," he spurts, breaking the unexpected pause in our conversation. "That was a shitty thing to say."

"It's okay. I understand how stressful it can be to run a business and to work with your significant other on top of it. Anyway, I just have a quick question about something."

"Shoot."

"Did you by any chance enroll me in the Bucky's Perks program?"

"The what?"

"The Bucky's Perks program. You know, so Bucky's Beans would text me coupon codes every day?"

"No. Why would I? Do you even drink their coffee?"

"No, but that's not the point. Are you *sure* you didn't give them my number as a prank? Because I think I might have to change my number if these texts don't stop soon."

"Ruthie, I'm a medical professional. I don't have time for shenanigans like that anymore." *He's so full of crap.* "Just call them and tell them to remove your number."

"I tried that."

"Try texting *end* or *stop*. That's how I got Redbox to stop texting me. I texted the word *stop*."

"Nope. Tried that too. In fact, I've responded with every possible combination of words you can think of, and nothing works. I keep getting texts from them every. Single. Day."

"Well, what did they say when you called?"

"The girl told me to log in to my Perks account and change my settings, but I don't have a Perks account, so I can't log into anything. And then she suggested I call Bucky's corporate offices in Madison, which I did, but they were closed, of course. So then I sent them a private message on Facebook, but no one responded. That left me no choice other than to post publicly on their page, but so far that hasn't yielded any results either." I take a deep, much-needed breath.

"Wow. You're pretty bent out of shape over this, huh?" He snickers and then chomps on something, most likely popcorn from Kwik Trip, which has always been his favorite snack.

"Tyler. It isn't funny."

"It's just some annoying texts, Ruthie. What's the big deal? Just ignore them." This is the same thing he said to me when he submitted my number to Catcall-A-Day. I have a momentary flashback of answering the phone and hearing hoots, hollers, and provocative whistles, as if a studio of construction workers had been gathered together to record the message.

I sigh, wondering if I might be blowing the texts out of proportion.

"I'll tell you what I think. I think you need something else to focus on, besides work. Have you considered throwing yourself back on the market? Joining an online dating site maybe?"

"Stop, Tyler. I don't feel like discussing this with you."

"Molli's sister just met a nice guy online, and Molli created her profile. I bet she'd be more than happy to set one up for you, too . . . Molli," he whispers. "Molli, Ruthie's on the phone and—"

"Tyler! Knock it off! Don't you dare wake her up for something so *stupid*. I'm not interested in online dating." While I'm going off on my brother, Sonia enters the room and side-eyes me as she heads to her purse hanging on the wall. Leave it to my brother to make me revert to my whiny teenage self and call him stupid in the presence of a coworker.

"Fine. But I'm not kidding, you obviously need something to occupy your time, so you stop getting so bent out of shape over something as silly as an unwanted text here and there. Go on a date, okay? I'm sure you have plenty of options to choose from at Posh." It's not even worth telling him about Mitchell, since that's obviously not going anywhere. "And when you do go on a date, make sure you put out the right vibe, one that says you're available. Don't be your weird self by talking about puzzles and saving the ozone. Brush your hair. And wear something other than workout clothes because—"

"Yeah, yeah, yeah. I got it. Thanks for the advice. Look, my break is just about over so I have to go."

"Maybe it was Adam."

"Who signed me up to receive the texts? No way. He doesn't have time for that with the way QuickForm is blowing up and his new baby . . ."

"Well, everyone is suing someone for something these days, so you could always sue them," he says, laughing. I laugh, too, but in the back of my mind I'm thinking of the message I received from the lawyer earlier this week.

"Good one. But, hey, I need to get going . . . Love you."

"Love you, too, Ruthie. Bye."

I stare at my phone for a few moments, contemplating my next move. Do I really want to seek help from a lawyer over some harmless text messages?

My phone vibrates alerting me of another message from Bucky's Beans.

That's it, I think, the feisty inner teen in me is cropping up again. I open Facebook Messenger and navigate to the lawyer's message.

Mr. Mancuso,

*On second thought, I am interested in hearing how you might be able to help
with the Bucky's texts. They won't stop, and I seem to be losing my sanity over
it for some reason. I've tried numerous things, so I'm not sure you'll be able to
help, but I guess it can't hurt for us to talk if the offer still stands.*

Thank you for your time.

Ruth Bateman

After I send the message, I remove the ice pack from my ankle and
hobble over to put it back in the freezer compartment of the break
lounge's mini-cooler. Then I pop a couple of Ibuprofen, determined to
make it through the last two hours of my shift. Hopefully it doesn't hurt
in the morning since I have to stand most of the day at the Wixleys'
cancer workshop.

I'm about to return my phone to my purse when it vibrates.

Hi Ms. Bateman,

*I'm delighted to hear that you've changed your mind and would like nothing
more than to help put an end to the text messages you've been receiving from
Bucky's. I am confident we will be able to help. Would you be willing to provide
me with your email address? Then I can send you an official letter detailing
what we know about the unsolicited messages and outline the information we'll
need from you before we proceed.*

Thank you, Ms. Bateman!

Sincerely,
Henry Mancuso
Attorney at Law
Benson Tillman Whitmore, LLP

"Well now, Mr. Mancuso, aren't you an eager beaver?"

I check the time, and laugh, imagining this lawyer sitting at his
computer on a Friday night, just waiting for people to respond to his

solicitous Facebook Messenger inquiries. But my laughter peters out quickly because it occurs to me that maybe he doesn't have anything else to occupy his time and attention.

Maybe he's lonely.

I shoot him a quick response that includes my email address and get back to work.

CHAPTER 14

Thursday, April 21
Henry

Still standing on my bed, I glance out the window and wonder if any of the condo residents across the river are watching me. One second, I'm watching a show on C-SPAN about the science and physics behind the conveniences of everyday life, and the next I'm reading a message from Ruth Bateman and jumping on my bed. Anthony is right. I am a nerdy lawyer.

Clutching my phone, I hop off my bed and retrieve the remote for my blinds from the drawer of my nightstand. As I hold down the button to close them, I scrutinize the mess I've made of my bed.

I'm straightening my sheets and comforter when my phone dings. Anxious to see if it's Ruth Bateman, I stub my toe, causing the nail to bend backward. But that doesn't stop me from pacing as I read the email that could set the Bucky's case into motion.

Hi again, Henry. (I hope it's okay if I call you that. Please feel free to call me Ruth.) My email address is ruthieb@gmail.com. Just so you're aware, I don't want to be involved with a lawsuit, nor do I want any sort of compensation from Bucky's. (I assume you don't do anything without the prospect of getting paid, so that's why I'm bringing this up.) All I want is for the texts to stop.

Have a good night and enjoy the rest of your weekend!
Ruth

"Okay," I whisper, as I make my way to my office. I have a habit of thinking out loud when I'm trying to solve a problem, and Ruth's comment about not wanting to be involved with a lawsuit has problem written all over it. "Maybe she'll change her mind when she sees how many others are receiving the texts . . ." I type as I talk. "Maybe she'll want to be more involved then."

I've gone over this case in my head dozens upon dozens of times, so I know exactly what the letter to Ruth should say. Within five minutes, I'm done, and the message is whizzing through cyberspace to her inbox.

Now, I play the waiting game. I kill time by cleaning my keyboard with short bursts of compressed air. Then I dust and straighten the items on my desk—a stapler, a statue of the Empire State Building (which serves as the perfect paperweight) from when my family drove to New York City when I was in eighth grade, a framed photo of my family from last Christmas, and a magnetic paperclip holder.

By the time eleven o'clock rolls around, I decide it's time to shut down my computer and head back to bed. Unlike me, Ruth Bateman must have better things to do on a Friday night than worry about unsolicited text messages from Bucky's Beans.

CHAPTER 15

Saturday, April 23
Ruth

"Good morning, Ruth. Your hair looks darling." Beverly leans in close enough that I get a whiff of the chai tea she's been drinking. "My, that's an interesting hair clip." She steps back, sipping from her Wixley Chiropractic travel mug, eyes smiling as she takes in the rest of my appearance.

"Thanks," I say with a smile. "I got it from my friend Sue's little girl, Eva."

The opaque jaw clip she's referring to, which has light pink unicorns etched into it, is in my hair because of a deteriorating charging cord that I've been meaning to replace for the past few weeks. My phone died in the middle of the night, which means no alarm went off this morning. Luckily, I woke myself up with ten minutes to spare before I had to be out the door. But in my mad dash to be on time to help Dr. Jackson and Beverly with setup, I threw my hair up as quickly as possible, hence the unicorn clip. I'm also wearing two different colored ballet flats, which Beverly has just noticed.

"Ruth, your shoes!" she exclaims.

"Oh, I know. My alarm didn't go off this morning, so I was in a hurry. But shhh," I say putting a finger to my lips. "If I own it, maybe other women will think wearing different colored shoes is a new thing." I tap a light gray satin flat out in front of me followed by a similar style in faded pink suede.

Beverly laughs. "I'm pretty sure you're the only person I know who could pull that fashion trend off with style, Ruth." She heads off toward the ballroom and calls over her shoulder, "One hour until show time."

That leaves me alone to set up the greeting area with a sign-in sheet, late registration forms, the handouts I put together on Thursday, and gift bags loaded with healthy goodies, supplement samples, and coupons for the family-owned nutrition store down the block from Wixley Chiropractic. I finish my job with about ten minutes to spare before check-in begins, so I take a seat and log into Facebook. I don't have any notifications, but I do see the post I've been anticipating for days. It's a photo of my former coworker, Elisha, and her new daughter, who was born in the middle of the night. I heart the post and congratulate her and her husband in the comments. I also ask her to let me know when she and the baby are ready for visitors. After marveling at the baby's tiny fingers clutching onto one of Elisha's fingers for a few more seconds, I check my email. I'm astonished to see that Henry Mancuso responded the night before, just minutes after I'd sent him my email address.

From: Henry Mancuso
To: Ruth Bateman
Date: Apr 22, 2016 at 10:25 PM

Good evening, Ms. Bateman.

Please see the attached letter regarding unsolicited text messages from Bucky's Beans. It outlines just a few key pieces of information we have compiled illustrating the company's disregard for TCPA regulations and details what your role would be if you agree to act as lead plaintiff in the lawsuit we hope to build. After you've had time to go over the information provided, please let me know if you are still willing to help with the case. Should you have any questions, do not hesitate to ask.

Best regards,
Henry J. Mancuso
Attorney at Law
hmancuso@bensontillmanwhitmore.com
350 E. Wisconsin Avenue, Suite 600
Milwaukee, Wisconsin 53202

Phone (414) 555-4242
Fax (414) 555-4241

I click to open the attached letter and quickly scan it. The fact that numerous FTC complaints have been filed against Bucky's seems significant and makes me more inclined to help, but I'm still not interested in suing. With less than five minutes before check-in for the workshop begins, I compose a quick reply to Henry letting him know that I'm willing to help by providing evidence to assist them with building their case. Surely the dozens of screenshots I have will help.

As I hit send, several guests approach the sign-in table, and I get to work checking them in. Two women set Bucky's Beans cups on the table in front of me as they fill out a few pieces of information. I can smell the combined scents of coffee and some herbal type of tea, and suddenly I feel bad.

Back when I was still involved with QuickForm, lawsuits were always a concern. Sure, we hired a good lawyer to handle all our waivers and signage for the various locations, but it was still impossible for Adam to not worry about something that could tarnish his dream. He was right to be worried, too, because a few frivolous suits cropped up each year. Interestingly, the only incident that occurred while I was still involved with the business that might have warranted a legitimate lawsuit was my own. I obviously didn't sue my own business, but we still suffered losses because my accident was a catalyst for the breakdown of our marriage. When I brought this very fact up to Adam, right before we signed the final divorce papers, he agreed but added that it also might have been a blessing in disguise for the business. Had others gotten injured due to the faulty weight bar collars, who knows what the monetary repercussions might have been? I didn't take offense to this revelation of his. After all, the process of Adam falling out of love with me and in love with all things QuickForm had already been complete for a long time.

"Earth to Ruuuuth." The sound of Stan Boyd's voice jogs me back to my check-in tasks.

"Oh, hi Stan," I say handing him a packet and a gift bag. "If you could move down to the next available spot and fill out a check-in form before you take a seat in the room that would be great. Just place your completed form in the pile at the end of the table."

"Sure thing, Ruth." He's about to leave but pauses. "You seem tired. I bet you wish you'd thought to use one of those Bucky's Beans discount codes, huh?" Laughing, he makes way for the next person in line.

For the next thirty minutes, I go into autopilot mode, seamlessly greeting and checking in one customer after another. But in the back of my mind, I wonder if maybe I should message the lawyer back to tell him I've changed my mind and don't want to be part of his case at all. As a former business owner, I'd hate to cause problems for Bucky's because of what might be an innocent glitch in their system. Besides, nothing will probably come of the lawsuit anyway, nothing other than people coming out of the woodwork with fake claims once word gets out that Henry Mancuso's law firm is taking the coffeehouse on.

When the timeframe for check-ins ends, I unlock my phone and navigate to Henry Mancuso's last email, which I just responded to. As I contemplate sending another message to back out of allowing Benson Tillman & Whitmore to use my screenshots, my Bucky's Perks text of the day comes through. Rolling my eyes, I shut my phone down so as not to be disturbed during the Wixleys' presentation.

CHAPTER 16

Saturday, April 23
Henry

"On your left!"

I glance behind me and reflexively hop out of the way when I see a biking twosome careening toward me. "Urgh," I mumble as I resume my bent-over position off to the side of the paved path overlooking Lake Michigan.

As sluggish as I feel, I'm glad I turned down Constance's invitation to work out with her this morning at QuickForm, but I should have been smarter than to think my usual Saturday morning run was a better idea. Normally I circle the trail I'm on a few times, logging approximately five miles in about forty minutes. However, forty minutes have passed, and I haven't even made it once around. I stand and decide to walk instead, chalking up my decreased motivation to a lack of sleep and the excessive amount of contemplating I've been doing lately.

Instead of following the path to where I can cross the street and make a beeline for the building my condo is in, I cut through some trees and end up in the square where the farmers' market is taking place. It will take me longer to get home, but I might as well meander to make up for the miles I won't be logging this morning.

Scattered among the fresh fruit and vegetable stands are vendors offering things like honey, flowers, homemade candles and lip balm, baked goods, quilts, and hand-knit sweaters and accessories. There are also food carts offering things like pastries, quiches, breakfast sandwiches, and burritos. I debate getting a feta and spinach quiche but then notice a Coffee Cave stand in the distance, and I don't have enough money with me for both.

I weave through the crowd, the Coffee Cave sign beckoning me. I grin, remembering all the times I studied at the company's one and only brick and mortar location, back when I was an undergrad. While my roommates partied, I studied. But I quickly learned that getting anything done while staying on campus was near impossible due to all the distractions, so I spent a couple weeks hopping from business to business, trying to find a place where I could focus. That's how I found Coffee Cave and its low-key atmosphere. They also offered free Wi-Fi and a student discount, and their coffee was much better than the likes of all the bigger, more commercialized coffeehouses like Bucky's, Caribou, and Starbucks.

As I take a sip of Coffee Cave's signature roast and turn to head for the sidewalk, my eyes are instantly drawn to the huge Bucky's Beans Coffee Roasters sign across the street. That's when my Apple watch pings, alerting me to a new email from Ruth Bateman.

From: Ruth Bateman
To: Henry Mancuso
Date: Apr 23, 2016 at 7:47 AM
Hi Mr. Mancuso,

Thanks for the information you sent last night. I'm shocked by the number of complaints you've found regarding the Bucky's Perks texts. Maybe this is why people are so ornery all the time. Perhaps they're tired of being spammed by Bucky's. Anyway, the texts continue to drive me bonkers, and the worst thing about it is I never signed up for the program!

To help with your case, I've attached several screenshots. The first is of my conversation with Bucky's via Facebook messenger. As you know, I continue to receive texts, despite the fact that my issue has been brought to the attention of their IT team. The second and third attachments prove that I've tried to unsubscribe with many different responses to the texts. I always get a reply that says: You are not opted in. The last three attachments are just examples of what the texts say. I have dozens more if you need them.

Whatever you can do to make these texts stop would be greatly appreciated. As a reminder, I do not wish to sue Bucky's, so hopefully the evidence I've provided here will be enough to help.

Good luck with the case!
Ruth Bateman

As I walk, I finish my coffee and contemplate my next move. When I get to the crosswalk that leads to my condo, I press the pedestrian button, toss my empty cup in a trash bin, and stew for a few more seconds over the conundrum I'm faced with. *Good luck with the case?* The only reason she would say that is if she thinks her role with this lawsuit is complete.

Suddenly, a thought perks me up.

If I can just get her on the phone, she'll agree to be the name on the suit. I know she will.

I have no idea where the thought came from, but something is telling me that Ruth Bateman is my plaintiff. When the signal to cross illuminates, I take off in a sprint, eager to view the screenshots she sent and to email her back to ask if she'd be willing to participate in a conference call with Whitmore and me. Maybe if I ignore the fact that she has not agreed to act as lead plaintiff, things will just fall into place.

~

From: Henry Mancuso
To: Ruth Bateman
Date: Apr 23, 2016 at 8:35 AM

Good morning, Ms. Bateman.

This is great material and exactly what we need. Thank you for your willingness to help!

Is there a time next week when you might be available for a conference call with myself and one of the partners at my firm? Mr. Whitmore is just as passionate about seeing this Bucky's Beans case through as I am, so I know he'd like to hear about your experience with the text messages and answer any questions you might have about our firm before we put together a formal complaint.

Best regards,
Henry J. Mancuso
Attorney at Law
hmancuso@bensontillmanwhitmore.com
350 E. Wisconsin Avenue, Suite 600
Milwaukee, Wisconsin 53202
Phone (414) 555-4242
Fax (414) 555-4241

After I hit send, I immediately think of a million different things I could have added to the email, but what's done is done. So now all I can do is wait.

And wait.

The last thing I do before I fall asleep is check for a response, and the first thing I do Sunday morning is the same.

It isn't until Sunday night when I'm in bed watching CNN that I finally hear back from Ruth Bateman.

From: Ruth Bateman
To: Henry Mancuso
Date: Apr 24, 2016 at 9:35 PM

Hi Henry,

I apologize for not getting back to you sooner. Sometimes I like to take a break from my phone on weekends. You should try it sometime. Or don't lawyers get weekends off? Just kidding. ;)

As for the conference call, unless it can take place after 6 p.m. Tuesday or Wednesday, the week ahead is pretty booked for me. I work for Wixley Chiropractic in Bay View, and we just hosted a workshop on cancer killers this weekend, so we have a schedule full of potential patients coming in for consultations and X-rays. (Consults are free this week if you're interested!) The only other day I might have time is on Friday, during my lunch break. Would any of those times work for you?

Ruth

When I finish reading, I crack a grin at her comment about lawyers and weekends. Then I scan her response a few more times. Potential clients don't usually crack jokes, and most don't use emojis either. Aside from her informality and inability to schedule the call during business hours before Friday, I feel positive about this email and imagine Whitmore will be pleased when I tell him about Ruth.

I click to respond, but then hesitate, her comment about me getting off social media striking a cord. I have been obsessing over this case lately. And a few weeks back it was a different case. Come to think of it, I'm always obsessing over one case or another.

I close my eyes and breathe deeply several times. Then I back out of the response window and silence my phone for the night. I've already told Constance several times this weekend that I'm just not feeling one hundred percent, so she should understand if I don't respond to a call or text from her.

CHAPTER 17

I turn into my old neighborhood shortly after five. This is my routine the third Monday of every month. I leave work an hour early, and head straight to my mom's house to pick her up for the monthly Parkinson's caregiver support group meeting at White Pines. Even though we're coming up on the five-year anniversary of my father's passing, we still attend the meetings to support those who supported us through the last several years of his life.

My mom exits my childhood home moments after I pull into her driveway. Even though she won't be meeting with a realtor to put the house on the market for another few weeks, my mind plays tricks on me, and I see a *For Sale* sign next to the messy Russian elm my mom always used to complain about. Every fall, our front yard would be littered with its tiny leaves, which are too small to be raked properly. During storms, branches of all sizes would inevitably end up on the walkway. My dad loved the tree, though, so my mom's wish to have it cut down was never granted. When my brother suggested it might be time to hire someone to remove it the fall after my dad died, all she said was, "We can't cut down your father's tree," and she hasn't said a word about how messy it is since.

"Hey, Mom," I say as she climbs into the passenger seat. She places her purse on the floor and situates an aluminum-foil covered casserole dish on her lap. "The tree's looking great. I love the flowers you planted around it."

She smiles. "Walter thought of that. He said it gives the house a little extra curb appeal."

"He's right," I say, mirroring her smile and glancing at the ring of flowers at the base of the tree one more time before pulling away from the curb. "So, how was your day?"

"Oh, you know, just a typical Monday. Walter and I had coffee on the deck and went for a walk. Then I volunteered at the library for a few hours before coming home to pack up a few boxes and make a treat for the meeting. Retired life is good. You?"

"Busy. The Wixley's cancer killers presentation on Saturday has drawn a lot of new clients. We're swamped with appointments this week. In fact, I felt guilty for leaving early today, but Beverly insisted I go."

"Oh, I just love her. You're fortunate to work for such wonderful people . . . and they're fortunate to have you working for them."

"Thanks, Mom."

My phone vibrates, but I ignore it since I'm driving. My mom, on the other hand, leans over to sneak a peek.

"You're still getting those texts?"

"Let me guess . . . Is it from Bucky's?" I ask, my eyes focused on the yellow light and slowing cars in front of me.

"Yep."

"Unfortunately, yes, but I think I found someone who can help me with that."

"Oh yeah? Who?" she asks, prompting me to fill her in on Henry Mancuso and all of his messages. As I'm telling her, it occurs to me that I might be trading in never-ending texts from Bucky's for constant messages from Henry. This makes me giggle.

"What's so funny, Ruthie? Matters of the law aren't something to laugh about. Are you sure this lawyer, this Henry Mancuso, is legit? You didn't give him your social security number, did you?"

"No," I say with a brief chuckle. "Besides, why would that be a big deal? That's what my student ID was when I was in college, so I'm sure if someone was going to steal my social security number it would have happened over a decade ago."

"I'm pretty sure identity thieves are much more cunning these days, Ruth," she says, producing a chuckle of her own. "So, what do you have to do to help this lawyer? And did he say whether a company has ever been sued for sending too many text messages before?"

"Well, I've already sent him screenshots of some of the texts and of the messages between Bucky's and me, but other than that, I told him I don't really want to be involved."

"What did he say to that?"

"Uhh . . ." Thinking for a moment, I realize he didn't say anything in direct response to that. "He asked if I can participate in a conference call with one of the bosses at the firm. Probably to ask me a few questions, I assume."

"What's the name of the firm?"

"Benson Tillmore . . . or Benson Whitmore. Something like that."

She doesn't respond but instead focuses on her phone, which is unlike my mom, who doesn't even use Google Maps and confuses the names of all the social media platforms, often calling them things like Facechat or Snapbook. Not wanting to invade her privacy, I keep my eyes on the road and wait for her to finish whatever she's doing. Two stoplights later, she says, "Ohhhhh," prompting me to side-eye her quizzically. "Your lawyer is quite handsome."

"What? What are you looking at? Oh, and he's not technically my—"

"I Googled his law firm. It's Benson Tillman & Whitmore, by the way."

"But what are you . . . how do you know what he looks like?" I ask, looking back and forth from my mom to the road.

"Because they provide profile pages for all their lawyers. See? Here he is." She flashes her phone at me, barely letting me get a look. "He has a Facebook account too, you know. I can't believe you didn't look him up, Ruthie. He could have been a scammer!" I'm beginning to wonder if Mr. Walter has been teaching my mom a thing or two about technology. "*My, my,*" she mumbles, clearly impressed. "He graduated from Marquette Law School, Summa cum laude. I don't know exactly what that means, but I bet it means he was a good student."

"Wow. Impressive," I say in a nonchalant voice, not wanting to encourage her to suggest I date the lawyer. I turn into the White Pines parking lot. "Okay, we're here. Time to stop stalking Henry."

She goes silent, and I can feel her eyes on me as I maneuver into a spot.

"You ready?" I ask, looking over at her as soon as I put the car in park.

"How long have you been on a first name basis with this lawyer who isn't technically your lawyer? Is there something you're not telling me?"

"No," I say laughing. "Of course not! That's just what I call him. We're both adults, and like I said, he's not my lawyer."

"The same can be said for Walter, yet you still tack Mr. in front of his name."

"Habit, Mom. I'm trying," I assure her.

She widens her gaze and raises her eyebrows a hair, as though she's just had an epiphany. "Maybe you could ask him on a date."

"Who?" I play dumb.

"The lawyer!"

"What? Why would you say such a thing? Come on," I say, reaching into the back seat to retrieve the framed sunflower puzzle. "Let's get going so we're not late."

"That's pretty, Ruthie," my mom says as we exit the car. Then she continues talking about her harebrained idea as we walk to the front door of the nursing home. "You're always saying you don't know where to find people to date. Well, here you go. This lawyer found you."

"Uh, yeah . . . but it's not like he found me on a dating site. Besides, can you see me dating a lawyer? Something tells me we might not have a lot in common." I raise my arms and glance down at my comfy, colorful fitness attire.

On the outside, I might be poo-pooing her suggestions, but on the inside, I'm wondering what Henry's picture on the law firm's website looks like. Sure, I've seen his profile picture on Facebook, but it was blurry.

"Of course, I can."

I sigh, the fingers of my free hand wrapped around the door handle. "Okay, so you have to promise you won't say anything else about the lawyer after we walk through these doors."

She purses her lips innocently.

"Mom?"

"Fine."

~

My mom and I have been attending this support group together for five years, so most of the faces are familiar, but there are always a few new ones too. The first thing we do when we enter the meeting area is greet the people we know and introduce ourselves to those who are new to us. Then I lean the framed puzzle against a wall for the time being, and my mom deposits her brownies on the goody table for the social hour to follow. After that, we take two empty seats next to our friends, Betty and Dave Collinson, who started waving as soon as they saw us approaching the seating area. My mom hugs Mrs. Collinson, after she slides in next to her, and I greet the couple with a friendly smile and wave.

When the meeting begins, and the chatter of the crowd dies down, I glance over at Mr. Collinson's shaking hands and watch as Mrs. Collinson reaches over and folds her hands around them. Then she leans over and gives him a peck on the cheek. The gesture brings tears to my eyes and causes my eardrums to throb, making it difficult for me to focus on what the guest speaker is saying about the non-motor symptoms of Parkinson's disease.

When my mom and dad first started attending these meetings nearly a decade ago, they used to just sit quietly and blend into the background during meetings. Then they'd depart with little more than a smile or nod to anyone who made eye contact. I was too busy with the startup of QuickForm at the time, so I only know how close my mom was to holing herself up in the house with my dad and never venturing into public again based on the late-night phone calls I used to receive from her. She was certain that no amount of moral support was ever going to help with the pain, anger, and guilt she was feeling every day. Pain over watching the love of her life lose his ability to take care of himself, anger because she just didn't think it was fair, and guilt because some days she just didn't want to get out of bed to help. But then she met Betty, who showed up at the house with a batch of her famous rhubarb crumb cake after my mom and dad missed two meetings in a row. My mom called me later that night, bawling her eyes out, to tell me that it wasn't just my dad who needed help and support from Tyler and me; it was her too. That was how Betty helped her. She made my mom understand that it was okay for her to ask for help without feeling weak or guilty and that it was normal and more than okay for her to have a shitty day once in a while. No one can care for a loved one who's reached the later stages of Parkinson's disease alone. Coincidentally, my accident occurred shortly after Betty's visit that night, so it couldn't have been timed more perfectly. It wasn't just my dad who my mom and this support group helped pull through some dark days.

Near the end of the guest speaker's presentation, my phone pings, garnering a stern look from my mom.

"Sorry," I whisper, as I remove it from my bag and get a glimpse of a name: Henry Mancuso. I'm tempted to see what he has to say, but I don't want to be rude to the speaker or any of the other attendees, so I silence my phone and return it to my bag.

When the meeting ends, chatter throughout the room commences as everyone moves to the tables displaying goodies and refreshments. My mom pours herself a cup of coffee, and I open Henry's message.

From: Henry Mancuso
To: Ruth Bateman
Date: Apr 25, 2016 at 5:15 PM

Good afternoon, Ms. Bateman.

Now it's my turn to apologize for the delayed response. Friday will work just fine for the conference call. We have you penciled in at noon, and it shouldn't take much longer than ten minutes. Is that okay? Or is there another time that would be more ideal for you?

As for weekends . . . Wait, what are weekends? Kidding.

Best regards,
Henry J. Mancuso
Attorney at Law

hmancuso@bensontillmanwhitmore.com
350 E. Wisconsin Avenue, Suite 600
Milwaukee, Wisconsin 53202
Phone (414) 555-4242
Fax (414) 555-4241

Surprise, surprise. Henry Mancuso made a joke.

"Is that an email from your lawyer?" My mom asks, leaning in to view my phone screen.

"Mom," I whisper, pulling my phone close to my chest.

She covers her mouth, apologetic for her blunder, but it's too late. Everyone around us heard the question and quiets, waiting for my response.

"Your lawyer?" Betty asks. Dave cocks his head, clearly interested in my answer.

"Oh," I say dropping my phone into my bag. "He's not actually *my* lawyer."

"Why did he email you then, Ruth? I thought all the legal junk with that ex-husband of yours and your quick workout business was finished."

I hesitate, glancing around the small group of friends standing in front of us. Most are coffee drinkers, but I have no idea if any of them are Bucky's customers. I'd hate to offend anyone by admitting that I might agree to be part of a lawsuit against the company.

"Go on. Tell them, Ruthie," my mom urges as she goes around offering brownies and napkins to people. She loves a small dose of drama as much as anyone.

"Okay, you've all heard of Bucky's Beans Coffee Roasters, right?" Nods and sips of coffee from Styrofoam cups all around. "Well, they have this program called Bucky's Perks, and if you sign up for it, you get discount codes texted to your phone. So, I've been getting these texts every day for almost two months now. But the problem is I never enrolled in the Perks program." I pause, opening the floor for questions, but all I get is more nods. And several people fall into other conversations or peruse the rest of the goodies at the table. So, I continue. "Anyway, I tried to unsubscribe from the texts in various ways, but nothing has worked. So, I finally posted on Bucky's Facebook page, hoping someone at the corporate office could help me, but that was last week and I'm still getting the texts. Meanwhile, I've been contacted by a lawyer who's putting together a lawsuit against Bucky's for being in violation of some federal consumer protection act."

"This lawyer, how did he find you?" Karl May, a man who'd become a close friend of my father asks. The two of them used to attend group therapy sessions together when my dad was still mobile.

"Facebook. He saw my post when he was searching for complaints about the Perks program."

Karl nods, satisfied with my answer, but his daughter, Rita, has a different reaction.

"I don't know, Ruth. Sounds fishy to me. How do you know this guy isn't a scammer?"

"That's exactly what I said," my mom nods in agreement with Rita as she looks around the circle, "but look at this." She steps forward and shoves her phone in Rita's face. Betty and another woman named Ruby Jones nose their way in front of the screen too.

"Mom, what are you showing them?" I ask, craning my neck to sneak a peek. But my mom and the other women are now hovered over the phone, so my only option is to wait patiently next to the men who've struck up a conversation. When I hear someone say the word *handsome*, I know exactly what they're looking at. "Mom! Are you showing them Henry Mancuso's picture?"

"Oh, Ruthie, he *is a* looker!" Ruby says, dragging her left foot as she backs out of the tight-knit gaggle of women.

I squeeze into the space she left behind. Sure enough, Henry's photo and bio on the law firm's website are displayed on my mom's screen.

"And it says here he's a runner!" Betty only looks over at me briefly before turning her attention back to the profile.

"I told her she should ask him out. After all, it isn't every day that a handsome, intelligent man shows up on your doorstep." She gives my upper arm a squeeze and says, "Figuratively speaking, of course."

"Yep, your mom is right," Rita says craning her neck to see Karl. "Don't you agree, Dad? Ruth should ask the lawyer on a date, right?"

I sigh, not even bothering to pay attention to Karl's response. "Ladies, if I do end up agreeing to work with Mr. Handsome there," I gesture toward my mom's phone, "then I certainly don't want to mix business with pleasure."

"Ladies, ladies," Dave says, harnessing the attention of everyone within earshot. "You're missing the point here. Based on what Ruth said, it sounds like this guy is putting together a class-action lawsuit. Ruth, are you sure you want to be part of something like that? Over text messages? We constantly receive unsolicited phone calls from telemarketers, and no matter how many times I ask them to remove our number, they still call! Nothing will come of being part of this except lost time that you spend helping this guy put together his case."

My only concern up to this point had been that I don't want to harm business for Bucky's, but now, Dave has me wondering if I'm blowing the texts out of proportion. After all, Bucky's IT department will most likely solve the issue in due time.

"Maybe if you didn't harass the poor people who call our house they'd be more inclined to remove our number?" Betty reclaims her spot next to Dave, and my mom and Rita rejoin the circle as well.

"I agree with Dave. All those class actions lawsuit lawyers are just a bunch of gold diggers who'll sue for the most ridiculous things," Karl adds. "I'd advise against signing anything, Ruth." He grabs a coffee carafe off the refreshment table. "Does anyone need a refill?" His hand shakes, prompting Rita to rush over and take it from him.

"Here, let me do that, Dad." As she tops off everyone's coffee, Ruby returns with her Aunt Cecily in tow.

"I was just filling my aunt in on this Bucky's Beans situation, Ruth." Shielding her mouth from Cecily, she adds, "She isn't too keen on big chain coffeehouses."

"Why are you doing that, Ruby? I'm right here!" Cecily looks right at me. "So, you're going to sue Bucky's Beans, huh?"

Grinning and amused, I shrug. "I'm not sure yet."

"Well, they should be sued for making such terrible coffee."

"Aunt Cece," Ruby says with a chuckle, "They can't be sued because of how their coffee tastes. I told you, they won't stop texting her, and it sounds like that might break some consumer protection law."

Ignoring her niece, Cecily continues as she makes pointed eye contact with all the older folks in the bunch. "Whatever happened to a nice, old fashioned cup of coffee? Black, with cream, or with sugar—none of this whipped mocha latte espresso nonsense."

"You're right, Cecily," Dave says with conviction. "Their menu is a bunch of horse hockey!"

"And their prices are outrageous." My mom chimes in.

"Highway robbery," Karl says, nodding.

As the discussion over class action lawsuits and coffee preferences continues, I quietly excuse myself to use the bathroom. I'd also like to respond to Henry's email but don't want anyone looking over my shoulder. I lean against the wall just outside the bathroom and compose a response. But I don't send it right away.

From: Ruth Bateman
To: Henry Mancuso
Date: Apr 25, 2016 at 6:20 PM

Hiya Henry,

Friday at noon it is. Please call me on my cell phone. 414-555-2122

Ruth

I respect Dave and Karl, so the things they said have me contemplating again if I should tell Henry I've changed my mind. Could he really be a gold-digging lawyer? And if this whole lawsuit is legit, would anything even come of it? Or would it be a waste of time like Dave said? Also, everyone in the room seemed to be uninterested in Bucky's coffee, but what about the company's loyal customers? I imagine there would be people who will think it's ridiculous that anyone would sue such a reputable company over text messages. I know I've rolled my eyes at more than a few class action lawsuits, but I always thought the plaintiffs sought out their attorneys; I never imagined it could have been the other way around.

I scroll down to reread Henry's email. Then deciding to go through with the conference call, I click send. Maybe hearing what he and his boss have to say will sway me toward a definitive decision.

Moments later, as I'm locking the door of a bathroom stall, my phone pings. It's Henry again.

From: Henry Mancuso
To: Ruth Bateman
Date: Apr 25, 2016 at 6:23 PM

Ms. Bateman,

That's great to hear. I look forward to speaking with you.

If anything should change with your schedule and you think you might be available at any other time during the day this week, please feel free to call us!

Best regards,
Henry J. Mancuso
Attorney at Law
hmancuso@bensontillmanwhitmore.com
350 E. Wisconsin Avenue, Suite 600
Milwaukee, Wisconsin 53202
Phone (414) 555-4242
Fax (414) 555-4241

"Wow. That was quick," I say as I tap out the unnecessary response and wonder if he's as attentive with someone he's dating as he is with potential clients.

CHAPTER 18

Monday, April 25
Henry

I click to send my final email of the day to Ruth Bateman then rub my hands together briskly as I survey my desk. Normally, I'd be in a mad dash to eliminate the clutter, but today was a phenomenal day, so instead I whistle Mozart's "String Serenade No. 13" as I take my time straightening and sorting. Not only has Ruth just confirmed our conference call, but I was also able to make some serious headway on the Memory Hub and DigiScan cases. We won our discovery motion for the Memory Hub case, and after today's DigiScan mediation, I think we may have the framework of a settlement agreement in place.

Movement on my computer screen causes me to look up and scan the details of an email that has just come through. The sender is Ruth Bateman, and the subject line says: *Wow. That was quick.* Smiling, I click the message only to find my last email at the top because she hasn't added anything new to the conversation.

"Hey, you," Constance says as she breezes in, the click-clack of her heels echoing through my office. "What are you smiling about over here?" She rounds my desk and gives my shoulders a squeeze.

"Oh . . ." I say, backing out of Ruth's email, "it's just this response I got from a client."

She leans in closer to the screen to get a closer look at my inbox. "Oh? Was it the one from Ruth Bateman?"

"Yep." I stand and make quick work of clearing off my desk.

"Aren't you getting a little ahead of yourself?" She leans against my desk and folds her arms.

"What do you mean?"

"I think you meant to say *potential* client, because she technically isn't our client yet."

I pause what I'm doing and shrug. "Well, she will be as of Friday."

Constance laughs. "So optimistic. I love that about you." She wrinkles her nose at me and picks up the Mount Rushmore statue on my desk. "You know I'm only playing devil's advocate. My uncle said the same thing today—that you'd finally found your plaintiff for the Bucky's case. He also said your future here is shaping up to be a bright one. Shall we have dinner tonight to celebrate a great start to the work week?"

Despite several invitations from her, I haven't spent time with Constance outside of work since Anthony's drunken appearance at my condo two weekends ago. This is partly because I've been feeling rundown, but also because I really don't want to lead her on, even if she says she's fine with keeping things casual. I value her friendship, though, so I owe her complete honesty.

"Constance, you know how much I enjoy doing things with you, right?"

"Yeah, of course. I enjoy doing things with you, too." She gives my forearm a little rub.

"I just need to make sure we're still on the same page as far as—"

"My God, Henry." She sighs. "How many times do I need to tell you we're good?"

"Sorry. I'm like a broken record sometimes, aren't I?"

"Yes, yes you are," she says, nodding emphatically. "So, are we grabbing a bite to eat?"

"Only if you're buying."

"Yay!" She hops upright and places my statue in the wrong spot, causing me to reflexively move it to where it belongs. Constance scrunches her face and laughs. "Geez, Henry."

"What?"

"Nothing. I just find it amusing the way you need to have your things just so."

I shrug and place the last loose document on my desk where it belongs.

"We need to get you a drink, so you can loosen up. I'll get my things. Meet you in the lobby?"

"Ten-four. Lobby."

CHAPTER 19

Friday, April 29
Ruth

The courtyard behind the chiropractic office is one of my favorite places. Even though it abuts an alley, Beverly has created a zen-like atmosphere complete with a fountain, benches, hummingbird feeders, and a gorgeous display of wildflowers, making it so cozy you barely notice when cars drive by.

My conference call with Henry and his boss is supposed to begin any minute, and I'm sitting on the same bench I sat on when Beverly interviewed me two years ago, the day before my final divorce hearing. I remember that day like it was yesterday.

I'd arrived an hour early for my interview, and had planned to ride my bike around the neighborhood, but when I stopped by Wixley Chiropractic so I'd know where it was, the garden drew me in. When Beverly pulled up in her Honda Pilot, I thought she was either a client of the Wixleys or another interviewee who'd arrived early and wanted to enjoy the garden as well. We got to talking, and after a few minutes she revealed her identity. Before I knew it, I was crying on her shoulder.

I hadn't cried since my father died, not even when the bones in my ankle and my Achilles tendon were damaged by a load of free-weights. Looking back, I think it might have been because part of me was relieved that I would have to take a break from all things related to QuickForm. Even throughout the chain of events that followed—my weight gain, my inability to be the business partner and supportive wife Adam was used to, Adam's affair—I didn't cry. The pain pills I'd become dependent on probably had a lot to do with my lack of emotion, but through therapy, I eventually realized how unhappy I was since my life with Adam had become all about the growth of our business. There really wasn't even an "us" anymore because we'd become business partners first and foremost. I was the one who took care of the day-to-day operations—the accounting, the employees, calls from franchisees—all while he socialized and traveled around recruiting new investors to grow the franchise. After my injury, when I needed him most, it became clear that our relationship as husband and wife, best friends, and lovers was over. I didn't tell Beverly any of this, though.

What I did tell her was that I was about to be newly divorced and looking for a fresh start. And when she asked why on earth I wanted to work for them when I could do so much more with my degree in nutrition, exercise, and health science, it hit me that I could never get back on the career path I'd been so in love with because of how intricately intertwined it had been with the demise of my marriage. That's when the unexpected flood of tears started.

Beverly hired me on the spot after asking one last question. *When can you start?*

My phone rings, pulling me from my thoughts.

"Hello?"

"Ms. Bateman? It's Henry Mancuso. How are you today?"

For some reason I expected him to speak quickly, maybe even jittery, like a used car salesman. Instead, his voice is smooth, deep, and measured. Friendly, but measured. Me, on the other hand . . .

"I'm fine, great. It's a beautiful day today. How about yourself?"

"I'm fine, as well. Thank you for asking. Just so you're aware, Mr. Whitmore is on the line with us."

"Hello, Ms. Bateman. Thank you for taking our call. It's a pleasure to meet you, so to speak," Mr. Whitmore says with a boisterous chuckle. He sounds like a televangelist, friendly and exuberant with a twinge of *please give me your money.*

"Nice to meet you too . . . both of you."

"If it's okay with you, Ms. Bateman," Henry continues, "I'd like to start with a recap of our communications up to this point."

"Sure, have at it," I say, standing to walk around the garden while we talk. I nod periodically as Henry describes how he came across my post on Bucky's Facebook page and how I contacted him via Facebook messenger, and then goes on to describe the progression of our email communications. He forgets to mention that he was the one who initially contacted me on Facebook, but I don't bring it up since the detail seems insignificant by the time he finishes.

". . . So, based on these screenshots Ruth sent, I believe we'd have a strong chance of making sure these text messages stop and seeing to it that Bucky's changes their text marketing system. That is, if she agrees to serve as the lead plaintiff of this case."

"Mm-hmm, yes, I agree." Whitmore's voice is subdued now, as if he's deep in thought. But for all I know, he could be reading a magazine, and this call is staged. "Ms. Bateman, you would be helping scores of individuals like yourself who've been receiving the same intrusive texts. And you'd be heading up a lawsuit that could set a compliance precedent in today's day and age of automated telephone marketing." He stops talking, but I'm busy processing what they're asking of me, so there's a brief silence.

"Ruth, do you have any questions?" Hearing Henry say my first name takes me by surprise. I wonder if it's a tactic to get me to warm up to the idea of helping him.

I clear my throat. "Would this hurt Bucky's Beans? I mean financially. Would it mar their reputation? Because I don't want to hurt anyone's business." Henry starts to respond, but suddenly other potential outcomes occur to me. "Would I be seen as a troublemaker and become a victim of cyberbullying? Could Bucky's Beans ban me from their stores? Not that I drink their coffee, but I do like having the option to purchase a cup of tea once in a while. I mean, they are everywhere . . ."

"Um, let's see . . ." Now it's Henry's turn to process. "No, I don't believe this case would hurt Bucky's Beans all that much financially. As for marring the company's reputation, cases like this don't tend to get a lot of media coverage. Law websites and those that report court news would most likely be the only places anyone would hear about it, and they'd have to search for it. So, no, I don't think it would do much to mar their reputation either. Though, I think they're actually doing that to themselves by utilizing a defective text marketing system. At one point, I thought there could be a chance they were unaware of the unsolicited texts their system has been sending, but after all the complaints I've found, I just don't believe that's possible."

"So, you're saying Bucky's is aware that they're sending texts to people who never signed up for the Perks program?"

"Exactly. Based on the sheer number of complaints I've seen, they have to know."

"Okay. And my other questions?"

"Right," Henry continues. "Would you be considered a troublemaker, and could they ban you? Umm, I can't say for sure, but I don't believe anyone would call you a troublemaker, and it would be illegal for Bucky's Beans to ban you from their stores."

"Oh," I say, suddenly feeling silly for even asking such a question.

"I'd like to echo Mr. Mancuso's responses, Ms. Bateman. You'd be helping a lot of people, and Bucky's probably wouldn't even blink at any ramification they may suffer. That's the nature of big businesses. If they don't obey the laws in favor of making money, they can't really complain if they get caught. And quite frankly, this is one of the worst cases of a company blatantly disregarding TCPA regulations I've ever seen."

"So, what do you think, Ruth?" Henry asks. "Are you willing to help us with the case?"

"I don't know," I say with a sigh. "Why hasn't anyone else agreed to help?"

"To be honest, most people brush me off when I contact them. I'm talking for any case I've ever been involved with. People just don't like to be bothered. They only want to complain and be heard, and then they're done. There are some who've considered helping, but ultimately, they end up saying they don't have time; they'll just change their phone number and be done with it. And then there are always a few who are professionals that troll company Facebook pages with frivolous complaints, just hoping some dirty lawyer will contact them."

"Not that we're dirty lawyers," Whitmore interjects.

"No. No, of course not," Henry chuckles. "We're legit, Ruth. We only pursue legitimate cases to serve the best interest of the public."

"Thanks for clarifying. I was about to hang up on you," I say, laughing.

"One last point, Ruth, and then maybe you need a day or two to think things over. I don't know what kind of service plan you have, but there are some people who don't have unlimited data plans, and some of those people are elderly and only have phones so they can talk to their grandchildren or make emergency calls. So, it isn't just a matter of receiving some annoying texts for them; it's costing them money they may not have. You'd really be doing these individuals a great service."

I'm no idiot. This sounds a lot like a Hail Mary speech, just in case I'm close to bailing on them. But there's something about Henry's voice that flips a switch in me, and I know I want to help. "What exactly do you need me to do?"

A car drives by, but I think I hear Henry breathe a sigh of relief before he says, "All we need at this point is for you to sign a formal agreement stating that you've agreed to hire our firm to represent you individually and as a potential representative of a class of similarly situated individuals."

"Okay. You've convinced me. Go ahead and send the form."

CHAPTER 20

Friday, April 29
Henry

"Well done, Henry, well done." Mr. Whitmore clutches my shoulder in one hand and shakes my hand with the other. Then he retreats to his ergonomic leather desk chair.

"Thank you, Bob. I'll be out of your hair now," I say, heading for the door.

"Oh, one more thing, Henry."

"Yes?" I ask, pausing in the doorway.

"Have you done some research on Ms. Bateman? You know, just to be certain we don't run into any snags?"

"Of course," I say, nodding and moving a few feet back into his office. I consider telling him that we have a mutual friend on Facebook but decide the connection is irrelevant. "As far as I can tell, her Internet presence is minimal at best. Web crawlers didn't return much on her."

"Well, that'll change," he says, nodding and tinkering around on his computer.

Indeed, it will. When I file the complaint against Bucky's next week, news of the lawsuit will spread like wildfire in the legal community. Then Google spiders will be all over Ruth's name for the duration of the case.

"Let's just hope she isn't prone to Googling herself." Otherwise I might have some damage-control to do, since some of the articles and corresponding comments are bound to be uninformed rubbish.

Mr. Whitmore shrugs, still focused on his computer screen. "It'll be too late for her to back out by then."

"Yeah," I say, running my fingers through my hair.

"Well," he says, smiling at me and tapping his hand once firmly on his desk, "Best send that engagement letter off to our new client ASAP."

~

I close the door to my office so as not to be disturbed while I type up Ruth's engagement letter. We have a standard template which simply requires a few pertinent details to be added, so this document won't take long to complete.

From: Henry Mancuso
To: Ruth Bateman
Date: Apr 29, 2016 at 12:44 PM

Hi Ruth,

Thank you for taking the time to speak with us.

Attached you will find the formal agreement which gives us permission to represent you and the class in a lawsuit against Bucky's Beans Coffee Roasters for the violation of the federal Telephone Consumer Protection Act (the "TCPA Litigation"). Please look over everything before signing and return it to me at your earliest convenience.

Don't hesitate to call if you have any questions!

Best regards,
Henry J. Mancuso
hmancuso@bensontillmanwhitmore.com
350 E. Wisconsin Avenue, Suite 600
Milwaukee, Wisconsin 53202
Phone (414) 555-4242
Fax (414) 555-4241

Attached - Formal Agreement re: Bucky's Beans Coffee Roasters Litigation

I scan the document for typos—top to bottom, bottom to top—then I email it to Ruth.

My next task while I wait for the signed agreement is to draft the class action complaint, which will be filed with the court and served on Bucky's, signifying the commencement of the lawsuit. Unlike the engagement letter, this document will take much longer to complete, even though I'll be creating it by making changes to an old complaint from a previous case.

Before I begin, I lean back in my chair and close my eyes to mentally go over all the details. When the conference call comes to mind, I think about Ruth Bateman's voice, which has a unique rasp to it. It's both charming and mesmerizing. She seems a bit goofy, too, just the sort of person I'd expect to inquire whether she'll be banned from a business because she's suing it. I almost laughed out loud when she asked that question.

My eyes snap open. Why am I thinking these things about her?

I sit up nice and tall and pull my chair in closer to my desk. Then I begin editing the complaint template that's up on my screen.

RUTH BATEMAN, on behalf of herself and all others similarly situated, Plaintiff, v. BUCKY'S BEANS COFFEE ROASTERS, Defendant . . .

CLASS ACTION COMPLAINT

Ruth Bateman, on behalf of herself and all others similarly situated, complains and alleges as follows based on personal knowledge as to herself, on the investigation of her counsel and the advice and consultation of certain third-party agents as to technical matters, and on information and belief as to all other matters:

I.
NATURE OF ACTION

1. Plaintiff brings this action for legal and equitable remedies resulting from the illegal actions of Bucky's Beans Coffee Roasters in negligently, knowingly, and/or willfully transmitting SMS text messages en masse to

Plaintiff's cellular telephone and the cellular telephones of thousands of other individuals across the country, without prior express written consent within the meaning of the Telephone Consumer Protection Act, 47 U.S.C. § 227 ("TCPA").

An unexpected yawn causes me to pause for a stretch. That's when my inbox pings. *Yes!* Ruth has returned the signed agreement. I send off a reply right away.

From: Henry Mancuso
To: Ruth Bateman
Date: Apr 29, 2016 at 1:15 PM

Hi Ruth,

Thank you for signing and returning the agreement so promptly. I'm putting together the formal complaint right now, and I just have a couple more questions.

Could you briefly describe the telephone call you had with the Bucky's employee regarding the texts? I can't remember exactly what you said about that conversation. Also, how many total messages would you estimate you've received since March? Would it be possible for you to take screenshots of your phone records dating back to when the Bucky's Beans texts began?

I hope to finish the complaint over the weekend for your review on Monday.

Thanks again, Ruth. Have a nice weekend.

Best regards,
Henry J. Mancuso
Attorney at Law
hmancuso@bensontillmanwhitmore.com
350 E. Wisconsin Avenue, Suite 600
Milwaukee, Wisconsin 53202

Phone (414) 555-4242
Fax (414) 555-4241

~

"Henryyyyy," Constance throws an arm over my shoulder. Grinning, I abandon my phone screen to look at her, our faces only inches apart. "You're so quiet tonight, and you've barely touched your Fat Tire. I thought it was your favorite."

"It is . . . I'm just not in the mood. I'd like to go for a run tomorrow morning." We're at a pub and grill with a few of Constance's friends and some of our coworkers. An uproarious bout of laughter diverts her attention for a moment before she turns back to me.

"I'd love to go for a run!"

I check the time on my phone and then turn the screen to her. "You're half in the bag, and it's nearly midnight," I say with a chuckle. "Are you sure you'll be up for that?"

"I'll be fine," she says, waving me off before she sips the last few drops of her extra dirty martini.

"You ready to go?" I ask, eyeing her empty glass on the table. The only reason I stuck around this long was to give her a ride home.

"Is that an invitation?" She raises a seductive eyebrow at me and walks her fingers up my thigh.

"Constance," I say, giving her hand a gentle squeeze before placing it in her own lap, "what about our conversation the other night? I thought we agreed to go the friends-only route for a while. You know . . . to see if either of us ends up wanting more."

"I want more now, Henry." She returns her hand to my thigh.

"That's because you're tipsy," I say, removing her hand again.

"Maybe, maybe not," she says, teasing.

I would want more right now too if I'd had as many drinks as she has. That's how things progressed beyond friendship between us in the first place. Alcohol consumption turns Constance into a blazing bundle of hormones when we're together. And what can I say? I was weak. But since the serious conversation we had when we went to dinner on

Monday night, things between us have been pleasantly chummy. Constance had mentioned her sister's upcoming baby shower and the way her mother has been pressuring her to commit to a steady relationship, and at first, I wondered if she was about to fess up to desiring more than our 'friends with benefits' setup, but then she surprised me by suggesting maybe we should eliminate sex from our relationship because she thinks she might be ready for something more. Scratch surprised; I was shocked. But then when we ordered a dessert to share, she tried to feed me a bite from her spoon. That got me wondering if maybe her suggestion to go back to being friends (minus the benefits) was a ploy to see how I'd react. The suspicion has faded throughout the week, but now I'm starting to wonder again if we've ever really been on the same page or if maybe we've been interpreting the same page differently all along. Or maybe I've turned to a new page, to the part where I actually do want more than casual sex, but just not with Constance.

"Hey, what are you two whispering about over there?" Constance's friend Tara asks, causing all eyes to turn our way.

"I'm sure they're just trying to decide whose place to sleep at tonight," Don Barron, who works in the accounting department at our firm, ribs. Like most people we work with, he suspects that Constance and I have spent time together behind closed doors—of the bedroom variety, that is. But we never came out and confirmed anything to anyone.

As everyone laughs at Don's joke, my phone pings notifying me of a new email. I unlock the screen, hopeful that it's the information I'd asked Ruth for this afternoon, because I'd really like to polish off the formal complaint for the Bucky's case this weekend.

"Henry," Constance says, her coy laugh tapering off, "why don't you just go? All you've been doing is checking your phone all night anyway. I can get a ride from someone else."

"Are you sure?"

"Yeah, Tara can drive me. Or Don even." She gives me a pressing stare, rekindling my suspicion about her 'let's go back to being just friends' idea.

I decide to assume positive intent and take her suggestion.

"Sounds good. Text me in the morning if you'd like to join me on my run. I'm thinking around eight."

"Yeah, sure. Sounds good, Henry," she mumbles as I stand and wave goodbye to everyone.

CHAPTER 21

Saturday, April 30
Ruth

I step out onto my front porch, pulling the door closed behind me. Early morning rays of sunlight splay across my front lawn, causing the dew-covered grass to shimmer. I enjoy the beautiful sight only for a moment before Winston notices me and starts yipping. It's his *hey, come say hi to me* bark in lieu of the ferocious growl he emits when strangers walk by.

"Good morning, Winston," I say as I approach the fence where his shiny black nose is poking through. I reach my hand over and he jumps up, tail wagging a mile a minute, so I can scratch the top of his head. The fence, like the grass, is moist with dew, so the sleeve of my fuchsia pullover becomes damp. "See you later, little guy."

I turn and make my way across the walkway that wraps from the front of my house along the side to the garage out back. As I round the northeast corner of my house where a cluster of daylilies are emerging, I pull my phone from my pocket to check my email. I haven't checked it since right before my conference call with the lawyers, so I'm certain I have some catching up to do.

A quick glance reveals about a dozen new emails: a Chase credit card statement, several notifications from Amazon, a newsletter from my mortgage lender, the latest Roadtrippers blog post, a survey from my dentist, a few messages that look like spam, and a message marked urgent from Henry Mancuso.

I delete the spammy-looking ones without opening them and then read the one from Henry.

. . . Could you briefly describe the telephone call you had with the Bucky's employee regarding the texts? I can't remember exactly what you said about that conversation. Also, how many total messages would you estimate you've received since March? Would it be possible for you to take screenshots of your phone records dating back to when the Bucky's Beans texts began? . . .

Henry Mancuso sure does have an interesting perspective on what constitutes as an urgent email. I click the arrow to respond.

From: Ruth Bateman
To: Henry Mancuso
Date: Apr 30, 2016 at 7:10 AM

Hi Henry,

Sorry, I didn't get back to you sooner. I don't check my email all the time, so you might want to text me if something urgent comes up. Just promise you won't blow my phone up like a certain company whose name rhymes with Lucky's Jeans . . . 414-555-2122.

Anyway, about the call I made to the Bucky's Beans located on Wisconsin Avenue . . . I explained to the gal that I never signed up for the Bucky's Perks text messages and that they kept coming even though I'd texted STOP several times. She told me that I would need to access my Perks account and change the text message settings. I then reiterated that I never signed up for the program, so I wouldn't be able to access an online account to change any settings. She then told me I'd have to contact Bucky's corporate offices. So I looked up the number online and called, but since it was a Sunday, they were closed. That's when I decided to contact them via Facebook. I assumed the issue would be resolved quickly that way. As you know, no such luck!

As for the number of messages I've received, I'm not sure, but I know it must be anywhere from three to four dozen (and counting), considering I receive at least one a day. Yes, I can send screenshots of my text records, but most likely not until my lunch break on Monday.

Enjoy your weekend!
Ruth

Now for more important things.

I don't usually go downtown on Saturdays because the farmers' market is on Sundays, but the weather is way too nice to pass up a bike ride on the Oak Leaf Trail. The sunshine also makes me long to run the Summit Stairway that leads down to Lake Michigan, but that's something I haven't attempted since I hurt my ankle. It will never be one hundred percent again, but my doctor has said there's no physical reason I shouldn't be back to doing all the things I used to do by now. So who knows? Maybe today's the day I get back to those stairs.

As I wait for the garage door to open, I slide open the hidden compartment built into my phone's case and check to make sure I have the essentials—ID, credit card, and some cash. Then I slip my phone back into my pocket.

I promptly remove my helmet from a hook on the wall and snap it in place on my head. Then I wheel my bike out into the alley as I reach into my pocket and press the button on the opener to close the door behind me. After I unzip the bag strapped just below my bike seat, it takes mere seconds for me to make sure I have all the essentials for my ride—patch kit, spare tube, CO2 inflator, and multitool. Before I hop on and pedal off, I remove the garage door opener and my phone from my pockets to add them to the seat bag too. I'm about to zip the bag when it vibrates, so I pull my phone back out. It's no surprise to see that Henry has already acknowledged my email. Smiling, I respond.

Don't you have a life outside of lawyering? :) I promise I'll get back to you with screenshots of my text records on Monday, but only if you stop working and enjoy your weekend. As your client, I insist.

I slip my phone back into the seat bag, then hop on my bike and pedal off toward the nearest entrance to the Oak Leaf Trail.

∼

It's almost nine, so the sun's grand entrance for the day is complete. Despite the chill in the late April air, sweat drips from my brow, and runs down my cheeks and upper lip. I wish my appearance was a result of running the stairs, but it's not because I only made it a couple of flights down before heading back up and running on the paved path instead. As I make my way diagonally across the clearing where the farmers' market takes place, I use my pullover to wipe my face and then rewrap it tightly around my waist.

When I reach my bike across the street, I remove my phone from a pocket of my pullover and stuff the pullover into the basket affixed to the handlebars of my bike. Before I return my phone to the bag under my seat, I unlock it to check the notifications. A few texts came through while I was running: one from my mom, one from Sue, and of course one from Bucky's Beans. And today must be my lucky day, because I also have an email from the Bucky's Beans IT department.

From: itservicedesk@buckysbeans.com
To: ruthieb@gmail.com
Date: Apr 30, 2016 at 9:13 AM
*Subject: Bucky's Beans Text Solution *ref#25-481126*

Hi Ruth,

We had sent this issue to our technical team who had contacted Imperial Wireless. Your information is not signed up in our system and we are not sending you the text alerts, rather they are forwarded to your phone number by Imperial Wireless. Unfortunately, since we do not know what number is being forwarded, we cannot suppress it from our system. It is for this same reason that when you reply STOP to the text message, the STOP is coming directly from your number, which the system doesn't recognize as a number within the database.

Please contact your carrier (Imperial Wireless) and inform them that you are receiving messages that are intended for a number that does not match yours. As this has been an ongoing issue between Clear Connect Wireless and Imperial Wireless, they should be familiar with your request.

We are sorry that this has happened, Ruth. Please know that we have done all that we could to research and resolve this situation.

Sincerely,
Mildred/Customer Relations Specialist

Note: This E-mail is sent with reference to Incident #481126. Kindly mention Reference Number 'ref#25-481126' for further E-mail communication in this regard.

So, they're telling me Imperial Wireless is responsible for the text messages? Seriously? I'm no technology expert, but I'm pretty good at recognizing a case of passing the buck. Unsure of the implications this message will have on the case Henry is putting together, I scratch my head and furrow my brow. Then, with a sigh, I shove my phone back into the seat bag and unlock my bike.

As I wrap the cable lock around the frame of my bike, I sense someone is looking at me. I glance up and inadvertently lock eyes with a man across the street. He's leaning casually against the wall between QuickForm Fitness and Bucky's Beans Coffee Roasters. We both look away within seconds, but I'm still picturing the stranger in my mind's eye as I start to wheel my bike down the sidewalk. White and gray athletic shorts, sneakers, a fitted gray t-shirt with a navy sweatshirt thrown over his left shoulder, black hair—short on the sides and medium length on top . . . Suddenly, I'm overcome by déjà vu. I've seen this man somewhere before, but where?

I stop pushing my bike and glance over my shoulder in his direction. He makes eye contact with me again, but only for a split second this time, then he looks to either side of him. I get the impression he's probably wondering why I'm staring, so I quickly look away, not wanting to come across as a total stalker. But I still can't shake the feeling I know him. I push my bike a few more feet and steal one last quick glance. Then it hits me.

I turn my bike around and wheel it back to the bike rack, so that I'm directly across from him again. Now he's looking down at his phone, so I can no longer see his face, but I'm certain it's Henry Mancuso.

I smile as I cross the street to meet my handsome lawyer.

CHAPTER 22

Saturday, April 30
Henry

Why is this woman staring at me again? I pretend to look at something on my phone, but I'm really using my peripheral vision to watch her.

Okay, fine, I admit she caught my eye with her colorful clothes and wild hair. But I only looked at her once and only for a few seconds, until she noticed. This is the third time she's looked in my direction now. *Could she be looking at someone else?* I glance to my right. There's no one on the sidewalk, and there's no one looking out the front windows of QuickForm Fitness. I glance to my left toward Bucky's. There are people going in and out, but no one is even close to me. Why doesn't she just hop on her bike and go? Oh boy. Now she's crossing the street.

Maybe she's just going to Bucky's for a coffee.

I can't help but glance up at her again. Her cheeks are flushed, and her curly golden hair is in even more disarray than it appeared to be from a distance. She waves as she reaches the middle of the street. Then she pauses to wait for a car to pass. I look around again, but there's still no one near me that she could be waving to. So, I hesitantly wave back, and instead of looking down at my phone again, I watch as she reaches the sidewalk and lifts the front tire of her bike onto the curb, pulling the rest behind her. My eyes linger on her toned upper arms long enough to make me wonder if she noticed. Then something occurs to me—the workout clothes, her flushed cheeks, her fit physique—maybe she worked out at QuickForm earlier and she's returning for something she forgot.

"Hi," she says.

A sense of familiarity tugs at me when I see her smile up close, but I can't seem to put my finger on how I could possibly know the woman standing before me. She looks like she hopped off the page of a trendy fitness apparel catalogue like Lululemon, Athleta, or Title Nine. Constance is always looking at these types of catalogues in the lounge at work, but she wears more subtle colors than this woman.

"Hi." I return her smile. "Do I know you?"

"Your name is Henry, right?"

I nod, glancing toward Bucky's again, expecting Constance to emerge with her drink any second. "It is. I'm sorry; have we met?"

"Ruth Bateman," she says, extending a hand over the handlebars of her red Trek.

Ruth Bateman?

"Oh!" I use a heel to push myself off the wall as I shove my phone into my pocket. "It's good to meet you!" I say, shaking her hand. "Sorry, I didn't recognize you. It's just . . ." I gesture toward the top of her head with both hands. "You're not wearing a hat like you are in your profile photo on Facebook. I mean, that's the only picture I've ever seen of you, and the hat makes it difficult to see your face, so . . ." I motion across the street to where she was standing when we first noticed each other. "You seemed familiar, but I wasn't sure . . ." I lie, suddenly paranoid that she may be wondering if I was checking her out earlier. Obviously, that would be unprofessional. She smiles and nods, seemingly amused by my rambling. Why am I rambling?

"I wasn't one hundred percent sure it was you either," she says, shrugging, "but I figured I should say hi, just in case. So . . . hi." She blows upward, forcing a curly lock out of her right eye.

"Well, I'm glad you did. It's nice to put a face to your name."

"So," she looks around and then points behind me, "what are you doing? Holding up the wall?"

"No," I say laughing. "I just worked out at QuickForm with a friend, and now she's getting a coffee." I glance toward Bucky's.

"And you waited outside because . . . of the lawsuit?"

"No. I just don't usually drink Bucky's coffee. It has nothing to do with the lawsuit. I'm more of a Coffee Cave kind of guy."

"Coffee Cave? I used to work there when I was a teenager!"

"Really?"

"Yeah." She nods and glances upward as if recalling memories from her youth.

"I used to study there when I was in college, but that was probably long before you worked there."

She pulls her head back in surprise. "Oh, I don't know Henry. I'm no spring chicken." When she smiles, her right eyebrow raises a hair. "So, how long have you been working out at QuickForm?"

"Eh, this was only my second time. I'd much rather go for a run, but my friend persuaded me to get a trial membership. Have you ever tried it?"

She hesitates, her smile faltering for the first time since our conversation began. "Actually—"

"Sorry it took so long. You wouldn't believe the line in there. And ehhhhveryone seems to be placing bulk orders to go . . ." Constance finally notices Ruth. She hands me a drink I didn't ask for, and then holds her empty hand out to Ruth. "Hi. Constance Whitmore."

"Hi. It's nice to meet you." Her smile returns in full force as she shakes Constance's hand. "I love your name. It's so . . . elegant."

"Why, thank you! That's sweet of you," Constance gushes. "So," she glances at me and then back at Ruth, "how do you two know each other?"

"Constance, this is Ruth Bateman, our new client and lead plaintiff for the Bucky's Beans case."

"Really? The two of you just bumped into each other? What are the odds? And right in front of Bucky's Beans, too," Constance looks back and forth from me to Ruth, laughing with surprise.

I shrug because I don't think it's odd at all. Chance meetings like this happen all the time, and we do live in the same city. "Ruth, Constance works for Benson Tillman & Whitmore, as well. She helped me with some of the initial research for your case."

"So, are you related to Mr. Whitmore, Constance?" Ruth asks.

"He's my uncle," Constance responds politely, but I suspect she thinks Ruth is being nosy by the way she purses her lips and sips her coffee afterward.

Ruth nods. Then she breaks the silence by asking Constance about her new Garmin watch, and they get to talking about the different features it has to offer. Normally Constance wouldn't be so chatty with someone she just met, especially a client, but Ruth is asking a lot of questions. As they talk, I can't help but compare the two. At five foot nine, Constance towers over Ruth who can't be much more than five foot two. Where Constance's curves fill out her conservative designer workout clothing, Ruth's toned physique is obscured by her brightly-colored sportswear. And then there's their hair. Constance's signature sleek, black ponytail appears cocktail party ready; whereas, Ruth's curly locks look like they're ready for a kegger.

"Henry?" Constance's voice halts my train of thought.

"Hmm?" I mumble, my eyes snapping up to meet hers.

"Are you ready to go?"

I glance at Ruth who's smiling at me, and suddenly I feel abashed for comparing her appearance to Constance's. Ignoring my increased heart rate, I do my best to act natural. "Sorry, I was just . . ." I point to my head and swirl my finger, "you know, thinking about work."

Constance rolls her eyes, and Ruth suppresses a laugh. Then she says, "I believe it. I've just met you, but all evidence leads me to believe you're probably always working or thinking about work. But I suppose I should be happy about that, since you are my lawyer." She laughs freely now.

"Well, it was nice to meet you, Ruth," Constance says, as she inches her way in the direction of my condo.

"Nice to meet you too!" Ruth looks at me. "Goodbye, Henry. Enjoy the rest of your weekend," she says as she hops on her bike and pushes off.

"Yes, you too, Ruth," I say, feeling rushed to get the words out before she really gets going. "Ruth, wait!"

She stops and looks over her shoulder.

"Henry, let's go," Constance calls lazily from the opposite direction of where Ruth is. I put up a hand, letting her know I need a moment.

"I should have the formal complaint ready for your review by Monday afternoon."

"Sounds good, Henry." She starts to turn back around.

"Have you heard back from the IT department yet?"

This time she doesn't just turn her head, but she wheels her bike around to face me. Then hesitates, as if pondering whether she wants to say what's on the tip of her tongue.

"What? You've heard from them?" I walk toward her, closing the gap.

"Just a little while ago. I wasn't planning to forward it to you until Monday morning . . . so you can enjoy your weekend."

"Why? What did they say?"

Ruth shrugs and then wheels her bike back around before hopping on and taking off. Wisps of stray curls float behind her.

"Can you forward it Sunday night?" I call out.

She waves without looking back.

I sigh and turn back toward Constance just in time to catch an eye roll.

CHAPTER 23

Saturday Night, April 30
Ruth

"Oh, no," I whisper, clutching the Princess Leia buns on either side of my head. "Don't die on me now, old boy."

I try not to be materialistic, but the thought of saying goodbye to my fifteen-year-old Honda Civic makes my heart ache. I'd saved up for it throughout high school and my first two years of college, and my dad had gone with me when I purchased it. It was one of the last times I recall him walking without his walker out in public. Years later, after QuickForm was up and running, Adam argued that I should trade it in for a shiny, new Lexus to match the one he was buying. I tried to reason with him that there were much better things we could spend our money on, but what I was really thinking was that I didn't need or want something so ostentatious. I never thought he would either.

I say a little prayer as I stare down the *check engine* light, then I give the key one last hopeful turn. Relieved when it starts, I sigh and pat the dash. "Atta boy."

As I back out of my garage, I wonder how many more times my old Honda will pull through for me. With May right around the corner, I figure I have roughly four months to shop around before a new car becomes a necessity, since riding around on a bike in Wisconsin during brisk fall months and bone-chilling winter months would be borderline insanity.

When I drive by QuickForm and Bucky's Beans on my way to Posh, I think about meeting Henry and Constance this morning. What an ideal couple—both dark and attractive, and both lawyers. My mom is going to be so disappointed when she finds out he's taken. I suppose I was, in a way, too. Besides the fact that he's nice to look at, I like the goofy vibe he puts out. The way he rambled when he first realized who I was and the way he was so eager to find out about the email from Bucky's IT department was quite amusing. I laugh as I picture him staring after me like a forlorn puppy when I rode away. Winston gets that look when Joan leaves him in the yard while she does maintenance work outside her fence.

~

"Hey there, Sunshine!" Marty looks up from the paperwork he's doing in his office.

"Hey, Marty," I say, taking a seat on the La-Z-Boy chair in the corner where he takes naps.

"Why are you early? You're here too much as it is."

I shrug and ignore his latest attempt to discuss cutting my hours. What I haven't told him yet, is I'd probably keep coming in even if he stopped paying me. "So, I noticed you're friends with Henry Mancuso on Facebook. Through college, I assume, since you both went to Marquette? How well do you know him?"

"Henry Mancuso?" He scratches the salt-and-pepper stubble on his chin. "I haven't seen him in years. Why do you ask?"

"You know those texts I've been getting from Bucky's Beans?"

He chuckles. "The ones that make you curse under your breath?"

I nod. "Anyway, he's been looking into Bucky's text marketing setup and contacted me when he came across a message I posted to their Facebook page."

"Aha! So, he does go on Facebook. I've tagged him in the past and tried to connect with him on there, but he never responds to anything."

"Maybe he just uses it for work purposes?" I suggest.

"Maybe. That actually does sound like Henry—all work, no play. So why did he contact you?"

"I guess what Bucky's is doing breaks federal communication laws."

"No shit. And what? Henry wants you to help him sue them?"

"I've already agreed to help. So now I'm just curious about him. That's all."

Marty leans back in his chair, fingers laced behind his head. "Henry Mancuso is a good guy. Wears his serious pants a little too often, but a good guy. A bit particular, too." Suddenly, a huge grin forms on his face, and he sits upright. "We were in the same fraternity, and he used to clean the house all the time. The guy would use Q-tips to clean the grout on his bathroom floor and around all the faucets he used." Marty starts laughing. "Some of the guys used to mess with him by doing things like adding vodka to his mouthwash and mismatching his socks. It drove him nuts. It was all in good fun though."

I smile picturing a frazzled college-aged Henry Mancuso. "So, he was a goody-goody?"

"Henry?" Marty's eyes widen. "I wouldn't say that. Not before he started dating this girl Tracey, anyway. Henry drank enough that first year to pack on the old Freshman Fifteen." He pats his stomach. "And the ladies sure did like him. But that was before—and after—Tracey. I still don't know exactly what happened with them . . . Anyway, you can trust him. He's a solid guy, and probably nothing less than a top-notch lawyer being the perfectionist he is. Tell him I said hi, would you?"

CHAPTER 24

Saturday Night, April 30
Henry

For probably the eightieth time, I look away from the book I'm trying to read and glance at my phone on the coffee table. I know it's a bad habit, one that appeases my constant need to stay on top of things, but the harder I try to focus on not looking at my phone, the more desperate I am to look. It's a vicious cycle.

I turn back to page ten and vow to not stop reading until I get to at least page twenty, but I only make it to fourteen before I look at my phone again. Maybe if I allow myself a few minutes to poke around on it a bit I'll be able to concentrate. After all, giving up a habit cold-turkey isn't always the most effective way to go. That's why they make nicotine gum and patches and those annoying vapor cigarettes. I don't even have to check my email. It could be a non-work-related Google search (I have been meaning to look up how to fix a Keurig that's still backed up after descaling) or a scroll through my Facebook feed. I haven't done that for a while.

Setting the Grisham book face down in my lap, I relent, picking up my phone and noting the time. I'll give myself five minutes.

Facebook, it is. Unsure where to start, I click on *Home* to view my newsfeed, then I scroll and scroll . . . and mindlessly scroll some more. Until I unexpectedly see a post from Tracey Mullins. A lump forms in my throat and slowly works its way downward, coming to rest in my chest.

My first inclination is to close out the app, because seeing Tracey's face brings back so many memories, mostly good, but it's the bad ones that creep their way front and center. There's the one of her picking me up at the San Francisco airport; she wasn't nearly as excited to see me as I was to see her. Then there's the one of her telling me we needed to "talk" when we were at dinner that night. Then everything else that followed happened in an avalanche. The long-distance thing wasn't working for her. There was that one guy who stood out from the group of friends she'd introduced me to; the looks they'd exchanged, the way he tried to hide the fact that he was staring at her all night long. I wasn't fooled, but the thing was, they weren't even trying to fool me, because they didn't plan to fall in love.

Until now, I'd forgotten about the night I friended Tracey on Facebook. I'd been out drinking with some friends and overheard a buddy's girlfriend say Tracey had gotten engaged. I couldn't believe she hadn't told me, but then I thought about all the times I'd refused her calls and texts after she told me Steven had asked her out. Even so, I decided I needed to hear it from her, but I no longer had her number. So I did what any desperate, drunk ex-boyfriend would do: I looked her up on Facebook. At some point, she must have accepted my friend request, but by then, I'd already begun the process of purging my resentment toward her from my system. It started with an undergrad named Rita, whom I'd just met the night I sent the friend request. She was followed by many others, some whose names I don't even remember.

As I stare at the photo she's posted of her family on a beach in Cabo San Lucas, I can't help but wonder if I hadn't refused her calls and texts for so long, if maybe things would have worked out for us in the end. Could I have been the man in the photo with her? Could those have been our kids?

We'll never know.

I press the screen, wanting to see something else, and my most recent searches appear. Ruth Bateman's name is third on the list. Still reeling from my sudden stumble down memory lane, I impulsively click her name.

Her profile looks the same as it did a few weeks ago when I first looked her up. For a second, I think about sending her a friend request, reasoning that Facebook messenger might be a useful way for us to communicate down the line. But then I realize what a preposterous move that would be since all our communication should really be handled via my email address with the firm. I back out of her profile to view my newsfeed.

The top post is by an old buddy of mine, Martin Meyer. We were frat brothers at Marquette and used to party together. Marty was always the life of the party, so it doesn't surprise me that he's utilized his MBA to open a successful bar in downtown Milwaukee called Posh. The post is about how his bar was voted in the Top Five of Milwaukee's best nightlife establishments. A bunch of our other frat brothers have liked the post, but I don't tend to 'like' stuff on Facebook, so I don't even consider clicking on the little blue thumb. Instead, I scroll on to the next post, which is by another college friend who shared Marty's previous post. I sigh, guilt kicking in for never having checked out Marty's bar, even though he's invited me to many events via tags on Facebook. I even missed the grand opening of Posh.

I glance at the time in the upper right-hand corner of the screen. It's a little after seven. Maybe I'll pop in while it's still early and catch up with Marty a bit before the place gets busy.

"No effing way!" Marty rushes out from behind the bar and gives me a full-on hug. If I hadn't lived with the guy for three years when we were undergrads, it might be weird. Then he grips my shoulders and looks me over at arm's length.

"Sorry," I say. "This visit is long overdue."

He releases my arms and waves for me to follow him. When we get to the end of the bar furthest from the front door, he points to an empty stool. I take a seat, and he slides in behind the bar, meeting me face to face. "So, where've you been, who've you seen, whatcha been up to? Wait ... hold that thought. What can I get you? Fat Tire?"

"Sure, sounds good," I say nodding.

He bends down and retrieves two bottles from a floor cooler and hands one to me. Then he raises the other. We clink them together and both take a sip.

"It's about damn time you stopped in here, Mancuso."

I nod, looking around. Large booths line the walls, and there's a dance floor, a second bar on the other side of the room, and stairs that lead to an upper level overlooking the dance floor. "This is a nice place you have here, Marty. I'm impressed."

"Well, thank you." He bows his head a tad. "But I didn't do it on my own. My wife Bridgette was in charge of the décor."

"Is she here?" I ask, glancing behind the bar. There are two bartenders serving customers—one male, one female.

"Nah. She's at home with our little ones." He reaches into his back pocket for his phone, and then shows me pics of his kids. Then we chat for a few minutes about how fatherhood is treating him. I'm in awe of how much Marty has matured until I remind myself we haven't seen each other for nearly eight years.

"So, Henry, what's going on in your life? Kids? Wife? Girlfriend?"

"Nope," I say shaking my head. "I was dating someone, but we recently decided—"

"Henry?"

Marty and I turn to look in the direction of a familiar, raspy voice.

"Oh! Hey! That's right." Marty looks back at me, smiling. "You and Ruth know each other."

Ruth? Wait, how does Marty know I know Ruth?

"Ruth? What are you doing here?" She moves along the perimeter of the bar then rounds the end, coming to a stop a few feet from me. She's wearing a fitted black t-shirt that says POSH, and I can't help but notice the way it hugs her lean curves. "Wait, you work here? I thought you worked at Wixley Chiropractic."

"I do, but I also work here part-time . . . even though upper management can be a real asshole sometimes." She widens her eyes and glances pensively at Marty.

"She's a barrel of laughs, this one," Marty says to me, chuckling.

"I'll be back," Ruth says. Then she rushes over to claim the tray of drinks one of the bartenders has just loaded up for her.

I don't even realize I'm staring after her until Marty slaps the bar a few times with his palm. "That's cool you're helping Ruth with those annoying texts. You'll have to fill me in on what laws they're breaking over at Bucky's so I don't make the same mistake if I ever implement text marketing."

"Yeah," I shake my head, incredulous, "you wouldn't believe the racket they have going on. Seriously, I'm shocked by their blatant disregard for TCPA regulations. But, let's not talk about that right now. I came here to talk about anything but work. So, how do you and Ruth know each other? Just through this place or . . ."

"High school. Wait, I take that back. We went to middle school together too. But we weren't really friends until we had world studies together our sophomore year. Yep, Ruthie Bateman. Everybody's best friend."

"So, she's your age?"

"What do you mean, my age? You're only two years younger than me!"

"Yeah, yeah, yeah. I know," I say laughing. "I just assumed she was younger than me. That's all."

"Pfft. You wanna know why she looks so young? It's because she doesn't have kids yet. When that happens, she won't have time to exercise and ride her bike all over town anymore. She probably won't even wash her hair anymore. You? I don't know why you look so old. What's with the gray hairs there?"

"What?" My hand shoots up to the side of my face where he's pointing. "I don't have any gray hairs."

Marty laughs and takes a sip of his Fat Tire. "I'm just messing with you, Henry. You don't look a day over thirty-five."

"That's how old I am."

"I know."

Smiling, I roll my eyes, and we both take a drink.

"So, how did you know I was working with Ruth?

"Because she asked about you."

"She did? When?"

"Tonight. Right before we opened. She noticed you and I are Facebook friends, and I guess she wanted to make sure the desperate lawyer who uses Facebook to drum up business was legit. I told her you were a total schmuck, of course."

"Piss off, Marty," I say, laughing. It occurs to me that it's been a long time since I laughed so freely.

Marty continues, ignoring my weak attempt at a comeback. "This whole thing is unbelievable. She asked me a few weeks ago if I signed her up to get text message coupons from Bucky's, and I had no idea what she was talking about. Now I'm sitting here with you after not seeing you for eight years, and you're representing Ruthie Bateman in a lawsuit against Bucky's Beans. Life sure is weird."

I nod and ask, "So how long has Ruth been working here?"

"A couple years, give or take a few months. I don't really need her, but she won't stop coming in even though I know she doesn't need the money." He laughs. "Whatever, though. She only comes in for three or four hours at a time, and it's nice having her around to chat with when it's slow. Plus, I can always count on her when someone calls in." He takes a sip of his beer, and I follow suit.

"Why do you think she works here if she doesn't need the money?"

Marty hesitates, looking in Ruth's direction for a second. She waves obnoxiously, and he waves back in the same manner. Then he looks at me with a shrug. "She just happened to be looking for a part-time job back when I posted on Facebook about being in a pinch to find a server . . . Anyway, what's going on with you?"

Marty and I spend the next couple hours catching up on the past eight years. We talk about old times, families, careers, 401K plans, the NBA playoffs, and all the shitty things about getting older. The only topic I gloss over is my sex life, but that doesn't stop Marty from reminiscing about when we *both* used to be "ladies' men." Of course, Ruth happens to show up to ask him a question during this part of our conversation, but if she heard anything, she does a good job of hiding it.

As the club becomes busier and the music grows louder, it becomes harder to hear, and Marty's ability to sit and chat with me dwindles. While he's busy taking care of business, I occupy myself by people watching and picking at the label on my warm bottle of beer. I wonder if Ruth might stop by again but try not to watch her as she works. It isn't easy, though, because there's something compelling about the way she spends a little extra time talking to every single customer, always with a smile on her face. It reminds me of the way she rattled off questions for Constance, who would normally find that irritating coming from someone she just met. Yet, Constance seemed to warm up to Ruth the longer they talked.

When Marty disappears for a third time and I decide it's time for me to head home, he returns with a fresh bottle of Fat Tire to replace the half-empty one I started with.

"No, no, no. You drink it," I say, handing the beer back to him. "I've got to get going." I practically yell so he can hear me over the crowd.

"Come on," he tries to convince me, "it's only ten!"

"Nah, I'm bushed," I say, standing and moving out behind my chair as I push it in. "And it's too loud in here for us to talk anyway!" He shakes his head and waves me off. Then he fixes his gaze to my right.

That's when I realize Ruth is standing next to me.

CHAPTER 25

Saturday Night, April 30
Ruth

"Hey, Marty!" I lean into the bar, squeezing in next to Henry, so I don't have to yell. "I'm heading out. I already told Beth."

"Yeah, okay." He nods. "I'll see you next week, unless you decide—"

"I'll be here Thursday."

"All righty. Sounds good," he says. Then he points at Henry. "You. Do not turn into a stranger again. Next time I invite you out, you're coming!"

"Done," Henry says, reaching over the bar for a parting handshake.

As he does, I look him up and down, stealing a glance at his rear end. He may be my lawyer and have a girlfriend, but that doesn't mean I can't look. As is so often the case, Henry's pictures on Facebook and the law firm's website are deceiving. Only with him, he's even better-looking in person than on the computer screen. He seems like a nice guy, too. A bit uptight, maybe, but nice.

After Marty disappears to help with a few orders, Henry pulls out his wallet and retrieves a five. He places it under his half-empty bottle of Fat Tire, and then turns to leave, coming face to face with me.

"You barely drank any of your beer," I say.

"Yeah . . . I'm not much of a drinker."

"Me either. Just on special occasions and sometimes holidays. Coffee or tea is more my speed."

"But not from Bucky's," Henry says.

My chuckle is cut short when I realize he isn't smiling. "Wait, are you serious?"

"Absolutely not," he says, his stone-faced expression morphing into a grin.

Laughing, I say, "Well, bye, Henry. It was . . . weird seeing you again."

"Uh . . ."

"Not that *this* was weird." I move a hand back and forth between us. "Just randomly running into each other twice in one day. That's weird. You know?"

He shrugs. "What makes you think this was random? Maybe I like keeping an eye on my clients, especially the new ones."

"Wha— Oh, you're funny," I say, with an inadvertent snort, garnering a chuckle from my handsome, sophisticated lawyer. I quickly straighten my posture and clear my throat. "Okay, then. I'll see you around, Henry." I turn to leave.

"Hey, I'll walk out with you."

"Okay," I mumble, glancing back.

As I navigate through the crowd, Henry follows. When he accidentally steps on my heel, he shouts out an apology and grips my upper arms for a few seconds.

"That's okay," I say over the noise of the crowd, acting like it's no big deal. And it isn't. Except for the tingle that rushes through my body. What was *that* all about?

When we get outside, Henry and I stand in front of Posh for a few seconds before either of us says anything. The sidewalk is bustling with people enjoying the nightlife downtown Milwaukee has to offer, and large groups cut around and between us. After they've all passed, we both take a step, closing the gap between us.

"Ruth?"

"Yeah?"

"Is there any chance you can forward that email from Bucky's IT department to me tonight?"

"Yeah, sure. Okay if I do it when I get home?" I ask.

"Of course . . . So, where's your car?"

"About half a block that way," I say, pointing and taking a few steps. "Well, bye, Henry." I only get a few feet before I hear footsteps behind me.

"I'll just walk you if that's okay," Henry says, falling in step next to me.

"Thanks," I say, smiling over at him. He returns the smile and shoves his hands into his pockets. Then we walk in silence the rest of the way.

As I open my car door, Henry calls out, "Don't forget to forward that email . . . and I'll send you the formal complaint on Monday."

"Sure thing, Henry. Buh-bye."

As I buckle my seatbelt, I watch Henry in the side mirror when he turns to leave. Then I switch to the rearview mirror and continue to watch as he walks back toward Posh. On the first turn of the ignition, my car sputters. *Crap.* I try again. An even weaker sputter this time. I lean my forehead against the steering wheel. "Why now? Couldn't you have not started at home?" Leaning back, I sigh and unlock my phone. I'm about to request an Uber when there's a knock on my window.

"Where to?" Henry asks as we buckle our seatbelts.

"Waukesha."

"Excuse me, did you say Waukesha?"

"I'm kidding!" Henry visibly relaxes when he realizes he doesn't have a fifty-minute round trip ahead of him. "I live on Bay Street. Just head south on Kinnickinnic and turn left on Bay."

Henry nods as he looks over his left shoulder and pulls away from the curb.

The interior of his Acura is impeccable.

"New car?"

"No," he says, slowing down for a yellow light. "I've had it for about a year. Why do you ask?"

"It's just . . . really clean."

"Thank you . . . I think." He gives me a sideways glance.

I glance back thinking, *Sorry, Henry, it's not a compliment. More like a diagnosis.*

When the light changes, I look out the window and press the pad of my index finger against the glass, leaving behind a smudge. I smile and wonder how long it will take him to clean it off. Then I remember what

Marty told me about Henry always cleaning their frat house, and I laugh out loud.

"What's so funny?" He asks.

"Oh, it's just something Marty said about you being compulsively clean when the two of you lived together . . . during your college days. I suppose cleaning must still be a hobby of yours?"

He shakes his head and laughs through his nose. Then he mumbles, "Marty."

I steal another glance at him. It's dark, but his face is illuminated by street lights and lights from the businesses we pass. Why does Henry Mancuso have to be so handsome? "Do you know where you're going?"

"It's been a while since I spent any amount of time in this area, but I know it well. I used to be a Cave Dweller, remember?"

"That's right, you said you did a lot of studying at Coffee Cave. So, you must know where East Bay Bowl is then?"

"I do, and there used to be a custard stand right there." He points as we drive by a recently built gas station. "At least they left the gathering green alone." He's referring to a small, grassy area with benches and picnic tables where people can sit and enjoy coffee or lunch from one of several trendy new cafes that have popped up in the area.

"Yeah, hopefully it stays that way. Did you know Bucky's was trying to buy that theater off of Superior so they could turn it into a multilevel store with views of the lake?"

"I had no idea. When was this?"

"Two summers ago, when I moved into the neighborhood. It was a hot topic among my neighbors because the theater has been around since a lot of them were kids, and they couldn't stand the thought of a big business, like Bucky's, moving in. The woman who lives next door to me put together a petition, and now the theater is considered a historic landmark."

"That's impressive."

"Yes, Joan is quite an impressive woman."

Henry slows down, almost stopping completely, as we drive by East Bay Bowl, but the car behind him honks.

"You okay?" I ask, as he speeds up quickly.

He nods, and cracks open his window. "I was just thinking about the last time I went bowling there."

"When was that?"

"Thirteen, maybe fourteen years ago."

"You haven't been bowling in fourteen years? How is that possible? You do know Milwaukee is the home of the Wisconsin State Bowling Association, right?"

"I didn't. But thank you for telling me. That's . . . good to know."

I laugh because I'm pretty sure Henry just proved he's capable of sarcasm, which makes me even fonder of him than I already was. "My family used to go midnight bowling at East Bay Bowl on Friday nights when I was a kid. It really wasn't midnight bowling though because it was the earlier family session, which started at nine. The real midnight bowling started at eleven."

Henry laughs. "My family went to the early midnight bowling session a few times, too, but then my brothers smuggled in a couple of cantaloupes one night because they wanted to see what would happen if they bowled the fruit down the lane. Any guesses?"

"Cantaloupe everywhere?" I grin.

He nods. "That was the last midnight bowling session we attended as a family. Pretty sure my brothers might still be banned."

"Are you a good bowler?" I ask.

"Define good."

"Let's go with anything over one hundred."

He chuckles. "I guess that makes me mediocre, at best. What about you?"

"Eh, I used to be pretty good, but only because my dad loved bowling, so we did it quite a bit when I was growing up. Even when my brother and I were both teens and preferred to hang out with friends when our parents went bowling, we still went at least once a year for my dad's birthday. Until he wasn't able to bowl anymore . . ." I pause, remembering the last birthday celebration we had for my dad at East Bay Bowl. Henry looks over at me, probably longer than he should since he's driving, but he doesn't say anything. "Anyway, it's been years since I went bowling. Not anywhere near fourteen, but still a long time. Probably too long."

"So, your dad . . . he's . . ."

"He passed away five years ago."

"I'm sorry to hear that, Ruth."

We drive in silence for a block before I snap out of the bittersweet reverie. "So, where did you grow up?" I ask.

"In Milwaukee," he says matter-of-factly. "My parents still live in the house my brothers and I grew up in, over by UWM." I recall his Facebook profile says he went to Shorewood High School, but I don't want to seem nosey by asking why he didn't go to a public high school in Milwaukee. "What about you?"

"Same. My mom still lives in my childhood home, too, over on the North Side, a few blocks from Wauwatosa. It's kind of funny, isn't it?"

"What?"

"That we've frequented the same places over the years but have never seen each other before, and now you're my lawyer. There's also the fact that we both know Marty. I went to high school with him, by the way." Keeping one hand on the wheel and his eyes on the road, Henry gives his head what appears to be a contemplative scratch but remains silent. "My house is coming up on the right, next to the one with the fence."

"You know, statistically speaking, we've most likely crossed paths but just never noticed each other. And never underestimate the power of Facebook when it comes to revealing coincidental connections," Henry says, pulling up to the curb. He smiles, propping his left forearm up on the steering wheel and turning his upper body to face me.

"Yes, Facebook certainly has a way of bringing people together, doesn't it? Thanks for the ride, Henry. I hope you didn't go too far out of your way."

"No worries. I live right over in one of those new condos along the Milwaukee River."

"But that's back where we came from! I should have just called for an Uber," I sigh.

"Honestly, it's not a big deal. I'll just take the gas money out of your settlement."

He remains stone-faced for a beat, and then we both laugh.

"Do you honestly believe there will be a settlement?"

"I do, but at this stage, your guess as to how much it could be would be as good as mine. I'm sorry you're still getting texts, by the way. That should stop shortly after I send the formal complaint to Bucky's."

"That'll be a relief," I say, unbuckling my seatbelt and opening the door so Henry can be on his way. "Bye, Henry."

"Ruth?"

I look at him, one foot out the door.

"Don't forget to forward that email from Bucky's IT department tonight."

"I won't," I say, chuckling and hopping out. I grip the upper corner of the door and turn, lowering my head slightly inside the car. "But I can handle a few more days of texts, and I'm sure everyone else on the list can too. So, I hope you don't plan to work on the case tonight." The only response I get is a shrug. "Thanks again for the ride."

"My pleasure. I'll be in touch."

As I make my way up the walkway to my door, the soft hum of Henry's car engine remains. He doesn't drive off until I get to my door. I want to look back, but I don't, because that seems too much like something you do after a date. And this wasn't a date.

Henry's my lawyer, certainly not a dating prospect.

CHAPTER 26

Saturday Night, April 30
Henry

I wait as Ruth makes her way up the walkway to her house but try not to make it obvious I'm watching her. As soon as she's inside, I get a better look at her humble brick abode, which is illuminated by motion lights. It's a ranch style home with a cozy front patio. The well-manicured wrap-around flower garden reminds me of projects I used to help my dad with during summer breaks when I was a teen. It's amazing what my grandfather's small family landscape business has grown into over the past couple of decades with the addition of a construction division.

The outline of a bistro table and two chairs on the patio makes me wonder if Ruth has a roommate. The thought doesn't linger long before I find myself wondering why her living situation has intercepted my train of thought and heat spreads into my cheeks. No sooner do I acknowledge the mild attraction I feel toward my new client when the motion lights turn off along with my inappropriate thoughts.

I compose myself and pull away from the curb.

As I drive down Kinnickinnic, making my way back toward downtown Milwaukee and my condo, I think about how much the area has changed. In addition to the disappearance of the custard stand, most of the storefronts have been renovated and the streets have been updated to include modern lamp posts, decorative planters and dog waste receptacles every few blocks. Bright mustard lines have also been painted to highlight the bike lane that leads all the way to the lakefront. Until now, I'd forgotten about the path. I clear my car's Trip A odometer, curious how far I am from my condo. If it isn't too far maybe I could try the route sometime when I go for a run.

At first glimpse of the East Bay Bowl sign on my right, my chest tightens the way it often does when something reminds me of Tracey. In response, I give my car a little more gas and watch in the rearview mirror as the bowling alley shrinks out of view. But no longer being able to see it doesn't prevent a sudden memory of the lot out back where Tracey and I used to park and make out before we'd go in to meet our friends. A smile grazes my lips as I recall the time Marty lined up a group of guys around the car to moon us when we came up for air. Marty. Always the ringleader. My smile fades when my thoughts shift to the last time Tracey and I went to East Bay. We'd rung in 2002 at their New Year's Eve Bash. A bunch of Tracey's friends were there, but the real draw for my friends and me was the drink special they were running. All you could drink from eight to midnight for two-thousand two cents. The souvenir pint glass is still on a shelf in my bedroom at my parents' house. Not only was that the last time I went bowling, but it was also the last New Year's Eve Tracey and I spent together because she left for grad school at Stanford that summer.

A honk from the car behind me alerting me that the light has turned from red to green interrupts my train of thought. It's perfect timing, really. Because this woe-is-me crap I've been experiencing over memories of Tracey Mullins is getting old. Although, I probably should have processed all this shit a long time ago. I lower my window and stick my hand out to wave a quick thank you as I depress the gas pedal.

When I get up to my condo, I take a quick shower to wash away the scent of Posh. It's nothing compared to when smoking used to be allowed in bars, but I still feel the need to rinse off what can be best described as stale beer. After I brush my teeth, I move through my apartment and make sure everything is spotless and tidy. Then I close the curtains in my bedroom, move the extra pillows on my bed to one side, turn off the lights, and climb under the covers.

I lie there and do my best to summon unconsciousness, but jumbled thoughts of nothing in particular keep me awake. I open one eye and glance at the digital clock on my nightstand. Eleven twenty-four. Then I open the other eye and stare at my phone. I checked my email shortly after eleven, right before I crawled into bed, but Ruth still hadn't forwarded the email from Bucky's IT department. Is it possible I dozed off for a moment and missed the ping?

I grab my phone, wiggle myself into a sitting position, and prop a pillow between the headboards and my upper back. Still no new emails. But I do have a Facebook notification alerting me that Marty posted the photo he took of us at Posh tonight. The photo caption says: *Had an awesome time catching up with this guy!* Along with fifteen other people, I click to like the post. When I do so, a friend request notification comes through, immediately followed by a text from Constance.

CONSTANCE: ARE YOU STILL AWAKE?

To respond or not? That's the question. If it were any of my other friends, I would find out if everything was okay given the late hour. But this is Constance, so I wonder if responding will only result in me having to turn down an alcohol-induced booty call.

I decide to poke around on Facebook a bit longer first, and I'm shocked when I see the friend request is from Ruth Bateman. Without hesitation, I confirm. Then as I'm about to click to view her full profile, I remember Constance.

ME: I AM. EVERYTHING OKAY?

I click over to Ruth's profile, and scroll to the first post that wasn't visible to me before. It's a picture of her and an older woman with the same shade of dark blonde hair standing in front of a picture of sunflowers. The picture, which was taken at White Pines Nursing Home, according to the tag, and was posted by a woman named Ruby Jones earlier this week. *White Pines Nursing Home.* I've heard of this place before, but I can't figure out where.

My phone pings.

CONSTANCE: EVERYTHING IS FINE. JUST LEAVING VINO 100 AND CURIOUS IF YOU'D LIKE SOME COMPANY...

ME: ALREADY IN BED.

I smack my forehead, realizing how she might interpret my response.

CONSTANCE: SO, IS THAT A YES THEN?

ME: LOL. SERIOUSLY, I REALLY AM IN BED, SO NOT UP FOR VISITORS. HOPE YOU HAD A GOOD NIGHT. DRIVE SAFE.

After about ten seconds with no response from Constance, I go back to Ruth's Facebook profile. As I scroll, I quickly learn two things about her: She likes colorful clothing, and she's even less active on Facebook than I am. Other than several scenic photos and about half a dozen shared posts about Wixley Chiropractic specials and workshops, Ruth hasn't shared much this year. The rest of the posts on her wall, mostly pics of her with other people, were made by others who tagged her. When I get to a photo of her with a man and the same woman who was in the sunflower picture with her, my gut tells me it must be her mom and brother, but I also catch myself wondering if it could be a boyfriend. I shake away the irrelevant thought, then scroll some more until I get to a video captioned *ALS Ice Bucket Challenge.* I press play, and Ruth, who's wearing a modest black one-piece swimsuit and a hot pink tutu, comes to life. I catch myself smiling at the sound of her raspy voice and laughing out loud when she pours the bucket of ice water over her head. Then, just when I think the video is over, someone off camera soaks her with yet another spray of icy cold water, sending me into another bout of laughter. The video ends with her threatening revenge on someone named Tyler, and again, I wonder if it could be a boyfriend.

My phone pings.

CONSTANCE: NIGHTY NIGHT <3

Attached is a close-up of her freshly glossed lips moving in for a kiss. I delete the text and go back to Ruth's profile. Several more scrolls bring me to a photo of her from last summer with a group of people wearing running attire and race bibs. The post says *White Pines represents at the third annual Lake Park 5K benefitting Parkinson's disease!* I click the photo and zoom in on Ruth. Her tank top says *Screw Parkinson's.*

White Pines Nursing Home. Now I remember. It was mentioned in Ruth's father's obituary. Suddenly I feel ashamed. Not only did I Google her before she even agreed to help with the Bucky's case, but then I pretended not to already know her father passed away five years ago when she mentioned it in the car. And now I'm nosing through her personal life on Facebook. What kind of attorney does this?

Wait a second. She friended me.

What if she's nosing around on my Facebook page too? Maybe I should unfriend her.

My phone pings.

From: Ruth Bateman
To: Henry Mancuso
Date: Apr 30, 2016 at 11:55 PM

Hi Henry,

Here's the email from Bucky's IT. It makes little sense to me, but I assume the information might change the scope of your case. Please let me know what you make of it, but no rush. It can definitely wait until Monday!

By the way, thanks again for driving me home tonight. It was nice chatting with you. And thanks for accepting my friend request on Facebook.

Enjoy the rest of your weekend, Henry!

Ruth :)

Grinning, I scroll down to read the forwarded email. A few lines in, my smile fades, and the thoughts racing through my mind about what a terrible, stalker of a lawyer I've been are replaced with one determined thought.

Bucky's Beans is in for one hell of a lawsuit.

CHAPTER 27

Sunday, May 1
Ruth

From: Henry Mancuso
To: Ruth Bateman
CC: Robert Whitmore
Date: May 1, 2016 at 12:08 AM

Good Evening, Ms. Bateman,

*The e-mail you received from Bucky's IT department only reinforces our desire
to proceed with this case. In its email to you, Bucky's essentially points its finger
at Clear Connect Wireless, saying that it (Bucky's) is sending messages to a
Clear Connect Wireless number, and that Clear Connect Wireless is then
automatically forwarding those messages to your Imperial number -- all
without Bucky's being able to identify the Clear Connect Wireless number
serving as the source. Bucky's explanation is untenable for several reasons.*

*First, based on our experience in this field, there is no question that the
sophisticated text messaging technology used by companies like Bucky's
provides detailed information relating to the forwarding numbers and ultimate
recipients of any text messages sent.*

*Second, even if Bucky's could not initially identify the Clear Connect Wireless
number through which the texts you received purportedly passed, your multiple
requests to opt-out would necessarily have been delivered back through the
same Clear Connect Wireless number en route to Bucky's. Therefore, Bucky's
would surely have been able to identify, and thus could easily have removed*

from its database, the Clear Connect Wireless number that Bucky's says is behind this problem.

Third, even in the unlikely event that Bucky's really has no way around this "ongoing issue" between Clear Connect Wireless and Imperial, the appropriate and responsible solution would have been for Bucky's to altogether stop sending text messages to Clear Connect Wireless cellular numbers, and thereby prevent the delivery of unsolicited text messages to Imperial cellular numbers. By not doing so, Bucky's unfortunately put its financial interests ahead of consumer privacy concerns.

I'll send you a draft of the complaint tomorrow.

Thank you,
Henry J. Mancuso
Attorney at Law
hmancuso@bensontillmanwhitmore.com
350 E. Wisconsin Avenue, Suite 600
Milwaukee, Wisconsin 53202
Phone (414) 555-4242
Fax (414) 555-4241

"Why the long face, Ruth?" Joan hollers from her porch. She couldn't care less that it's not even seven a.m. yet and that our neighbors are probably all still snug in their beds. I descend my front steps and walk over to the fence, just so I don't have to yell. She meets me, most likely anticipating an earful of drama. "So? What is it? Is Dr. Jackson cheating on his wife? Is that slime bag ex-husband of yours trying to get you to take him back?" She motions with a swift scoop of her right palm for me to spill the nonexistent gossip.

"No and no," I say chuckling. "I was just reading an email from my lawyer, Henry Mancuso." I raise my chin and enunciate his name in a stately manner.

"Your lawyer?"

Nodding, I say, "Remember those texts I've been getting from Bucky's Beans?"

"Goddamn frou-frou drinks," she mumbles with contempt and shakes her head.

"Well, it turns out I'm not the only person who's been receiving them, and what they're doing is against the law. So now I'm helping this lawyer put together a class action lawsuit against them."

"Good for you, Ruthie! You make those corporate bigwigs pay for thinking they're above the law!" Joan yells so loud Mr. Johnson over on the other side of her asks through an upstairs window if we can keep it down, but Joan waves him off. "I never complain when I hear him in his garage sawing and drilling and hammering away. You'd think he was carving up a dead body in there the way he only does it late at night." She rolls her eyes and yells at him to quit eavesdropping and to shut his window if our visiting is bothering him. Then she turns back to me. "Wait, you never answered my question. Why the long face when you were reading the email from your lawyer?"

"Oh . . . it's nothing really. The email just wasn't what I expected."

"Bad news?"

"No, not at all. Good news, actually, from what I understand anyway. The email was just sort of dry and . . . impersonal." I'm saying this more to myself than to Joan, since she has no knowledge of the recent chance encounters I've had with Henry.

"Well, not everyone is as outgoing and personable as you are, Ruth. In fact, most people are schmucks. Besides, that's the kind of guy you want representing you. Someone who's focused and on the ball, always one step ahead of the enemy and ready to pounce."

"Yeah," I say, shaking my head, "you're probably right. Well, I better get going so I don't miss out on the really fresh stuff. Do you want me to get you some beets?" The last time I made beets and offered some to Joan she went on for days about how much she liked them.

"That would be wonderful. And I could use some real maple syrup if you see any. Thanks, Ruth."

"No problem, Joan," I say as we both turn to leave.

I spend most of the time riding to the farmers' market wondering why Henry's email was so formal without a hint of the friendly demeanor I saw in him over the weekend. Did I cross a line by sending him a friend request on Facebook? If so, why did he accept? Does he feel as though he crossed a line by driving me home? Or is it possible that our coincidental meetings have him wondering if I'm actually a spy for Bucky's sent to sabotage the case . . .

Okay, Ruth. Time to get a grip on reality.

Maybe you're just being sensitive because you have an inappropriate crush on your lawyer.

Ding, ding, ding! We have a winner!

Smiling, I shake my head. I've had enough introspection for one day. For the rest of the ride to the farmers' market, I enjoy the scenery and the cool breeze on my face.

It's a little after eight by the time I get to the market square, which is just down the road from Bucky's and QuickForm where I usually lock up my bike. Since it's later than I usually arrive, I opt to leave my bike near a bench overlooking the lake, right off the path that winds around the square.

I head to my favorite vegetable stand and snag a few beets for Joan before perusing everything else. After I've filled my bag to the rim with fresh asparagus, potatoes, green onions, mini crusty Tuscan garlic rolls, and nectarines, I purchase a bouquet of fresh peonies and a cup of coffee from the Coffee Cave stand.

As I weave my way through the stands on the way back to my bike, something at a crafty knickknack stand catches my eye. It's a sign with a paisley neon border that says CREATE TIME FOR YOURSELF in black block letters. Displayed in front of the sign are dozens of wooden eggs standing on end.

"Would you like to hold one?" The man behind the stand asks. He has short well-kept dreadlocks and is wearing a white bohemian style tunic.

"Sure," I say, setting my coffee down on the ground. "What do they do?"

"These are Zen Eggs. Just focus on how it feels in your hand, then channel that concentration into recognizing your emotions, desires, and intuition."

"Okay," I say, not so sure I get it. I choose a walnut colored one and expect it to just feel like your average everyday smooth wooden egg (because those are everywhere, you know), but something about the texture, the shape and the weight of this egg is calming.

"I work a desk job during the week . . . believe it or not." He fingers the dreads on top of his head. "And I keep one of these on my desk. When I'm feeling stressed or overwhelmed or just not centered, I do this." He tilts a honey colored oak egg all the way to the left. "Then I watch, and I breathe." He releases the egg. It pops back upright and wobbles back and forth, quickly at first, until it slows to a complete stop. The movement only lasts for about ten seconds, but it's long enough to make me feel a strong sense of . . . Zen. Amazed, I look at the egg in my hand and then at the man. "Close your eyes," he says. "Smell it."

I do as he suggests, inhaling the fresh, rustic scent of the magical egg. It smells like clarity.

My eyes pop open. "How much is it?"

"Thirty-three, or you can get two for sixty."

"I'll take that mahogany one too," I say pointing and then retrieving the cash from my bag.

When I get to my bike, I hang my bag over the handlebars and place the bouquet of peonies in the basket. Then I take a seat on the bench, Zen Egg in one hand and coffee in the other. I roll the smooth egg around in my palm, and watch people enjoying the beach below. Some are walking, some are jogging, and some are reading. There's a couple taking turns throwing a ball into the water for their dog to retrieve. There are sounds all around me, but the only thing I'm focused on is the waves rolling into shore.

I glance down at the egg in my hand and watch as I close my fingers around it and grip it tight. Then I stand and toss my empty Coffee Cave cup into the nearest waste bin, and place the Zen Egg into my sling bag, which I tighten diagonally around my chest.

As I stand at the top of the Summit Stairway for the second day in a row, I remind myself that I'm not as fit as I was before the accident, so I just need to pace myself. When I first get going, I move slowly. But little by little, as I become reacquainted with the feel of running the stairs, I speed up. My ankle throbs a little, but I keep going because I'm too stubborn to turn back at this point. Before I know it, I'm at the bottom looking up, and it's quite a treat to see how far I've come.

When I get back to the top, I walk in circles around the bench with my hands on my hips for a few minutes until the rapid pounding in my chest slows and the dull ache in my ankle fades.

CHAPTER 28

Monday, May 2
Ruth

I'm working on some billing for the chiropractic office when an email comes through from Henry.

From: Henry Mancuso
To: Ruth Bateman
CC: Robert Whitmore
Date: May 2, 2016 at 10:45 AM

Hi Ruth,

We're almost done with the complaint and I'll send it to you soon. In the meantime, I think I may have figured out why you aren't able to opt out of the messages. Every Imperial Wireless number has a "behind the scenes" Clear Connect Wireless number that is used when Wi-Fi isn't available. It is likely that Bucky's is sending unsolicited texts to your Clear Connect Wireless number, and that your opt-out requests are being sent from the Imperial Wireless number. If that's the case, we need to determine your phone's Clear Connect Wireless number. Here's how you do that:

1) Open the phone app.
2) Bring up the number pad.
3) Enter ##3282# on the number pad.
4) Tap Data Profile.
5) Under Username is an E-mail address. The numbers to the left of the "@" in the address is your Clear Connect Wireless number.

6) Tap the Home button to dismiss the information screen.

Once you find your Clear Connect Wireless number, please let me know what it is so I can include the pertinent allegations in the complaint. There are probably tons of people in the same boat as you who use Imperial Wireless and other similar carriers with secondary numbers who cannot opt out. This will be an important case because it will expose this problem, get it fixed for everyone, and prevent it from happening again. I'll send you the complaint shortly.

Thank you!
Henry J. Mancuso
hmancuso@bensontillmanwhitmore.com
350 E. Wisconsin Avenue, Suite 600
Milwaukee, Wisconsin 53202
Phone (414) 555-4242
Fax (414) 555-4241

I finish up the billing and a few other housekeeping items that need to be taken care of at the beginning of each month. Then I find my phone's secondary number and email it to Henry.

From: Ruth Bateman
To: Henry Mancuso
Date: May 2, 2016 at 11:30 AM

Hi Henry!

Here's the number you asked for: 262-555-0640.

I hope you enjoyed the rest of your weekend. I got the coolest thing yesterday at the farmers' market. A Zen Egg. Ever heard of those things?

Ruth :)

Right before I'm about to send the email, I reread it and realize it would probably make Henry think I'm a flake. Just because he was nice enough to drive me home last night doesn't mean he wants to know about my Zen Egg. So, I delete a few things, doing my best to mimic Henry's formal tone.

From: Ruth Bateman
To: Henry Mancuso
Date: May 2, 2016 at 11:30 AM

Here's the number you asked for, Henry: 262-555-0640.

Thank you!
Ruth

Satisfied, I click send. Then I log into MailChimp and get to work on the Wixley Health & Wellness Chiropractors monthly newsletter. I only make it as far as choosing a template before my phone pings.

From: Henry Mancuso
To: Ruth Bateman
CC: Robert Whitmore
Date: May 2, 2016 at 11:42 AM

Thank you for the quick response, Ruth.

As a quick test, do you mind if I send a text to your secondary number to see if you receive it?

Henry J. Mancuso
Attorney at Law
hmancuso@bensontillmanwhitmore.com
350 E. Wisconsin Avenue, Suite 600
Milwaukee, Wisconsin 53202
Phone (414) 555-4242
Fax (414) 555-4241

I reply with a simple *nope* and go back to composing the Wixleys' newsletter, but I'm interrupted again moments later.

414-555-3423: Hi Ruth, this is Henry Mancuso. Please let me know if you receive this message.

Me: Got it!

414-555-3423: Great. This is a huge breakthrough for our case. Stand by, I'll explain via email.

I begin typing a response but then pause. I've never been too keen on electronic correspondence in lieu of talking to someone, so I delete the few letters I just typed and press the tiny receiver next to Henry's cell number.

CHAPTER 29

Monday, May 2
Henry

"Hello?" I answer, the number on my screen vaguely familiar.

"Hi, Henry. It's Ruth."

I can hear the smile in her voice.

"Oh, Ruth! I thought I recognized this number," I say, followed by a brief chuckle.

"Sorry to catch you off guard like this. I'm just not a huge fan of emailing and texting back and forth when you can pick up a phone and call someone." I'm about to agree with her, but she continues. "Anyway, what's the big breakthrough?"

"Okay, so you received the text I sent to your hidden Clear Connect Wireless number, which someone else who was previously assigned to the number enrolled to receive Bucky's texts, but when you responded your text came from the 414 number instead of the hidden 262 number. This explains why you can't opt out."

"Wow, nice work, Columbo."

"What was that?"

"You know, the private eye? Columbo? Never mind."

"Oh! Yeah, I know who you mean. My grandma used to watch that show when I was a kid . . . Um, anyway, I'll add this information to the complaint as soon as we get off the phone and will hopefully send it over to you by this afternoon."

"Sounds good, Henry. Thank you so much for your help with this. Marty was right; you are a top-notch lawyer."

"I appreciate you saying that, Ruth, but this whole case wouldn't be possible without your help. So, thank *you*."

After we hang up, I get right back to work, determined to live up to my status as a top-notch lawyer.

CHAPTER 30

Monday, May 2
Ruth

After I hang up with Henry, I program his number into my phone, just in case. Then say goodbye to the Wixleys' final patient of the morning and lock the front door.

"Was that the lawyer you were chatting with just now?" Beverly asks as she enters the waiting area with a weighted harness strapped to her forehead, indicating she's just been adjusted by Dr. Jackson.

"It was. How did you know? You were all the way over in the warm-up area."

"Just a hunch." She tweaks an eyebrow.

"What do you mean?"

"Oh nothing, you just had the same look on your face that you had when you told Jackson and I about running into him this weekend."

"What look?" I ask, incredulous.

"A look I like seeing on you," she says smiling. "One that tells me you might appreciate more about this lawyer than just his legal expertise."

I shake my head at her. "I'm just glad someone is finally going to make these annoying texts stop." I hold up my phone to show her the text that has just come through from Bucky's. Then I duck down to grab my salad out of the mini fridge behind the front counter.

"I'm just telling you what I see," she says, holding her palms up.

Her sly expression makes me smile.

"I'm taking my lunch out back," I say, inching my way down the hall. "Holler if you need anything."

"Nah, we won't bother you. Enjoy those daylilies. They just started blooming."

As soon as I sit down, an email from Henry comes through.

From: Henry Mancuso
To: Ruth Bateman
CC: Robert Whitmore

Date: May 2, 2016 at 12:10 PM

Sorry to bother you again, Ruth, but I forgot to mention what we've discovered about hidden Clear Connect numbers. Apparently, they can change at random. This is probably why you suddenly started receiving the texts— because the previous subscriber to your current Clear Connect number was most likely signed up. According to an expert in cell phone forensics we consulted, Bucky's and other companies that use text marketing are aware when numbers change and are supposed to stop texting a number when it is reassigned. In this case, Bucky's clearly failed to do that, and the result has been disastrous. They need to change their policies and practices, which is what your case should motivate them to do.

I just thought you should know all the facts.

Stand by . . . I'll send the complaint soon!

Best,
Henry J. Mancuso
Attorney at Law
hmancuso@bensontillmanwhitmore.com
350 E. Wisconsin Avenue, Suite 600
Milwaukee, Wisconsin 53202
Phone (414) 555-4242
Fax (414) 555-4241

I click to reply and remove Robert Whitmore from the CC line.

From: Ruth Bateman
To: Henry Mancuso

Date: May 2, 2016 at 12:14 PM

Thank you for the extra information, Henry. Have you had lunch yet? If not, the complaint can wait. ;)

Ruth

I click send and then dig into my chicken, strawberry, walnut, and goat cheese salad. I don't even swallow the first bite before I grab my phone and send an additional reply to Henry.

From: Ruth Bateman
To: Henry Mancuso
Date: May 2, 2016 at 12:16 PM

Just wanted to clarify, I wasn't asking you to lunch. Only making sure you don't forget to eat, since you're so wrapped up with this Bucky's case, as well as others I'm sure.

Ruth

～

It's close to six, and I'm about a block away from home when I receive another email from Henry.

From: Henry Mancuso
To: Ruth Bateman
CC: Robert Whitmore
Date: May 2, 2016 at 5:55 PM

Ruth,

Sorry for the delay, but I was not able to complete the complaint to my satisfaction. I will be sure to send it over first thing tomorrow morning.

Regards,
Henry J. Mancuso
Attorney at Law
hmancuso@bensontillmanwhitmore.com
350 E. Wisconsin Avenue, Suite 600
Milwaukee, Wisconsin 53202
Phone (414) 555-4242
Fax (414) 555-4241

I delete the email, and another one from Henry pops up. This one is in response to the one I sent only to him.

From: Henry Mancuso
To: Ruth Bateman
Date: May 2, 2016 at 5:56 PM

I thought you might like to know that I ate lunch today. Thank you for the friendly reminder.

Henry

I think he's trying to be funny, but it's cheesy. Even so, I catch myself smiling and wonder what Beverly would say if she saw me right now.

$\backsim$

Tuesday, May 3
Ruth

Normally, I don't mind walking in the rain, but the downpour that's just now starting to taper off has me wishing my car wasn't in the shop. It's heavy enough that my pants are wet from splatter even though I'm wearing a raincoat and rain boots and carrying an umbrella. To make matters worse, the sky is dark and dreary, and I've already jumped twice due to thunder.

When I let myself in through the back entrance of the chiropractic office and flip the switch to turn on the lights, nothing happens. Then, after I remove my coat and creep my way down the hall toward the front desk, I trip over the ream of copier paper that was delivered right before I left the day before, causing me to fall to my knees and smack my forehead against the counter. I roll over onto my back and laugh, reminding myself that days like these need to happen once in a while, the whole yin and yang thing and all. Something good must be in store for me.

That's when my phone pings, and the screen lights up. I remain on my back and reach over to where it landed about a foot away from me.

From: Henry Mancuso
To: Ruth Bateman
CC: Robert Whitmore
Date: May 3, 2016 at 6:48 AM

Good morning, Ruth.

Attached you will find the complaint, which we are confident will result in the cessation of texts to your cell phone and will further cause Bucky's to fix the same problem affecting countless other people across the country. It may take a bit longer for Bucky's to agree to implement the changes that will fix the problem for everyone else, because they will need to totally change the way they are doing business by removing numbers from their system that are reassigned from one subscriber to another (particularly Imperial Wireless-based Clear Connect Wireless numbers), which is what happened to the Clear Connect Wireless number that you are currently assigned. For that reason, the primary relief we are seeking in the complaint is "injunctive relief," which will prohibit Bucky's from continuing to operate its texting program without making those changes.

We hope to file the complaint this afternoon, so please let us know if it looks good or if you have any questions.

Regards,
Henry J. Mancuso
hmancuso@bensontillmanwhitmore.com
350 E. Wisconsin Avenue, Suite 600
Milwaukee, Wisconsin 53202
Phone (414) 555-4242
Fax (414) 555-4241

I smile and wonder if this is my something good, meaning that the texts from Bucky's will soon be a thing of the past, not the momentary tug in my chest when I saw that Henry had emailed me.

Another ping. Another tug.

From: Henry Mancuso
To: Ruth Bateman
CC: Robert Whitmore
Date: May 3, 2016 at 6:50 AM

Ruth, please read this version of the complaint instead. I corrected a typo in the other version.

Thanks,
Henry

Another ping. This time it's an email from Henry's boss.

From: Robert Whitmore
To: Henry Mancuso, Ruth Bateman
Date: May 3, 2016 at 6:54 AM

Hi Ruth,

Further to Henry's email, now that we'll be suing Bucky's, you should not talk or write to Bucky's about your situation from this point forward. Henry will be in direct communication with you and will let you know what Bucky's has to say and we'll keep you fully informed throughout the process. Thank you for entrusting us with your case. We look forward to working with you.

Regards,
Robert W. Whitmore
Attorney at Law
rwwhitmore@bensontillmanwhitmore.com
350 E. Wisconsin Avenue, Suite 600
Milwaukee, Wisconsin 53202
Phone (414) 555-4233
Fax (414) 555-4241

I pry myself off the floor, open the blinds, and reset the breaker. Right when the lights turn on, Beverly and Jackson arrive. We all greet each other and scramble to take care of last-minute details before patients begin arriving at seven.

After I unlock the door and fire up my computer and the sign-in scanner, I send a text to Henry before I have a chance to consider better judgment.

ME: I'M GUESSING THIS MEANS YOU SHOULD PROBABLY STOP LOITERING IN FRONT OF BUCKY'S BEANS?

CHAPTER 31

Monday, May 2
Henry

It's seven fifteen when I return to my desk after a brisk walk around the office. It's been months since I've arrived at the office earlier than six, but I had to finish the Bucky's complaint. If it weren't for my colleague Luke coming down with some sort of stomach virus yesterday, which meant I had to take his place in court, I would have had things squared away then. But never being one to shy away from wearing myself thin, I jumped at the chance to take on the extra task. Of course, that meant dragging myself in at five thirty this morning. Now I can check in on the DigiScan case while I wait for Ruth to respond.

I sink into my chair and lean back with my eyes closed, then I take a few deep breaths. I know I'm over-worked, but I also have faith that all my hard work will pay off soon. My status as a partner at the firm is almost certain. I just have to ensure the cases I'm currently working on, the Bucky's case being the most crucial, reach desirable outcomes.

If I visualize it, it will happen.

My eyes snap open and I hop back into action, waking up my computer screen with one hand and reaching for my phone with the other. A text notification from about twenty minutes ago flashes across the screen, and I recognize Ruth's number. I read her message and surprise myself by chuckling.

Maybe it's because I'm sleep deprived, or maybe it's because I'm close to overdosing on caffeine, but I type a response.

ME: I DON'T THINK HOLDING UP THE WALL COUNTS AS LOITERING. BUT YES, I'LL HAVE TO ABANDON MY POST UNTIL THE CASE IS SETTLED. LOL.

Then, against better judgment, I send it, and add Ruth's name and number to my list of contacts. I rub my eyes with the thumb and index finger of my left hand, bringing them together to squeeze the bridge of my nose with a sigh. Now I better send something more definitively work-related, even though the ball is in Ruth's court to return the signed complaint.

From: Henry Mancuso
To: Ruth Bateman
Date: May 3, 2016 at 7:30 AM

Ruth,

Do you have any edits to or questions regarding the complaint? If you think it looks good, we can get it on file today. Otherwise, feel free to email me so we can discuss—

Maybe it would be more convenient for us to talk . . .

Otherwise, feel free to give me a call so we can discuss any issues you might have with it.

Thanks,
Henry

I do my best to focus on other things, but I fail miserably at resisting the urge to constantly check my email and my phone. Finally, a little after eight, an email from Ruth pops up. I reach for my mouse.

"Good morning!" Constance breezes in and sets a cup of coffee from Bucky's Beans on my desk. "Black. Just the way you like it." She smiles, crosses her arms, and leans a hip against the corner of my desk.

"Constance, seriously?" I look from her to the Bucky's cup and back.

"Oh, Henry, just because *Ruth Bateman* is suing Bucky's Beans doesn't mean *you* can't enjoy a cup of their coffee now and again," she says, making light of my reaction.

"Fair enough, but I'd rather not. It just doesn't feel right." I swivel my chair and open a door on the credenza behind me to retrieve a bag full of the QuickForm supplements that were at my apartment. I close the cabinet and hand the bag to her as I swivel back toward my desk. "Here you go. It's all in there."

She peeks inside, and then looks up at me, a pursed reflective grin on her lips. "Henry?"

"Yeah?"

"Have you . . ." She stands upright and tightens her folded arms a bit. "How have you been feeling lately?"

"Fine," I say with a shrug. "Whatever was making me feel so sluggish has passed, and I'm right back in the swing of things."

"I guess what I mean to say is . . . do you think we'll go back to doing anything more than just having lunch together during the work week and working out together? Not that I don't love going on runs with you and forcing you to go to QuickForm with me." Her grin turns mischievous for a second. "But I kinda miss hanging out with you. You know, in a social, more intimate setting." She puts a hand on my forearm.

"Constance . . ." I pause, giving her an earnest look. *Just be honest with her.* "I'm happy with where we stand right now. I thought you were too."

"I am." She pulls her hand back to her side and nods, as if trying to convince herself. "Sorry, I know we've already discussed things." She holds up the bag. "Thanks. I'll stop over one of these days and get all my shoes, so you don't have to bring them here."

"I don't think a big enough bag exists," I say, chuckling.

She laughs and ruffles my hair, which she knows I hate, and grabs the cup of coffee with her empty hand. Then her gaze falls on my computer screen. "Looks like you've been emailing Ms. Bateman a lot. How are things going?"

"Wonderful," I say, minimizing the email window. I'm not sure why I do so, and judging by the way Constance wrinkles her brow, she's not either. "As soon as Ruth gives us the A-OK on the complaint, I can send it over to Bucky's corporate and get this snowball really moving."

"Good. That's great. Let me know if there's anything I can do to help." She eyes my computer screen one more time, and then clip clops her way toward the door. Just when I think she's going to leave, she turns, gripping the doorway. "Henry, if you ever decide you're ready for something more than friendship, let me know . . . because I'm interested."

Constance has never come right out and said she's interested in more than just a casual relationship with me, so I'm taken by surprise, especially since she's chosen to reveal her true interest at work.

"Okay. I will."

Okay? But what else can I say?

She smiles. "All right. I'll see you later then."

"Yep, for sure."

As soon as I can no longer hear Constance's heels, I maximize the email window and open Ruth's message.

From: Ruth Bateman
To: Henry Mancuso
Date: May 3, 2016 at 8:07 AM

Looks good, Henry. Thank you!

By the way, I only sent you the page I had to sign. If, for some reason, you need both, let me know and I'll resend.

Ruth :)

I click to reply.

From: Henry Mancuso
To: Ruth Bateman

Date: May 3, 2016 at 8:20 AM

Thanks, Ruth. The signed page that you sent is all we need. I will keep you posted with all developments after we file.

I hope you have a great day.
Henry

After I send the email, an odd sensation settles in my stomach, but I can't figure out why. I ponder for a minute whether it could have something to do with what Constance said. Maybe I shouldn't say I feel nothing because that's not entirely accurate. I really do like Constance and I think we'd get along well in a more serious relationship, but there's something missing. Something I think I should feel in my gut . . . or in my heart.

Nope. The odd sensation definitely isn't because of Constance.

CHAPTER 32

Thursday, May 5 – Late afternoon
Ruth

Thursday afternoons are usually slow at the chiropractic office, and today is no exception. I've already completed my duties for the day and given the front office, the kiddie play area, and my desk a thorough cleaning, so I hop on Facebook to kill some time. As I'm scrolling through my news feed, a message pops up from Elisha, my former QuickForm coworker.

Ruth! Thank you so much for messaging me about the baby! Sorry I'm just getting back to you—the last two weeks have been quite an adjustment, but I think we've finally figured out this whole parenting gig. We'd love for you to stop by and meet her, but we're leaving Sunday for my husband's parents' house in Sturgeon Bay and will be there for two weeks. Should we plan for a visit when we return? Or, and I know this probably isn't ideal for you but figured it's worth throwing out there, Eliana and I are meeting some of the girls at QuickForm on Saturday. If you're up for it, I know everyone would love to see you. Either way, can't wait for you to meet Eliana! ~Elisha

Without hesitation, I click to reply.

Hi Elisha! I'm glad to hear things are going well. Two weeks from now would work, but I was just looking at the new pics you posted this morning, and OMG, that little girl is too precious! I need to meet her ASAP! So, you can expect to see me on Saturday at QuickForm. What time should I arrive?

As soon as I send the message, a text from Bucky's pops up.

"Seriously?" I say under my breath.

"Hey, Ruth?"

I jump and swivel my chair toward the sound of Beverly's voice, clutching my chest dramatically. "You scared the bejesus out of me!"

"Sorry about that." She puts her hands up, laughing. "Since it's so quiet this afternoon, I was wondering if you wouldn't mind looking over this outline for our next workshop and letting me know what you think."

"Of course!" I say, accepting the handwritten outline from her. "I just have one thing I need to take care of." I place the stack of papers on my lap and screenshot the text.

"Is that another text from Bucky's?" Beverly asks, glancing at my phone. "I thought those were supposed to stop by now?"

"They were," I say with a shrug.

"Hmm, sounds like a great reason to call your lawyer . . ." she says as she turns and heads down the hall, glancing back with raised eyebrows just before she disappears into her office.

Laughing, I swivel back around and move Beverly's workshop outline from my lap to my desk. Then I tilt my Zen Egg all the way to the left before leaning back, phone in hand, to ponder whether to call Henry or not. When the egg comes to a standstill, my phone pings alerting me to a new email.

From: Henry Mancuso
To: Ruth Bateman
Date: May 5, 2016 at 4:20 PM

Hi Ruth,

Just checking in to see if you've received any texts from Bucky's since yesterday. Also, feel free to let me know if you ever want updates. As promised, I'll keep you informed about all major developments as they occur.

Thanks,

Henry

This is either perfect timing or Henry is psychic and sensed I was about to call him.

From: Ruth Bateman
To: Henry Mancuso
Date: May 5, 2016 at 4:25 PM

Hi Henry,

Funny you should ask. I just got one a few minutes ago, and I also got one yesterday.

By the way, I think you might be psychic, because I was just about to call you. Meaning, I picked up my phone right when your email came through. Now that's what I call service. ;)

Ruth

The front door sensor chimes as a family of four new patients enter. I greet them and escort them to the warm-up area. As I'm demonstrating the pre-adjustment exercises they need to do, I hear the faint sound of a ping from my phone and silently scold myself for wanting to rush back to my desk to see if it's a response from Henry. After I answer a few questions about proper form, I return to my desk and scoop up my phone, eager to satisfy my curiosity.

From: Henry Mancuso
To: Ruth Bateman
Date: May 5, 2016 at 4:36 PM

Oh wow. Well they should end very soon, and permanently, because we delivered the complaint to Bucky's HQ yesterday. Please let me know if you receive any more.

*Perhaps we should touch base on Monday. Are you available for a quick
phone call?*

Henry

Why yes, I think I should be able to squeeze you in, Mr. Mancuso.
Suddenly, the chorus to "Call Me" by Blondie is playing in my head.

CHAPTER 33

Saturday, May 7
Henry

Even though most of my muscles have been adequately stimulated, my mind is numb from the mechanical nature of the QuickForm environment. At least when I go for a run or do quick sets of pushups or pullups on my lunch break, I'm in control of my environment. Then again, maybe that's partly why I don't love choreographed workout routines.

I'm stretching my IT bands purely to kill time while I wait for Constance to finish the back and ab routines when I see Ruth walk through the front door. She's holding a yellow gift bag with a baby elephant on it. I'm about to head over to greet her when there's an outburst of squeals from a few employees who are congregated around a table in the seating area by the Nutrition counter. They all rush toward Ruth for hugs, revealing that the table is covered with gifts and one woman is holding a baby. So now the gift bag in Ruth's hand makes sense. What I don't understand is why these women are having a baby shower here.

When the group of women move back to the table and continue what appears to be a baby shower/reunion of sorts, I continue to stretch and pretend not to be eavesdropping.

I'm far enough away that I can't hear everything they're saying, but I do make out bits and pieces, mostly baby related, but things that I'm certain are directed at Ruth, too. *You look great . . . It's been too long . . . Why don't we ever get together? . . . Things haven't been the same without you.*

Is it possible Ruth used to work here? Right when the thought crosses my mind, two QuickForm employees who've just gotten done assisting clients, rush out from behind the counter and give Ruth quick hugs, then they return to their posts. Ruth smiles after them, and that's when she sees me and waves. I smile and wave back, then bend to pick up my water bottle, not because I'm thirsty but rather to create the illusion that I wasn't just watching her. When I stand up, bringing the bottle to my lips, she's already on her way over.

"You again," she says stepping in front of me and putting her hands on her hips. Her hair is piled on top of her head in an unruly manner just like it was last Saturday when I met her for the first time, and a pleasant earthy scent reminiscent of an Aveda spa emanates from her.

I lower the bottle, revealing a grin. "No, it's you again."

"Milking your free trial membership, huh?"

"Something like that," I say, laughing. Then I nod toward the group of women. "Interesting location for a baby shower."

"It's not really a shower, just a quick celebratory gathering . . . This is where we all met, and Elisha, the one with the baby, works here."

"So, you used to work out here?"

She nods. "You could say that."

I look at her quizzically.

"I used to own it." She scans our surroundings and then mumbles, "My ex-husband still does."

"So, the guy on the franchise pamphlets and in the intro video? He's your ex-husband?"

She nods uncomfortably, and then glances over her shoulder at the group of women.

"Wow, that's impressive." I have so many questions but hold back, remembering the look on her face when we first met on the sidewalk right out front and I asked if she ever worked out here before. "Hey, I meant no offense when I said I'd rather go for a jog than work out here. I just prefer being outside, you know?"

Ruth chuckles. "Henry, no offense taken. I'm not really a fan anymore either."

"Are you ready?" Constance gives my hip a subtle bump with her own. Then she sees Ruth. "Oh, Ruth! I can't believe we're running into you again. Are you here to give QuickForm a try?"

"No," she says shaking her head. "I'm just here to deliver a gift and catch up with some friends. It was nice seeing you again . . . Constance, right?"

"Yes, that's right. Good memory," Constance responds. Then she looks at me. "Funny running into her again, isn't it?"

"Yeah," I say with a shrug. "I mean, it's a public place, but I guess so."

"Well, I'm going to get back to my friends." Ruth points a thumb over her shoulder. "Henry, I'll talk to you on Monday then?"

I feel Constance's eyes on me as I nod.

"Feel free to call anytime between noon and two," Ruth says as she turns to leave.

"Will do. Bye, Ruth."

"See you, Henry." She waves as she walks away.

I take a drink of water as Constance watches Ruth until she gets to her friends. "That was interesting."

"What was?" I start walking toward the QuickNutrition counter where I know Constance will get a shot of vitamins. She follows.

"She just seems overly comfortable around you . . . as if you're old pals or something."

"I'm not sure what you mean, but if she does feel comfortable with me, I'd say that's a good thing considering we're working together on the Bucky's case." But I actually think I know what Constance means, because I do feel a sense of comfort around Ruth too. Which is odd, because I barely know her.

"I suppose . . . Hey, why do you have a conference call set up? I thought the complaint was done and you're just waiting on Bucky's to respond."

"I just wanted to touch base. You know, find out if she received any texts over the weekend and update her on what to expect moving forward. That sort of thing." I take a sip of water, attempting to mask my bullshit.

"Oh . . . okay," Constance says turning her attention to the vitaminista.

I sneak a peek over at Ruth and find her looking at me.

We both look away.

CHAPTER 34

Saturday, May 7
Ruth

I've been sitting at my dining room table staring at a sea of colorful puzzle pieces for at least fifteen minutes but still haven't managed to find one match. Usually I can complete the border for a five-hundred-piece puzzle in that amount of time, but tonight I can't seem to focus.

It was wonderful seeing Elisha and her new daughter and all my other QuickForm friends, but it was also hard. They all knew me before my accident, and they all worked with Adam's new wife, who now oversees the Madison area locations. But memories from my past life with Adam weren't the hardest thing about seeing those women today, nor was it seeing the baby, which surprised me. Turns out it was hearing about everyone's significant others. I certainly don't need to be in a relationship to be happy—been there, done that—but it is something I hope for. That certain level of intimacy. The feeling of being with someone who makes my insides quiver and knowing that I make their insides feel the same way. I suppose it didn't help that Henry Mancuso was there, while I'm on the topic of quivering insides. Too bad he's my lawyer, and too bad he has a girlfriend.

Finally, I locate a match. And then another. And just when I think I'm on a roll, "Call Me" by Blondie starts playing, and all I can think about is Henry and that last look we gave each other today at QuickForm.

I pick up my phone and type his name into the Google search bar. Then I delete it. I repeat the process two more times before actually going through with the search.

Dozens of results pop up. The first page is filled with social media and professional profiles, such as on LinkedIn and the one from his firm's website. Most of the rest are links to legal website articles or filed court documents. It isn't until page five that I find a link to the website for Mancuso Construction and Landscape. I click on the site, curious if the web crawlers made a mistake linking Henry to the site. At first glance, it's a nice website for a family-owned and operated business that was established in nineteen seventy-two. They offer both construction and landscape design. I click the *About Us* tab, and several photos appear on the screen. The first one is of an older man and woman sitting and three men standing behind them. One of the men is Henry, and another seems familiar to me, but I can't quite place whether I know him or not. Maybe it's just because he looks like a younger, taller version of Henry. The third man is taller than Henry, too, but he has light brown hair and a much bulkier frame. The next photo is of everyone in the first picture, minus Henry, and their names and company titles are below: Anton Mancuso (President/Owner), Penny Mancuso (CFO), Robert Mancuso (Construction Division Manager), Anthony Mancuso (Landscape Division Manager). Then there's a third photo of Anton Mancuso Sr. and Sofia Mancuso and much younger versions of the rest of Henry's family. Henry looks about fifteen in the photo, and he's holding a shovel. His younger brothers, both who now tower over him, are wearing hard hats. Seeing this adolescent version of Henry warms my heart, and I have an overwhelming urge to text him to say how much I love the photo, but I can't, because that would be weird. Crazy stalker client weird.

For God's sake. What am I doing? This isn't like me to look up people online. In fact, I've never looked up a guy online before.

My phone vibrates, startling me and prompting me to close the browser. Then I accept the incoming call from Sue.

"Hello?" I say softly.

"Hey, what are you doing? Why do you sound weird?"

"Um, nothing. Why? What are you doing?" I take deep, measured breaths, still feeling a bit guilty for stalking Henry.

"Oh, you know. Sitting on my couch drinking the one glass of wine

I'm allowed per day and waiting for the littlest critter to wake up for his eleven o'clock feeding."

"What's Stuart doing?"

Sue snort laughs. "He's passed out on the recliner. Good times, good times. This is exactly why you need to get yourself out there, so I can live vicariously through you!" I hear her sip her wine.

"Sorry, Sue. My drinking days are over."

"I'm not saying you need to go out drinking. I'm saying you need to go out and get yourself laid. Do you know how long it's been since Stuart and I have done it? Two. Weeks. And I know it's been, at least fifty times that for you."

"Last I remember, you said you guys were still at a healthy four times a week."

"Yeah, that was before the littlest critter came along. And even if he wasn't built to survive on four hours of sleep a night, my boobs are so swollen they hurt even if I lay real still and let Stuart do all the work. It only takes the slightest movement, though." She winces, and I laugh. "So, what's going on with you? The last time we talked you'd agreed to help some lawyer sue Bucky's Beans for sending you too many text messages."

I sigh. "So, about the lawyer . . ." I feel the need to confess the inappropriate crush I have on Henry. It might as well be Sue.

"Yeah? What about him?"

"I just Googled him."

"So? I'd Google him too if I were you, just to make sure he's not some crook."

"No, I mean I Googled him because I want to know more about him . . . I also friended him on Facebook."

"Ooooooh. See? You're so deprived of sex that you're fantasizing about some lawyer you've never met."

"Actually, I've met him. Three times."

"What? When?"

I fill Sue in on how I recognized Henry on the street outside QuickForm last weekend, and about how we ran into each other again today when I dropped off the gift for Elisha's baby. I save the kicker for last.

"And when was the third time?"

"He stopped in at Posh last Saturday night. Turns out he and Marty were frat brothers at Marquette."

"And you've never seen him there before?"

"No, I guess Marty hadn't seen him for like five years."

"So you're telling me that this lawyer, who only found you after you —a person who never complains—posted a public complaint on Bucky's Facebook page because they've been texting you coupon codes you never asked for; then you run into this lawyer who you've never seen before on the street in front of the business you used to own and the business the two of you happen to be suing; then he shows up at your part-time place of employment because he's friends with your boss? And you run into him again today?"

"And now I can't stop thinking about him."

"Wow. It sounds like serendipity to me."

"I don't think so, Sue. He has a girlfriend."

"Whaaat? How do you know this?"

"I met her too."

"What's his name?"

"Why?"

"Because I want to see what he looks like."

I laugh and tell her Henry's name. Then I sort through puzzle pieces while I wait for her to look him up.

"Damn. I can see why you can't stop thinking about him. So, what are you going to do?"

"What do you mean?"

"What do you mean what do I mean? Are you going to ask him out or what?"

"No, of course not! He's my lawyer, and I told you, he has a girlfriend."

"Who cares and so what?"

"Um, I do, and are you kidding me? I'd never go after another woman's man."

"How do you know for sure they're dating? Did he introduce her as his girlfriend?"

"Actually . . . no, I don't think he did."

"See? So, ask him out."

"Even if they aren't dating, he's still my lawyer."

"Give me a break, Ruth. It's not like he's your divorce lawyer."

I ponder this one. "I don't know. I guess I'll see how I feel when the case is settled."

"Couldn't that take months?"

"Exactly. If I asked him out and he turned me down that would be awkward . . . for months."

"Or you could start getting laid by a hot lawyer now instead of waiting months."

I ponder this one too.

"Oh, Ruth, I have to get going. Brenton is awake. Keep me posted about the lawyer . . . not the case, the sex."

"Goodbye, Sue," I say with a chuckle.

~

Sunday, May 8
Ruth

It's a little after seven, and I've just locked up my bike on the rack across from QuickForm and Bucky's. Today, I plan to attempt the Summit Stairway again before I get my haul from the farmers' market. When I get to the other side of the road where the path to the stairs begins, I bend over to tie my shoe.

"Ruth?"

I glance up and squint through an eyeful of sun. "Henry?" He reaches a hand down to help me up. "Are you following me?"

"I think I'm the one who should be asking you that. After all, you *are* on my side of town," Henry says, releasing his grip on my hand.

"Thank you," I say with a laugh. I take in his attire. "Out for a run?"

He nods. "You?"

"Yep, I'm going to run the stairs before I get a few things from the farmers' market."

"The stairs?"

I nod toward the path entrance behind him. "That path connects to another when you get about halfway. That one leads to eight flights of stairs that wind all the way down to the beach. Or you can just cut across the market square to get to the top, but today you'd have to weave through the farmers' market."

"Oh, okay, I know the ones you're talking about."

"And you've never used them?"

He shakes his head. "Not a fan of the beach."

"Well, you don't necessarily have to go to the beach. Most people just run up and down for the exercise. It's a great workout. Do you want to join me? I mean, unless it's not okay for us to . . ." I gesture between us.

"Fraternize?"

I nod.

He laughs. "It's fine. I mean, it's just a run, right?"

"Does that mean you're interested? In the run, I mean," I stutter.

Oh, Lordy.

Henry does a poor job of suppressing a grin. "Sure, let's go."

When we get to the top of the stairs, I take a moment to stretch.

"So how often do you run these?" Henry asks, craning his neck to look over the edge at the dozens of stairs that lead down to the beach.

"To be honest, last weekend was the first time I ran them in over three years. So, I'm not going to be moving very fast."

"Well, I've never run them, so we'll go slow together . . . Why three years?"

I hold up my bad ankle for a second, and then set my foot back on the ground, leaning forward for a hamstring stretch. "I could hardly walk, let alone run, for months after a bad accident damaged the bones and tendons in my ankle. Then, even when I could, I still didn't due to a bad case of the woe-is-me's." *Too. Much. Information.*

His eyes move from my ankle, coming to rest on my face. I'm expecting him to ask about the accident, but instead, he says, "At least you're back at it." Then he nods his head sideways toward the entrance to the stairs. "Shall we?"

Maybe he just wants to respect my privacy. After all, we barely know each other.

We start out slow, next to each other at first, but then I pick up speed, and Henry falls behind. I don't stop or slow for him, though, because I can still hear his footfalls behind me. The stairs are wide enough to accommodate people going up on our left, as well as those who want to pass in either direction, sort of the way driving on the freeway works. I've counted the stairs dozens of times, so I know there are exactly one hundred twenty. I also know that we'd have to go up and down all eight flights fifteen times to travel about a mile, so when I get to the bottom, I turn and head back up. When I pass Henry halfway up the first flight, I put my hand up for him to high five. He does so hesitantly.

When I get to the bottom for the eighth time, I jog in place as I wait for Henry who still has a full flight to cover.

"Are . . ." He gasps for breath, "we done?" He asks when he gets to the bottom.

"Why? Do you need a break?" I ask sarcastically.

"Maybe . . . just . . . a short one." He bends over and clutches his knees. "Not going to be moving very fast, huh?"

I stop jogging and start stretching. "Well, I wasn't. You were just going exceptionally slow."

He glances up at me and cracks a grin. Then he stands and looks back at the stairs, his breathing pattern much closer to normal. "I think it's amazing that you run those things."

"Come on," I say, reaching over and giving his sleeve a tug. Then I head toward Lake Michigan.

Henry waits a few seconds and then follows, tiptoeing gingerly across the sand. When we're a few feet from the water's edge, I stop and remove the sling bag draped snugly across my chest, dropping it on the sand. Then I slide off my sneakers and bend over to remove my socks, sticking one into each shoe.

"What are you doing?" Henry asks.

"Going in. Are you coming?"

"I . . . uh . . ."

I wade into the brisk water, leaving Henry to catch his breath and ponder what he wants to do. When I'm in up to my calves, I turn to find him standing there watching me with his hands on his hips. "Isn't it cold? It's got to be what? Sixty something?"

"It feels nice," I say, bending slightly to arc my hand through the water in front of me.

"How do you plan to dry off your feet so you can put your socks and shoes back on?" he asks.

"I hadn't thought about it," I say with a shrug, wondering if there's more to his hesitance than worries over wet feet. Then I roll up the legs of my capris so that they're above my knees and wade in a little further. When I glance back at Henry, he's scratching the back of his head and looking up and down the shoreline. "Is that really what you're standing there thinking about? How you're going to dry off your feet if you get them wet?"

"No, not just that," he mumbles. "I don't particularly like the feel of wet sand between my toes, so I'm thinking about that too."

"Haven't you ever dipped your feet in the lake before? Or when you were in college, didn't you and your buddies ever come down here and jump in? Perhaps a little skinny dipping with a girlfriend?"

He shakes his head and a hint of a smile appears. "Yes, of course I've dipped my feet in the lake before. But, no, I've never jumped in, and I've never gone skinny dipping in there. Why, have you?"

"Who lives this close to a Great Lake his whole life and never goes skinny dipping in it?" I kick a little water in his direction, causing him to take a step backward even though the spray didn't land anywhere near him. "It's just water and sand, Henry. It'll eventually dry and fall off if we sit here long enough. Or we could just carry our shoes and socks up, and our feet will be dry by the time we get to the top." A horrified expression flashes across his face, telling me that walking up without shoes is just as foreign a concept to him as going in the lake on a whim. In response, I laugh and splash more water in his direction. This time he crosses his arms and smirks but doesn't move except to glance down at the few drops that land on his gray t-shirt. "You're lucky you're my lawyer, Henry," I say, exiting the water and taking a seat on the sand next to my bag and shoes. "Otherwise, those water spots on your shirt would be a lot bigger than the sweat stains under your armpits."

"Is that so?" He asks, crouching next to me to retrieve some rocks. He pauses to make eye contact with me before standing. Then he moves within a couple feet of the shoreline, careful not to step on wet sand. As he skips the rocks across the water, I grab a handful myself and join him.

CHAPTER 35

Sunday, May 8
Henry

As Ruth and I walk back up the stairs, I process everything I've learned about her since yesterday. She used to own QuickForm Fitness; somehow she injured her ankle over three years ago; she comes to the farmers' market every Sunday; she prefers to ride a bike or walk instead of driving a car; she's prone to jumping into lakes; she's unaffected by wet sand on her feet and hands, between her toes and fingers, on her face and in her hair; the top right portion of her upper lip curves up a little higher than the left when she smiles; and she's terrible at skipping rocks but looks adorable while doing it . . . *Okay, Henry, time to think about something else.*

I clear my throat.

"Are you okay?" Ruth reaches over and places her hand on my forearm for a second, causing my heart to palpitate even faster than the obscene number of stairs we're in the process of ascending. For the tenth time.

I take a deep breath and let it out as I say, "Yeah, I'm good. All this exercise will have me sleeping like a baby tonight."

She smiles at me, and we forge ahead with only two flights to go.

How is it possible that I've lived in this city my entire life, yet I've never been up and down these stairs? It's not like I didn't know about them. And how is it possible that I've never been in Lake Michigan as an adult? Sure, I went in when I was a kid and my parents used to take my brothers and me on beach outings, but those were planned excursions, and I knew I was going to get wet.

"Well, we made it," Ruth says as she pulls her right leg up behind her, touching her heel to her butt. "You should stretch your quads."

She says it with such an authoritative tone that I follow her lead, pulling my left heel up behind me. But I don't do it as gracefully as she did, and I have to hop a few times before I catch my balance. Ruth laughs and switches legs.

"So, how did you and your ex come up with the idea for QuickForm?"

She shrugs and begins twisting back and forth at the waist as I switch to my right quad. "We both have a love for working out, especially the strength training aspect of it. So, we combined everything I'd learned while obtaining my nutrition, exercise and health science degree and his expertise in business and finance to come up with the rapid rotation concept that is QuickForm. Just like starting any business, it wasn't easy, but things happened to work out because people were looking for an ala carte way to strength train whenever their schedule allowed." She stops twisting. "It's not for everyone, but it really does offer a full body workout if you do the complete circuit."

"Are you trying to get me to convert my trial membership?" I joke.

She smiles and then pulls her phone out of her bag and checks the time. "I have to go. Otherwise I'm going to miss out on the fresh kohlrabi."

"Kohl-what?"

She gives me a mock disappointed look. "You've never had kohlrabi?" I shake my head. "Henry, Henry, Henry. Follow me," she says, turning to cut through the thick brush that abuts the square where the farmers' market is taking place.

So, I follow her and enjoy more than just a cup of coffee from the farmers' market. Afterward, I walk Ruth across the street to where she has her bike locked up, right across the street from QuickForm Fitness and Bucky's Beans where I saw her for the first time.

"Thanks for fraternizing with me, Henry," she says as she removes her red bike from the rack. She turns it to face east. My condo is west.

"Thanks for inviting me to fraternize with you."

"So, you'll give me a call tomorrow then?" she asks, quickly adding, "About the case."

"Yes, I'll call tomorrow afternoon . . . about the case."

"Great. I'll talk to you later then, Henry . . . Bye." With one last smile, she hops on her bike and pedals off. She doesn't get very far, though, before stopping, reaching into the reusable shopping bag in her bike's basket, and pulling out a kohlrabi. She turns and says, "Think fast," as she tosses it to me. Then she hops back on her bike.

As Ruth rides off, I stare at the strange vegetable in my hand and wonder when I'll see her again. Or maybe the question is *will* I see her again? If I don't show up at the farmers' market or Posh when she's there, the odds probably aren't that good. Unless I follow through with adding her neighborhood to my running route. I checked, and it's only about three miles from downtown. But if Ruth sees me run past her house, that could be awkward. I certainly don't want to look like a stalker, but that's exactly what I'm beginning to feel like. Ruth is my client, after all.

At least I maintained some semblance of professionalism when I opted not to go in the water, even though Ruth kind of had me wanting to. What kind of lawyer frolics around in Lake Michigan with a client? Then again, what kind of lawyer accepts a friend request on Facebook from a client?

CHAPTER 36

Monday, May 9
Ruth

"Yes, Mom, I'll tell them . . . Well, the run isn't until July thirty-first, so we have plenty of time to place the order, and people have plenty of time to invite friends and family to join us. . ." Stan Boyd is at the counter adding his name to the interest form for our next workshop on ketogenic eating. When he's done, I wave to him and smile as I continue listening to my mom rattle off the names of people in our Parkinson's caregiver support group who still haven't confirmed whether they're participating in the Fourth Annual Parkinson's Walk/Run that's coming up, but instead of leaving, he waits for me to get off the phone. "We'll just have to make an announcement at the next meeting to remind people . . . Okay, I'll talk to you later this week . . . Love you, too . . . Bye."

As soon as I end the call, Stan says, "I wasn't eavesdropping or anything, but I overheard you say something about a Parkinson's run?"

"Yeah, it's happening at the lakefront on July thirty-first. My mom and I are on a team, and our goal is to raise ten thousand in sponsorship donations."

"Wow, that would be amazing!"

"Why? Are you interested? Anyone is welcome to join us."

"Maybe. My fiancée Val's uncle has Parkinson's, and she's the runner, not me, so I'll ask her. If not, I'll definitely make a donation."

"Thanks, Stan. That's so kind of you. And just so you know, you don't have to be a runner; people walk too. Just let me know within the next two weeks, if you could. We'd like to sign the team up before early registration ends."

"Will do, Ruth," he says with a wave.

"See you, Stan!" Beverly calls as she enters the front office. "Okay, Jackson can handle adjustments for now," she says turning her attention to me. "Are you okay with waiting a few minutes for me to take over for you up here, so I can use the restroom?"

"Of course, I am! You know that."

"Well, I also know you have a hot phone date with your lawyer, so . . ."

"A hot phone date? Really? That's some wishful thinking and quite a stretch," I say, laughing and checking the time. "Oh, before you go, on behalf of my mom and the rest of our White Pines team, thank you and Dr. Jackson for agreeing to sponsor us at the Parkinson's walk."

"Of course, Ruth," she says, smiling humbly. "I just wish we were available to participate."

While Beverly is gone, I tidy up my desk and slide my phone into my pocket, so I'm ready to head out to the courtyard as soon as she returns. Henry is supposed to call in a few minutes.

"All right, hon," Beverly says as she rushes back into the room. "Go on. Skedaddle."

Her timing is perfect because my phone rings as I'm walking down the hall toward the back door.

"Hello?"

"Hi, Ruth. It's Henry. How are you?"

"Couldn't be better," I say, smiling. "Yourself?"

"Good, overall, but I've got to be honest with you . . . my quads are killing me."

"Oh, no! I'm so sorry." I reach the courtyard and take a seat on one of the benches.

"No, no, no. It isn't your fault. Clearly, I need to run those stairs more often."

Just name the day and time . . .

"So, about the case . . ."

"Right, the case. I received two texts yesterday and another this morning. Will those count toward the settlement, if there is one?"

"Wow, that's just . . ." Henry sighs.

"What?"

"Well, Bucky's was served with the complaint last Wednesday, and it's disturbing to me that they haven't yet removed your Clear Connect Wireless number from their database. This makes me think they must not have hired counsel yet or they haven't given your number to their marketing team for removal. Either way, their casual lack of response is infuriating. So as soon as they make an appearance in the case, I'll call their attorney and demand that the messages cease immediately, if you're still receiving them at that point. In the meantime, please forward those messages to me as proof that you're still receiving texts even after we filed the complaint. They'll be very helpful to our case, and yes, they will absolutely count towards the settlement, because it demonstrates that Bucky's has no sense of urgency in putting a stop to their harassing conduct. It's a compelling fact that we can use to explain your experience and the experiences of the class members to the judge." He pauses and takes a few deep breaths. As he does so, I do my best to mask my own heavy breathing. Henry is even more attractive when he's in lawyer mode and all fired up.

After a few seconds, I hear papers ruffling. "So, what's the next—"

"You know what, Ruth? I'd like to confirm whether Bucky's has hired counsel, but I'm not at the office at the moment, so I need to make a quick call. Can you hold, or can I call you back?"

"Um, sure. I can hold, but I only have about ten more minutes."

"Great, don't go anywhere." When the line goes quiet, I close my eyes. Lulled into a trance-like state by the warmth of the sun on my face, I nearly fall off the bench when Henry returns. "Ruth? Are you still there?"

"Yeah, what'd you find out?"

"So, here's the deal. Bucky's hired a woman named Sonya Donovan with a law firm in Madison, and I've just reached out to her to ask if her client could kindly remove your number from its database ASAP. She seemed receptive, saying she'd reach out to Bucky's right away and ask them to do so. Hopefully that does the trick."

"Thank you, Henry," I say, wondering if Bucky's lawyer might think Henry is nuts the way he's all up in arms over a few lingering texts. After all, I'm sure there are much more serious things Bucky's could be sued over. I also wonder what it would be like to witness him in action on a case about something more important.

"No problem. That's what I'm here for."

"Don't take this the wrong way, but do you get all fired up like this with every case? Or do you have some sort of vendetta against frou-frou coffee drinks? Wait . . . have you been hired by Coffee Cave to take out their biggest competitor? I promise, I won't say a word to anyone."

"What?" He laughs. "Sorry to squash your conspiracy theories, but I just don't like when people or companies break the law. Even the mildest infraction gets me fired up." As if it's an afterthought, he adds, "But, I also really want to help you."

"Well, thank you, on behalf of myself and Coffee Cave."

He emits a single chuckle. "Let me know right away if you get anymore texts, okay?"

"Will do, counselor." I pause, trying to come up with something to say that might prolong our conversation, but nothing comes to me. "Okay, then . . . thanks for calling, Henry."

"Sure, no problem. I'll let you know about any new developments, but it could be a while before there's anything new to report."

"Sounds good."

"Okay, talk to you soon then. Bye."

"Bye, Henry."

CHAPTER 37

"Can you please put that thing away, Henry?" My mom gives my phone a stern look, her expression softening when her eyes meet mine.

"Sorry, I'm just browsing through some TCPA settlement news." I'm not lying about what I was looking at, but I'm also not disclosing the full truth. I've never been interested in any aspect of my family's business. If they need advice about dealing with consumer complaints, I'm their guy, but talking about electrical power standards and trenching techniques makes my eyes glaze over.

"Dude, no offense, but no one knows what you're talking about," Anthony says with a smirk.

"Now, now Uncle Tony, Wyatt and Alex are learning that if you don't have anything nice to say you probably shouldn't say anything at all," my sister-in-law chides. Anthony and Lori usually get along great, but Anthony kept Robert out a little too late after work on Friday, even though Lori had dinner plans with a friend from high school. Apparently, she still hasn't forgiven him.

"Mommy," my nephew, Alex, says as he rises to his knees on his chair to whisper something in her ear.

"Sure, buddy, I'll ask him," Lori says. "Hey, Uncle Henry?" She asks, pulling my attention away from the blog post notification I've just received from Arbitration Nation.

"Yeah?"

"Alex was wondering if you'd be willing to be a special guest during career week in his classroom. All you'd have to do is show up and tell the kids why you wanted to be a lawyer and what you like about it.

Then you get to eat some cookies afterward." Alex grins at the mention of cookies.

"Hey, I thought I was going to his class for career week," Robert interjects.

"No, Daddy, we're supposed to invite someone who does a job we want to do."

"Is that so," Robert says with a mock frown. Lori and my mom giggle, and I roll my eyes prematurely at what Anthony is sure to add to the discussion.

"Little Buddy, are you saying you want to be a lawyer like Uncle *Henry*?" Anthony asks, incredulous.

Alex nods excitedly.

"But I thought you wanted to build houses like Gramps, your dad, and me. Remember all the fun tools we get to use?"

Alex shakes his head and smooths out his polo shirt. "Yeah, but I want to wear nice clothes to work and use a phone and computer for tools."

This makes the whole family laugh, even Anthony.

"Sure, Alex, I'd be happy to be your guest. I'll even wear a nice suit that day," I say with a wink.

With that, everyone stands and helps carry things into the kitchen. Even Alex and Wyatt help by throwing napkins in the garbage and returning the butter and Parmesan cheese container to the fridge. When the table is cleared, my mom and I are left alone in the kitchen while everyone else retires to the basement to play ping pong and pinball.

"So, how's—put that phone away, Henry."

I sigh, grinning like a kid who's just been caught with his hand in the cookie jar, and place my phone face down on the counter. Then I grab a Clorox wipe to clean the counters and stove while my mom finishes loading the dishwasher.

"Thank you," she says. "Having a conversation with you is much nicer when you aren't constantly looking at your phone. Now, how's work? How's . . . what was her name? Constance?"

I laugh, silently cursing Anthony and his big mouth. "Work is good, and so is Constance, who's a great *friend* and workout partner, by the way."

"Oh," she mumbles, sounding disappointed. "So, nothing exciting is going on in your life then?"

"Well, I'm not sure you or anyone else in this family would consider it exciting, but I finally delivered the formal complaint to Bucky's Beans." Sighing, I continue. "So now the ball is in their court, and Ruth and I just have to wait to hear from their attorney."

"Ruth?"

"Yeah, she's the lead plaintiff in the case." I throw away a used Clorox wipe and retrieve another.

"How did you find her?"

I chuckle, and before I know it, I'm filling my mom in on everything about Ruth from seeing her public post on the Bucky's Facebook page and running into her on the street to finding out she works for Marty and driving her home. My mom is beyond shocked when I tell her about running into Ruth again at the lake the previous weekend. By the time I get to how sore my legs were earlier this week, she and I are sitting across from each other at the kitchen table, and the tea kettle is whistling, even though I don't recall her filling it with water or turning on the stove.

"So now we wait," I say with a shrug.

My mom gives me a silent grin, then gets up to make her tea. "You know, Henry," she says, her back to me, "I haven't heard you talk this in depth about anything other than work in a very long time."

"What do you mean? Everything I just told you was about . . ." And suddenly I realize what she means. ". . . the Bucky's Beans case."

She returns to the table with her tea cup and saucer and grins as she tears the corner off a packet of Truvia, adding the powdered sweetener to her tea. Then she grabs the string hanging over the edge of her cup and bobs the teabag as she continues, a you're-not-fooling-me look on her face. "Henry, we don't beat around the bush in this family, so I'll just say it. I think you like this woman, but for some reason you're afraid to do something about it."

"Mom," I say, rolling my eyes. "She's a client." She stares at me blankly as she cautiously takes a sip of her tea, so as not to burn her tongue. "It would violate the rules of professional conduct if I dated a client." Still nothing. "I could lose my job."

"Why? It's not like you're a criminal defense attorney and she's on trial for murdering her husband. You're trying to stop Bucky's Beans from sending her text messages. Not that that's not a worthy cause, Henry," she adds as an aside. "But let's get real here. You just talked about this woman for at least ten minutes straight, and I'm pretty sure you smiled a few times. I just think you should explore what's causing those smiles."

"I already know," I say with a shrug. "She's funny and kind of odd. Quirky. That's a good word for her." I nod, proud of myself for coming up with the perfect adjective to describe Ruth.

She emits an exasperated sigh. "Oh, Henry. Is there some rule against you asking her to lunch? Surely you lawyers take clients to lunch, right?"

I shake my head. "No, not technically, but I'm pretty certain it would be frowned upon by my colleagues." What I fail to be forthright about is the situation with Constance, which might help my mother understand. But I already feel lousy enough for not being able to reciprocate Constance's feelings for me, so I don't feel like discussing it right now.

"You know, when you were a kid, you loved going to the beach. Granted, you hated the feel of wet sand on your feet, so you insisted on wearing water shoes the entire time."

I nod.

"Remember that trip we took to Florida the summer before you turned twelve?"

"Of course. Robert and Anthony threw my shoes out the car window on the Interstate when we were on our way to dad's cousin Al's house. They've been pains in my ass since birth."

"Henry," she scolds, a hint of a grin on her lips.

"Sorry," I smirk. Not sorry.

"Anyway," she continues, "Remember how you almost didn't go scalloping with us because you didn't have your shoes to walk across the sand?"

I smile and nod slowly, picturing Cousin Al's house along a canal that leads to the Gulf of Mexico. The place had been built right before we visited, so you had to walk across a stretch of sand to get to the dock that led to his boat. Those water shoes were the only shoes I had that day, and my father refused to drive all the way back to our hotel in Orlando or stop at a store to buy me a new pair. It was near the end of our trip, and he was fed up with my aversion to sand between my toes.

"But then, at the last minute—"

"I took off running across the sand as you guys were about to pull away from the dock because I was desperate not to have to stay behind and play pinochle with Aunt Edna for three hours."

My mom and I both have a good laugh over the memory of Aunt Edna and her love of teaching us kids how to play old-school card games. When our laughter dies down, my mom's expression turns serious.

"And you ended up having the time of your life diving down into the water and swimming with the giant turtles and exotic fish. *And* you caught the most scallops."

Warmth spreads throughout my body when I close my eyes to get a better view of the memory through my mind's eye. That was the first time I ever swam in the middle of the ocean, and the first and only time I've ever been scalloping.

"Just think, if you'd never ran across the sand to the dock, you wouldn't have experienced any of it. Anyway, that's one of my favorite memories of you."

"Yeah," I say opening my eyes and sliding my chair back to stand, "It's one of my favorite memories too." I bend over and give my mom a kiss on the cheek. "I have to get going. I have some work to do."

My mom stands, too, and grabs her tea. "I suppose I'll go down and see if anyone wants a ping pong lesson."

When we exit the kitchen, my mom says goodbye to me and heads toward the basement, while I head toward the front door. As I'm about to enter the living room, I pause outside my old bedroom, which has been converted into a sewing room. However, some items from my younger years remain in the closet and on my old bookshelf, although most of the shelves have become overflow space for my mom's vast paperback collection. She used to reason with my dad that a book addiction is much better than a shoe or alcohol addiction. That usually shut him up.

Starting at the bottom, I scan the tall bookshelf, which almost reaches the ceiling. All my old high school yearbooks are there, along with many of my old grad school textbooks—ones my mom keeps asking me to go through. About three-quarters of the way up the shelf, there are less books and more memento type things, such as old framed photos of me from when I tried various sports as a kid, a certificate from when I competed at the Badger State Spelling Bee, and a few tokens from family road trips. I pick up my Empire State Building statue, and when I do, my eyes fall on the pint glass in the corner behind it. I quickly set the statue on the corner of my mom's sewing table and reach for the glass. Etched onto it is the East Bay Bowl logo, along with *HAPPY 2002!* I was so upset when I first found out Tracey was dating someone new that I threw out anything that reminded me of her, including pictures, ticket stubs, and articles of clothing. This glass is the only thing I kept.

"Hey, what are you doing in here, Henry?" Anthony barges in and throws an arm around my neck, putting me in a headlock.

I lose my grip on the glass and it falls to the wood floor, cracking in several places and denting the floor.

"What the hell, Anthony?" I yell, shoving him away from me.

"Sorry," he says, his hands up in the air. Then he follows my gaze and looks down at the broken pint glass. "At least it didn't shatter," he says, bending to pick it up. He hands it to me.

"Thanks a lot." I say without even looking at him.

"Are you heading out?" he asks, as if nothing has happened. But what do I expect? Anthony has no idea about the memories I associate with this glass.

"Yeah, I have work to do."

"All right, then. I'll probably see you next week." He walks across the hallway into the bathroom.

When I get outside, I pause before getting into my car. I took the pint glass with me but have no idea what I plan to do with it. I can't even use it now with all the cracks in it. Sighing, I walk over to the recycling bin along the side of my parents' garage and toss the glass inside. It didn't take nearly as much strength as running across the sand, but at least it's a step.

CHAPTER 38

Sunday Morning, May 15
Ruth

I'm making my fifth ascent up the stairs at the lake when I see a familiar face looking down at me, causing my heart to skip a beat. When he realizes I've spotted him, he waves and walks over to the entrance of the stairs. He looks different, the hair on his head taking on a slight curl near the tips and his facial hair slightly longer than five o'clock shadow length. As I draw closer to him with only a few steps between us, I nearly trip over my own feet and he hops forward breaking my fall. In that moment, every suppressed hormone in my body rages, preventing me from uttering the words on the tip of my tongue. *Thank you. Can we kiss now?* It's probably for the best.

"Hi," he says grinning down at me.

I glance down at his hands on my upper arms, to the left and then quickly to the right, causing him to release me and take a step back onto level ground. Clearly, reading minds is not Henry's forte.

"Hi." I smile back, placing my hands on my hips, thumbs facing out. "Are your quads ready for another workout? Or are you just out for a regular old wussy run?"

He laughs the way he always does when I say something ridiculous. "Nope, I took a wussy run yesterday. Today I'm back for more of this." He nods toward me, which actually translates to the stairs behind me I'm sure, but a girl has a right to her fantasies.

"Well, okay then. Let's go." I turn and start making my way down. Within seconds, Henry is right beside me, and he stays there for five and a half round-trips up and down.

"That makes ten for me. I think I'm done," I say, pausing at the bottom and leaning forward to catch my breath. I expect Henry to do the same, but instead he walks about five feet out onto the beach and stares at the water. I slide my feet out of my sneakers and remove my socks. Then I reach down to grab a handful of rocks. When I get to Henry's side, I hold out my open palm, revealing the rocks. "I'm going to dip my feet in the water."

He takes the rocks from me and follows me to the shoreline. I walk right past the point where the dry sand becomes wet, and he stops as I expected he would. Then he hurls one of the rocks I gave to him, and it hops five times across the surface before it disappears into the lake.

"How'd you learn to do that so well when you hate water?" I ask with a smirk.

"I don't hate water." He grins and skips another rock. "I hate the thought of cold, wet sand on my feet." He holds eye contact with me and continues grinning. Then he does something unexpected.

Henry drops the rocks in his hand, bends over, and unties his shoes. He gingerly removes one shoe and one sock, and then stuffs the sock inside the shoe. He pauses for a second with his bare left foot hovering above the sand, and then he puts it down and quickly removes his other shoe and sock. I watch silently, secretly wanting to laugh at the uncomfortable expression on his face, and I bet myself that he's going to change his mind and run for the pavement any second. But he doesn't. Instead, after straightening his sneakers so that they're resting neatly side by side, he walks across the wet sand and joins me in the water.

I look over at him and say the first brilliant thing that comes to my mind. "You're in the water."

"Yeah, I am," he responds with a goofy half grin. "Now what?"

"Now we make the most of it," I say, reaching both hands into the water and splashing him.

His eyes widen as does his grin, and he splashes me back.

~

"So, what are your plans for the rest of the day?" Henry asks.

I've just placed my goodies from the farmers' market into the basket on my handlebars. I was pleasantly surprised when Henry stayed to stretch with me after our jaunt into the lake. And then I was even more surprised when he joined me as I walked through the farmers' market. Granted, he was distracted by his phone a few times, but it was still nice to have him around. When we first started walking around we were dripping wet, and Henry had goosebumps all over his arms because he'd given me his sweatshirt. Now we're just damp and probably both smell mildly like wet dog.

"This was it," I say, running my fingers through my unruly hair as I pull it up into a bun on top of my head. A short strand falls over my left eye, and Henry reaches out to push it behind my ear. Now I have goosebumps. "What about you?"

"Oh," he says glancing down at his phone, "nothing much. I have a crazy week ahead of me at work, so I think maybe I'll relax with a book or crossword puzzle. Unless . . ." He furrows his brow and runs his fingers through his hair.

"Unless what?"

"Unless you'd like to grab lunch or an early dinner?" His furrowed brow straightens as his eyebrows rise quizzically.

"I'd like that, but . . . I don't mean to pry, but would Constance be okay with that?"

"Constance?" The furrow in his brow returns. "Uh . . . she and I aren't dating," he says, shaking his head. My heart starts racing, but I sense there's more based on his expression. "I mean, we were for a while, but now we're just friends. And colleagues, of course."

And suddenly my thoughts begin racing after my heart. *Hold on! Wait! What about the fact that he's your LAWYER?* "But . . . is it okay for us to have lunch? I mean, can we . . . ?" I don't even know what I mean to say, so I simply gesture at the distance between us.

Henry's gaze falls to the ground. Then he purses his lips and his chest begins heaving. After a few seconds, he looks up, his eyes resolute. "It's just lunch. It's fine."

"Oh . . . okay, great. Where should we go?" I blurt, before the opportunity is lost.

"It's only about ten-thirty. How about if we both shower, and then I can meet you at your place at one? Would that be enough time?"

"Plenty," I say, pulling my bike from the rack.

"Great, I'll see you then."

We smile at each other, him backing away and me getting on my bike, then at the same time we both turn and leave.

During my entire ride home, certain moments circulate through my mind. Seeing him looking down at me while I was running up the stairs, him catching me when I tripped, the disgusted look on his face when he ran across the wet sand (that one makes me laugh), the way he removed the loose strand of hair from my eye, and his heaving chest.

Instead of suing Bucky's Beans, I almost feel like thanking them for introducing me to Henry.

CHAPTER 39

Sunday Afternoon/Evening, May 15
Henry

"What are you doing, Henry?" I whisper to myself. I've been sitting in my car in the underground parking garage of my condo for the last five minutes, contemplating whether I should cancel on Ruth. I know I've been walking a fine line by talking to her and seeing her on a casual level, but a distant voice inside my head keeps telling me it's fine. Why though? I should know better.

I look down at the text I started when I got out of the shower. I've keep typing and deleting. Currently, it says *Sorry, Ruth, but something came up* . . . I lean my head back, sighing heavily and closing my eyes. When I do so, I picture Ruth and me standing in Lake Michigan, and suddenly it occurs to me that I never once thought about the rocky sand between my toes when we were splashing each other. Afterward was another story, but even then, I found myself distracted from my discomfort simply because any breaks in our conversation were few and far between.

It's just lunch. And who's going to know anyway? I think, my eyes popping open. Then I completely delete the text I began composing over an hour ago and start my car.

~

Paranoia rears its ugly head again when I make my way up Ruth's walkway and feel eyes on me. But a quick glance to my left reveals the source, and my increased heart rate slows. A spry-looking woman with a long white braid hanging over her shoulder peers at me from behind dark boxy sunglasses that are way too big for her face. I wave, and she gives a curt nod before going back to watering her flowers.

Seconds after I ring Ruth's doorbell, the door flies wide open, and Ruth extends an arm, inviting me to enter. "Hey, Henry. Come on in." She closes the door behind me and says, "I just have to do something with this hair. As you've probably noticed it leads a life of its own." She shrugs, pointing to her blonde afroesque do. "Make yourself at home."

"Thanks," I say, not really looking at her because I'm nervous.

She scurries off, leaving me alone in her living room. It's cozy with a natural stone fireplace, hardwood floors, and earth-toned walls and draperies. And her furniture is an interesting collection of mismatched pieces.

I walk through to the attached dining room where there's a large table covered with puzzle pieces grouped by color. The box cover for the one-thousand-piece puzzle is propped upright to reveal what the final project will look like: a waterfall surrounded by a tropical landscape. I begin searching for pieces to complete the brightly colored flowers in the foreground.

"I'm ready," she says cheerily as she enters the room.

When I look up at her, my breath hitches. I don't know if it's because of the flattering white dress she's wearing or because of the way her hair is pulled back so that not a single strand is out of place, but it takes every fiber of my being to not imagine what it would be like to kiss her. Realizing that I'm on dangerous ground, I fake a cough and look away quickly and slide a few puzzle pieces around on the table as panic mode sets in. Asking Ruth to lunch was a very bad idea.

"Do you like puzzles?" she asks as she steps up to the table and begins sliding pieces around too.

I greedily inhale her spa-like scent before shifting a step to the left, increasing the space between us. "Sure. But I haven't completed one in at least twenty years." We both stop sorting and look at each other. "I remember one year for Christmas, when I was seven or eight, I got a five-pack of Disney character puzzles. I worked on them for hours on the floor in our living room until they were all complete."

"How many pieces was each puzzle?" Ruth asks.

"I don't know for sure. Maybe fifty?" I say laughing. "I'm color blind, so I kind of suck at puzzles."

"But you were also a kid, so I'd say doing five puzzles on Christmas morning was quite an accomplishment."

I take in her smile and the delicate features of her face. "Shall we go?" She nods, and we make our way outside.

I figure we'll just decide where to go once we hop in the car, but when we reach the sidewalk, she asks, "Are you okay with walking to a nearby bistro?"

My thighs are screaming for me to make up an excuse for why we should drive, but I know Ruth would much rather walk, so I say, "Absolutely. You lead. I'll follow."

~

"That food was amazing," I say as I hold open the door of Wallflower Bistro for Ruth. "I never knew brussels sprouts could taste so good."

"Aren't you glad you decided to try them?" Ruth asks, raising her eyebrows at me.

Nodding, I say, "Thanks for forcing the first one into my mouth."

"Anytime. Hey! Let's stop here." Before I can respond, she's opening the door to Second Chance Consignment.

"All righty then." This time Ruth holds the door for me as I enter the small thrift store next to the bistro. "Thank you . . ." My voice trails off when I see how different it looks inside than I expected. Most resale shops I've gone to have been unorganized and cluttered with items that have been discarded for good reason. Games with missing pieces, shirts that are stained or missing a button, incomplete dish sets. But this place is organized like a big box store. Aisles are labeled, and merchandise is staged so that you'd never guess you were in a thrift shop if someone blindfolded you and shoved you inside.

Before I can ask if there's anything in particular she's looking for, Ruth heads for aisle two, which is labeled *Crafts, Costumes, Clothing*. She's still walking fast even after all the stair running this morning and the walk to the bistro. I smile, wondering why she's in such a hurry.

"Can I help you find something, sir?" a gangly teenager with shaggy hair asks.

"No, thank you, I'm just here to browse."

When I enter the aisle, I find Ruth sifting through the clothing in a section labeled *NEW*. She's already holding a few items in her non-sifting hand. Suddenly I have a flashback of going clothes shopping with Constance one time. She took forever to decide on items to try on, and then took even longer trying on the items she chose. I vowed to never step foot in a store with her, and possibly any woman, ever again. Granted, Constance is an admitted shopaholic. Could Ruth be one too?

"Whatcha got there?" I ask, trying to sound nonchalant even though a mini red flag is beginning to rise in my head. Of course, a red flag like this would be nothing compared to the one that overshadows every interaction Ruth and I have.

"Just a few tops. One for my mom, who never buys herself anything, and two for my friend Sue, who's three months into nursing." She looks me in the eye. "Can you imagine how annoying it must be to give birth and still not be able to wear your favorite shirts because your boobs are three times their normal size?"

"No, not really," I say laughing. "So why the mad dash into the store?"

"Because today is the second Sunday of the month, and that's the day they put out all the new stuff." She leans in and whispers, "I only know that because the owner used to work out at QuickForm. So, shhhh." She puts a finger to her lips.

"Mum's the word."

"If you don't mind, I'd also like to get some yarn for a few knitting projects I need to start."

"You knit?"

She nods. "Not well though. And not fast either. That's why if I hope to finish scarves for my family for Christmas, I need to start soon."

"I don't mind at all. In fact, I'd like to take a look around. Find me when you're ready to go?"

"Sure." She smiles and heads to the opposite end of the aisle where the yarn must be located.

I turn and exit the aisle the way I came, and walk slowly down the main aisle, browsing the signs. Ruth's clothing purchases have inspired me to buy something for someone else, too, so I turn down aisle six. When I get to the books, I scan the shelves for any author that I've seen my mom read, but then it occurs to me that if I get one by an author I know she's read, there's a good chance she'll have already read it. So I change my strategy and look for a book I think my mom is unlikely to have read and settle on a tattered copy of *Fifty Shades of Gray*.

"Are you buying that?" Ruth's shocked voice startles me. I turn to find her wearing a straw hat with a wide flowing rim, the most ridiculous festive red, white and blue sunglasses with stars sticking out at the corners, and a coral colored boa, which is wrapped around her neck a few times.

"Are you buying those?" I ask equally as shocked.

"No," she says, "unless you think these glasses make me look younger. Then maybe . . ."

I shake my head at her, my cheeks beginning to ache from smiling so much this afternoon. "I thought I'd get this for my mom."

"Ohhh, no you don't." She takes the book from me and hands me her yarn and shirts. Then she places the sunglasses on top of the hat she's wearing and begins browsing through the books.

"This one. You should definitely get her this one."

"*The Time Traveler's Wife*," I read, as we trade items.

"Trust me, she'll love it," Ruth says, her eyes migrating to something behind me and narrowing.

"What's wrong?" I turn to see what she's looking at, but she's already reaching onto the shelf behind me to retrieve a glass that's out of place.

"I hate when people don't put things back where they belong. You ready?" I glance down at the glass in her hand and can't believe my eyes. It's a vintage East Bay Bowl pint glass just like the one I threw in the recycling bin at my parents' house the night before. "I'm just going to put this and these other things back real quick before we check out. Hey, are you okay?"

"You're not going to believe this."

"What?"

"I used to have that exact same glass."

"Really? From East Bay Bowl?"

I nod. "Remember how I told you I haven't been bowling for at least thirteen years?" Now she nods. "Well, the last time I went bowling was the night I got a glass exactly like that one."

"What happened to it?"

I reach out with my free hand and she gives me the pseudo memento. Then I examine it as I answer her question. "It broke. Last night at my parents' house when I was there for dinner. My little brother startled me when I was holding it, and I dropped it." I shake my head in disbelief.

"This must be a sign. Don't you think?"

"A sign of what?" I ask.

"Duh, Henry. That you should get it . . . to replace the one that broke."

I squeeze my eyebrows together, contemplating, because I've never really believed in signs. "Nah, it's just a glass." I look back up at Ruth, with the ridiculous hat on her head and the corny boa wrapped around her neck, and my smile returns.

By the time we get back to Ruth's house, it's nearly six. Part of me hopes she'll invite me in as we stand on her porch outside her front door, but I also know that I have chores to do to prepare for the crazy busy week I have ahead of me.

"So," I say to Ruth.

"So," she says back.

"I have an extra crazy workload this coming week, so I may not be able to make any social calls. But don't be surprised if you hear from me about the case."

"I have a busy week ahead, too. I'm covering for someone at Posh on Tuesday, and then Thursday is my last day."

"It is? But you seem to really enjoy working there."

"I do, but I think it might be time for me to cut Marty loose."

"I'm sure he's quite sad about it, despite what he might tell you. Anyway, I better get going. I have about a million things to do and only two hands to do them with." The way I hold up my hands might seem cheesy if I was with someone else.

"Thanks for lunch. Next time it'll be my treat."

I would never allow Ruth to buy me lunch, but I nod in agreement anyway. "Okay then," I say clapping my hands once. "I'll be in touch this week . . . And you can be in touch too, of course . . . If you want." I slowly walk down her front steps, looking back over my shoulder with a wave.

"Henry?"

"Yeah?" I spin back around.

She takes a few steps so that she's at the edge of the porch looking down at me on the walkway.

"Was this a date?"

My heart rate spikes as I open my mouth to respond. but Ruth continues.

"Yikes, that was probably a stupid question, right?" She sighs, oblivious to how wrong she is. "It's just that . . . it's been a long time since I've felt this kind of connection with someone. So, I guess I'm sort of hoping it *was* a date . . . I mean, it sure felt like one." I nod, because there's nothing I was thinking of saying that she hasn't just said. "You know what, though? If this was a date, there was only one thing missing that would have made it perfect."

"What?" I ask, dazed, probably because of the sudden increase in blood flow to my brain, as well as another specific area of my body.

She takes a deep breath, her chest rising slowly and falling even slower. Just when I think she's never going to take another, she blurts, "A kiss." Then she looks to her left and to her right, as if she can't believe the words that just came out of her mouth. I can't help but laugh because this funny, attractive, confident woman can be so incredibly odd at times. But I love it.

Ruth turns, about to disappear inside and leaving me wishing I'd given her that kiss. Then she pauses, does an about face, and rushes down the stairs, coming to an abrupt stop so that we're only inches apart. Before I even have a chance to process the war that's raging inside of me, she leans up and kisses me. When I open my eyes a split second later, she's already headed back up the stairs. Just before she enters the house, she looks back over her shoulder and says, "There. Perfect."

CHAPTER 40

Saturday, May 21
Ruth

I've just returned from a run through my neighborhood, during which I found my mind wandering to thoughts of Henry. It's been six days since our first "date," but I haven't *really* heard from him since. Sure, we exchanged dozens of emails throughout the week, but they were all strictly related to the case. It turns out Bucky's admitted in their response to the complaint that someone who previously had my number signed up for the text messages, and Bucky's "forgot" to remove the number from its system when it was reassigned to me. When I read that email, I knew I was in for a slew of others, because I've learned that Henry likes to be thorough, and this small admission of guilt from Bucky's had him all fired up. The next handful of emails revealed: Bucky's didn't even have consent from the previous subscriber to send the texts, because said subscriber checked a box on the signup form saying "no" to text messages, yet Bucky's sent them anyway; Bucky's pulled a cheap move by filing a motion asking the court to delay the proceedings for a few months to wait for a ruling from the U.S. Court of Appeals for the District of Columbia, which their attorney believes could impact the case favorably for them; and Henry will be filing an objection to their motion in addition to a declaration stating that I continued to receive text messages even after the complaint was filed, which will highlight just how lackadaisical Bucky's counsel has been towards this widespread problem. Henry assured me several times that the motion they filed is an obvious delay tactic, and the court is not likely to grant the request for a stay.

Henry's emails were friendly, as usual, but I found myself

disappointed that there was nothing personal in any of them. No "how are you?" or "how is work?" or "hey, would you like to run the stairs with me again next weekend and make out on the beach afterward?" I was well aware that my thoughts were irrational considering one of his bosses was copied in every email, but that didn't stop me from thinking them. I was tempted to text him several times, but I didn't want to add any distractions during what he even said would be a crazy busy work week for him. But that's not the only reason I've held back. I also can't stop thinking about the kiss I planted on him. What was I thinking?

Instead of showering right away, I'm busy putting away the old mementos I picked up from my mom's house last night. One of the items is a Niagara Falls puzzle. I'll never open the box again, but the puzzle is a reminder of my dad, so I open the cabinet where I store all my unopened puzzles and squeeze it in on the top shelf. As I rise from a crouched position, my phone vibrates. I run to the living room where my phone is on the coffee table next to the three small boxes of items I'm going through. When I see who it is, I do a quick happy dance before answering.

"I was wondering when you'd return from planet work," I answer casually. "Welcome back." I'd rather eat a centipede than let on that I'm paranoid about the kiss.

His soft chuckle makes my insides twirl.

"How are you, Ruth?"

"I'm great. Had a nice run this morning," *during which I thought mostly about you*, "and now I'm just sorting through some old childhood mementos I picked up from my mom's house last night. How are you?"

"Good," he says, an upbeat tone to his voice. "I just got back from a run myself . . . Hey, I feel like I should apologize for not reaching out at all this week. I mean, I know we emailed back and forth a lot about the case, but that doesn't really count. I just have a bad habit of letting work take over every aspect of my life sometimes. I don't even think I got home earlier than eight any day this week. So, anyway . . ."

"Henry, you don't have to explain. I get it. Now that I'm not receiving the texts anymore, the Bucky's lawsuit is usually the last thing on my mind, but I know that's not the case for you. I wish I could be of more help than just signing and returning documents every few days."

"Oh! Speaking of documents, in response to those written discovery requests we served yesterday, Bucky's has said they'll produce thousands of pages regarding text transmissions under the Perks program, which we expect will be very helpful for the case. And as far as Bucky's motion to delay the case—"

"Uh, Henry . . . it's Saturday. Can you tell me about all this on Monday? Please?"

"Oh, yeah." He clears his throat. "Sorry . . . So, what are you up to after you're done with your sorting?"

"Oh, I don't know. I was thinking about working on that puzzle you saw on my dining room table last weekend."

"Would you like some help?"

"From you?" I say, giving him a hard time over his puzzle solving skills, or lack thereof.

"Yes, from me," he laughs.

~

"Here, these look like they belong in this area," I say sliding a handful of pieces over to Henry's corner of the waterfall puzzle.

"I'll do my best," he says, grabbing a couple pretzel twists from a bowl and eating those while he uses his free hand to move the pieces around.

Music is playing softly in the background. Other than that, we've been working quietly for about thirty minutes now.

"So, do you do puzzles a lot?" he asks. I imagine he's probably wondering if this is the most fun he can expect to have on a weekend if we end up dating long-term.

"If I say yes, are you going to think I'm the most boring person on the planet?"

"Not a chance," he says, shaking his head and winking at me.

"Okay then," I say laughing. "I pretty much always have a puzzle on this table."

He nods and grabs another pretzel. "What do you do with them when they're done?"

"Sometimes I just take them apart and save them, so I can do them

211

again. But I also glue and frame them, like those." I point at the wall behind me where three large puzzles of famous paintings by Monet, Van Gough, and Degas are hanging.

"Those are puzzles?" He stands and moves behind me to examine the puzzle art up close.

"Yeah. Isn't it crazy how you can't even tell from a distance?"

"Wow," he whispers and then sits back down.

"Most of the ones I frame I donate to nursing homes and rehabilitation centers."

"Amazing," he says under his breath. "When did you start doing puzzles as a hobby?"

"My dad used to do puzzles all the time, and he always had one in progress on an old card table in our basement." I look up from the section I'm working on and smile to myself. "In fact, one of my earliest memories is of my brother and me working on a train puzzle with my dad. He was showing us tips for finding matches." I shrug away the memory and go back to searching for one particular piece. "Anyway, besides the fact that puzzles remind me of my dad, I also like the sense of accomplishment I feel after going through the ups and downs of putting together one that's mammoth sized. The border is usually no problem, but then there's everything inside—that's where the real challenge begins. Sometimes there's that little speck of indigo thrown in among a sea of chartreuse, and you have to sift through all the chartreuse pieces until you find the right one." I look up at Henry and find him staring at me with his chin propped up on one palm. "Do you want to see something?"

"Sure." I stand and walk over to the lowboy cabinet against the wall behind him. He stays seated but turns to watch me open the four doors, revealing dozens of puzzle boxes. Some are open, and some aren't. "Wow. Excuse my language, but that's a shit ton of puzzles."

I laugh and am about to close the last door when Henry stops me.

"Hey, can I see that one?" He's pointing at the five-thousand-piece Niagara Falls puzzle I just put away this morning.

"Yeah," I say, curious. I remove it from the cabinet and hand it to him.

"Now *this* is a mammoth puzzle," he says, eyes wide. "It's open," he continues, looking up at me. "How long did it take you to complete?"

"That one has never been completed." He tilts his head inquisitively. "I don't think I've told you this, but my dad had Parkinson's disease. After he developed the hand tremors, I started visiting regularly to help him with his puzzles. He'd do most of the searching, and then I'd snap the pieces into place. That puzzle was the last one we ever worked on together. We were only half done with it when he developed aspiration pneumonia and had to be admitted to the hospital. He never returned home again after that."

We stare at each other in silence for a moment, tears forming in my eyes. That's when "American Girl" by Tom Petty comes on, and the corners of my mouth turn up in a smile.

"Why are you smiling?" Henry asks.

I grab the puzzle from him and put it back in the cabinet. Then I hold my hands out to him and give him a gentle tug when he takes hold. "What are we doing?" he asks.

"Dancing," I say, pausing at the speaker to turn up the volume, and then pulling him into the living room.

I come to a stop on the pseudo dance floor in front of the fireplace and begin moving to the music. My eyes are closed for a few seconds, and when I open them, Henry is barely moving, and his cheeks have taken on a pink tinge.

"Henryyyyyy," I coax. "Surely you can do better than that. I mean, who doesn't get the urge to dance with wild abandon when they hear this song?" I grab his hand and take the lead, giggling quietly, because it appears that Henry doesn't have even an ounce of rhythm.

Near the end of the song, there's a loud knock, prompting Henry to still. We both glance at the door and see Joan's face in the window.

"Can you please turn this down a little while I see what my neighbor needs?" I ask. He nods as he makes his way to the speaker on the lowboy, and I rush to open the door.

"Hey, Joan! Come on in," I say, opening the door wide enough for her to enter.

"Oh, no thanks," Joan says, staying put on the porch. But she leans her head inside to get a look at Henry who's returning from turning the music down. "Sorry to bother you . . . I see you have company."

"No problem. What's up?"

"Just wondering if you have some baking soda I could borrow. I'm making zucchini bread."

"Yes, of course. I'll get it for you right away. This is Henry, by the way. He's the lawyer who's working on the Bucky's Beans case. You remember how they were texting me?"

"Is that so? Are the two of you having a business meeting then?" She gives me a knowing look, which I pretend not to see.

"Henry, this is my neighbor, Joan."

"It's a pleasure to meet you, Joan." He extends his hand, but Joan hesitates before shaking it.

"I'll be right back," I say, rushing off to get the baking soda. While I'm gone, I overhear bits and pieces of their conversation, which is basically Joan badmouthing Bucky's Beans and other big companies like them who "will do anything to make a buck." Henry mentions the petition she started to keep Bucky's out of Bayview, and he laughs a few times.

"Here you go, Joan!" I say shuffling into the room.

"Thanks, Ruth."

"No problem."

"Nice to meet you, Henry."

"You too, and again, it's really impressive the way you've worked to keep the bigger companies out of the neighborhood."

"Yeah, well, I grew up three blocks from here. And someone has to stand up for the small business owners," she says, turning to leave. "Oh, Ruth?" She looks back just as she's about to descend the porch stairs.

"Yes, Joan?"

"Maybe he should join you when you come over for that dance lesson we talked about." With that, she turns and leaves.

I smile at Henry, and he asks, "Am I really that bad?"

CHAPTER 41

Thursday, May 26
Henry

I'm pacing my office, iPad in hand, reviewing patent case law relevant to the Memory Hub suit when my phone vibrates. I hustle over to my desk, certain that it has to be Ruth responding to the text I sent this morning or the message I left during my lunch break. Instead, it's a message notifying me that my dry cleaning is ready for pickup. Sighing, I back out of the message and open mine and Ruth's ongoing text thread. I scroll through about a dozen texts dating back to Sunday when we spent the entire day together. It started with us running the Summit Stairway and ended with us grilling salmon and vegetable skewers at her place, followed by a make-out session on her couch. How I managed to refrain from tearing off her clothes is beyond me, and I'm jonesing to pick up where we left off. But my workload this week is demanding, as usual, so I haven't seen her since. To make up for it, we've been texting each other regularly. That's why her silence today is unusual.

I try to go back to my case law research but can't seem to make it more than a few minutes without checking the time. It's nearly two, so Ruth would have had a chance to respond by now. Before I waste any more time reading the same two sentences over and over, I put my iPad to sleep and walk over to the door. Then I peek inconspicuously into the hall as I slowly close it. I'd hate for someone to walk in on me without warning while I'm doing what I'm about to do.

When I get back to my desk, I grab my phone, lower myself into my chair, and hunker down behind my computer screen. Since I've already texted Ruth and left her a message, I don't want to try either again and be *that* guy. Instead, I open the Facebook app on my phone and navigate to

Ruth's profile. I'll be *that* guy instead. Ruth hasn't posted anything, but I'm surprised to find two posts on her wall made by other people today. The first is by a woman named Ginny Bateman and says: *My thoughts and prayers are with you guys today, Ruthie.* And the next is from a man named Charles Bateman. It says: *I still miss him every day, Ruth. Love and comforting thoughts to you, your mom, and Tyler.* From what I can tell, Ruth hasn't reacted to either of the posts, but dozens of others have. Most have simply clicked the thumb, heart, or sad face, but some have commented with sentiments similar to those conveyed in the posts themselves.

I sit slumped in my seat, suddenly overcome by melancholy. Now I understand why Ruth most likely hasn't been in touch with me. These posts obviously have something to do with her dad. But what exactly is the significance of today? I wish I knew so I could be there for her.

But why can't I regardless?

I back out of the Facebook app, and type Wixley Chiropractic into my browser. As soon as the business information pops up, I press the phone number to connect.

After three rings, an unfamiliar voice answers. "Hello! Wixley Chiropractic. This is Gemma. How can I help you?"

"Uh, hi, Gemma. May I please speak with Ruth Bateman?"

"Oh, I'm sorry, but Ruth isn't here today. Can I take a message? Or if you're a patient here, maybe Beverly can help. I'm just filling in for today."

I want so badly to ask this woman why Ruth isn't there, but that would probably seem odd. "No, no message. Thank you. Goodbye." The moment I end the call, there's a knock on my door. "Yes?" I call out loud enough that whoever's on the other side should hear.

The door opens about a foot, and Constance pokes her head inside. "Hey, it's time for our weekly meeting with the paralegals. Are you coming?"

Crap. I've been so preoccupied this afternoon with wondering why Ruth hasn't responded that I completely forgot about the meeting. Without thinking, I do something I've never done before. "Actually, I'm not feeling so well." Closing my eyes, I squeeze my forehead and sigh heavily.

"So you're going to skip the meeting? Really?" Constance asks, her shock obvious and completely warranted considering I've never once missed work due to illness.

I glance up at her with my eyelids half open. "Yeah. I think I need to head home. Will you please cover for me?"

"Yeah, of course. You've never gone home early in all the years we've worked together, so you must feel pretty horrible. Do you want me to stop by later with some soup or something?"

"Nah, I think I just need to go to sleep. Thanks though." I fake cough for effect, causing Constance to shield her nose and mouth with her hand.

"You better get out of here before you get everyone else sick too. I hope you feel better soon," she says, backing out of my office and closing the door.

I promptly lower my head and bang it a few times against my desk. *What* has come over me?

∾

It's just after three when I knock on Ruth's front door. After about ten seconds and no sign of her, I think about leaving and just waiting patiently for her to call. But I didn't skip out of work for nothing, so I knock again, harder this time. Finally, I hear movement from inside, and shortly after, the door opens a crack.

"Henry?" Ruth widens the gap she's peeking through but not nearly enough to welcome me inside, causing my stomach to drop.

"I just . . ." I say, raising my shoulders and my palms for a second before slowly lowering them. "I'm sorry. I shouldn't have come here. You clearly need some space." Shaking my head, I rake the fingers of my left hand across the side of my head as I turn to leave.

"Henry, wait." When I turn to face her again, the door is now wide open, and Ruth is in full view. Her hair is sticking out in all directions, much wilder than I've ever seen it before. And her eyes are puffy and bloodshot. She pulls the long drapey sweater she's wearing closed to conceal the leggings and tank top she has on underneath. Then she crosses her arms. The next words out of her mouth are music to my ears. "Do you want to come in?"

"Yes, of course," I say, nodding.

When I get inside, I stand awkwardly, unsure whether it's okay for me to hug her or kiss her the way I want to. But Ruth puts my mind at ease when she moves in for a hug after closing the door. It feels different from others we've shared, though, because there's nothing sensual about it. Instead, it's as if she's counting on me to support her or keep her from falling.

"I'm sorry I haven't contacted you today," she says, the side of her head still planted firmly against my chest.

"It's okay. I'm sorry I showed up unannounced," I caress her back as I speak, "but I was concerned because it's not like you to not respond. Unless it's the weekend and I'm asking about something related to the Bucky's case, that is." I squeeze my eyes shut, cringing at my mention of the case, even though I wasn't really mentioning the case per se. Surprisingly, Ruth snorts and smiles up at me. Then she grasps my hands and pulls me over to the couch. We both take a seat, and she turns to face me with one leg bent in between us.

"Henry, today is my dad's birthday. He would have been sixty-six."

"Oh . . . Ruth, I'm so sorry." I reach out and rub her shoulder, my arm resting along the back of the couch.

"It's okay," she says, shaking her head, a faraway look in her eyes. Then she glances up at me and smiles. It's only half the size of a typical Ruth Bateman smile, but it still cuts right to my heart. "I'm not usually like this on his birthday, you know? It's just that for the first two after he died, my mom, my brother and I went bowling, because that's what he liked to do on his birthday. In fact, I believe he only missed celebrating at the bowling alley one year since my brother and I were born, and that was because he had his appendix removed the day before. Anyway, I thought it was going to become a tradition, but then years three and four, my brother couldn't make it. And now this year, neither can my mom. So it might seem silly, and I know it isn't true, but I feel like they've both moved on. And I just feel sad." She gives me another half-smile. "I'm glad you stopped by."

"Me too," I say, smiling back.

We readjust ourselves so that she's leaning against me with my chin resting on her head and my arm is around her. Then we sit in silence, I wonder if there's any way for me to cheer Ruth up, even if it's just a little bit. Then I get an idea.

"Ruth?"

"Yeah?" She turns slightly and looks up at me.

"Can I take you somewhere?"

"I don't know . . ." she responds, pensively. "Where?"

"East Bay Bowl?"

"Really?" she asks, sitting upright and turning completely sideways to face me. Her smile is slightly bigger than it was before.

"Yeah, of course," I say, nodding. "It'll be fun."

Based on her growing smile, I expect her to jump up, ready to go, but instead she looks me up and down. "Are you sure you want to bowl in your work clothes?"

I look down at my dress pants, shirt, and tie. "Sure, why not?" I say, loosening my tie and pulling it over my head.

With a shrug, Ruth says, "You'll be the sharpest dressed bowler there." Then she jumps up and makes a beeline for the dining room. Right before she disappears down the hallway to her bedroom, she calls over her shoulder, "I just have to do something with this hair."

We're bowling on lane six, which happened to be Ruth's dad's favorite lane. Ruth has no idea why, it just was. Coincidentally, it's the same lane Tracey and I bowled on the last time I was at East Bay Bowl, the night of the New Year's Eve party. As Ruth and I take turns—her getting mostly spares and strikes and me getting mostly splits—I keep wondering when nostalgia is going to kick in. By the sixth frame, when I still feel nothing more than happy to see Ruth having a good time, I make a conscious decision to stop wondering. And to my surprise, it isn't that hard.

"Would you like me to bowl this next one with my left hand?" Ruth asks, mocking me and my score, which is currently a whopping fifty-four. She's standing at the edge of the lane waiting for her ball.

"No, no, no, no, no," I say, shaking my head. "Don't you dare, Ruth Bateman. I can still beat you fair and square."

She suppresses a chuckle. "You know we only have four frames to go, right?"

"Hey, I never said I could beat you fair and square *this* game. You just wait until I'm warmed up," I say, feigning seriousness.

"So you're telling me you want to bowl a third game? You sure are a glutton for punishment, aren't you?" she asks, shaking her head and smiling as she retrieves her ball. When she gets her third spare in a row, I clap despite the playful banter we just engaged in.

By the end of the game, the score is one sixty-seven to eighty-one.

"As you can see from my score, I'm warmed up now," I say, cracking my fingers. "Ready for another round?"

"Nah," Ruth laughs, "I think I'm done. Are you hungry?"

I glance up at the large bowling pin clock on the wall. "It is almost six. I could eat. What do you feel like?"

We both sit and begin removing our bowling shoes.

"How about pizza?" Ruth asks.

"Sounds perfect," I say, even though I'm not fond of pizza. But I would have agreed to anything Ruth suggested.

While we wait for our East Bay Bowl specialty pizza, we play a few arcade games and a mean game of air hockey. As we battle for game point, I'm distracted for a moment when our pizza is placed on the table next to us, and Ruth scores. She only gloats for a few seconds before sidling up next to me and indicating with her finger for me to bend down and give her a kiss. I feel lost in the moment until I hear voices approaching us, causing me to pull back and scrutinize the faces passing by. It's the first time all evening I've felt paranoid that someone from work might see us.

"Are you okay?" Ruth asks, glancing from me to the group of college-aged-looking men and women, and back again.

"Yeah, I'm fine. Should we eat?" I ask, clapping my hands once and rubbing them together.

We climb onto the high stools at the table where our sausage, mushroom, and onion pizza is waiting for us. Without a word, we both grab a piece and start eating.

I'm only half done with mine by the time Ruth polishes hers off. She then takes a sip of water and grabs another piece. But she doesn't start eating it right away. Instead, she says, "Henry?"

I finish chewing and swallow the bite that's in my mouth and then use a napkin to wipe the corners of my mouth. "Yeah?" I ask before taking a sip of water.

"Thank you for bringing me here. It was exactly what I needed today," she chuckles, "but I'm sure it was the last thing you planned to do with your afternoon."

"My pleasure. It was a lot of fun." I smile and eat the remaining corner of my first slice of pizza.

Ruth is about to start on her second piece, when she pauses and says, "Hey, I meant to ask you when we were at my house. Did you get out of work early today?"

I hold up a finger to indicate that I need to finish chewing. "Sort of .. . Well, not exactly," I say wiping my mouth again. "To be honest, I was worried about you, so I uh . . . said I wasn't feeling well."

Ruth's eyes widen, and a smile stretches across her lips. "Henry. Mancuso. You played hooky from work?!"

Grinning, I close my eyes for a second. When I open them, I say, in all seriousness, "There was something much more important that needed my attention."

Ruth doesn't say anything. Instead, she reaches across the table for my hand and gives it a squeeze. Then she smiles and turns her attention back to her second slice of pizza, and I reach for another myself.

While we eat, we talk about random things like vacations our families took when we were kids, places we'd like to travel to, and where we would go if we could snap our fingers and be there in an instant. Ruth chooses Hawaii, and without really thinking, I choose Washington D.C., to which she scrunches up her nose. After that, she tells me about how she never did things like play arcade games and eat pizza with her ex because he was always on a strict low-carb diet, which for some reason, meant she was too. They also never ate or drank anything (other than water) after seven p.m. and were always early to bed and early to rise. For ten years she lived an uber-healthy lifestyle but didn't do much of anything that wasn't related to QuickForm.

Before dismissing the topic of her QuickForm days, she says "What's the point of life if you never enjoy yourself?" I don't say it out loud, but I think I'm just now learning the answer to this question.

When Ruth is off getting a box for our leftover pizza, I sip my ice water and pull my phone out of my pocket. I haven't checked for new emails or texts since I went to the bathroom about an hour ago. I'm about to click on a new work-related email when an obnoxious ringtone causes me to look over at the group of men and women that passed us earlier. They're sitting at a table across the room, eating pizza and drinking beer, but none of them are really talking to each other. Instead, two of the women are taking selfies, one of the men is on his phone, and the remaining woman and man are staring down at their phones on the table. Suddenly it occurs to me that I don't need to check the email that's pulled up on my phone right now. Whatever it's about can wait until the morning.

"You ready?" Ruth asks as soon as she arrives back at our table and begins loading the remaining three pieces of pizza into a cardboard carryout box.

"Yep," I say shoving my phone back into my pocket as I hop off my stool and reach for the box Ruth just placed on the table. I watch as she puts on her sweater and slings her bag over her shoulder, causing strands of her hair to break loose from the bun on top of her head. I revel in how beautiful she looks without even trying. But I'm quite certain she's even more beautiful on the inside.

We take our time walking back to Ruth's house, so it's close to sunset when we turn onto her block. Ruth has been kicking a rock since we passed Second Chance Consignment about five blocks ago, and she keeps kicking it in front of me and telling me to kick it back. My brothers used to do this all the time when we were kids, and it used to annoy the crap out of me. But every time Ruth does it, I chuckle, because I never imagined I'd fall for a woman who has something in common with Anthony.

As we make our way up the walkway to her house, Ruth asks, "So, are you feeling better?"

"Wha— Oh," I say laughing, "Yeah, much better."

"Thanks again, Henry."

We're on her porch now, and we're facing each other.

"Anytime," I say, pulling her in for a hug. But instead of allowing me to wrap my arms around her, Ruth plants her hands on my chest and looks up at me, her eyes and lips imploring me for a kiss.

When our lips meet, our bodies meld, and I sense we could be on the brink of taking our relationship to the next level. Without warning, the realization causes me to freeze. Literally.

"Henry?" Ruth asks, pulling her head back slightly. "Are you okay?"

I want so badly to resume our kiss and for her to invite me in, but not today. Not on her dad's birthday. "Yeah, I'm fine," I say, smiling down at her. Then I step back, taking hold of her hands as she removes them from my sides. "I should go, Ruth. Thank you for a fun afternoon."

"Are you sure you don't want to . . ." She releases one of my hands and points a thumb in the direction of the door.

"I wish I could, but I need to go in extra early tomorrow morning to make up for the hours I missed today. How about a movie tomorrow night?"

She smiles and nods. "Sure. Sounds good."

I lean forward to give her one last peck. Then I turn to leave but don't let go of her hand until I reach the edge of the top step and absolutely have to. When I get to the end of the walkway in front of Ruth's house, I glance back to find her watching me from just inside the house. She waves, then slowly closes the door, leaving me to imagine what would have happened had I gone inside.

CHAPTER 42

"How do you like it?" I ask Beverly, holding up a t-shirt design for our team to wear at the Fourth Annual Parkinson's run. The circular graphic is of six hands with fingers spread and touching in the center. Above the graphic it says *Together We Can.*

"I love it, Ruthie!"

"I do too. Do you believe it was designed by a thirteen-year-old girl? She's the granddaughter of a patient over at White Pines."

She puts an open hand to her chest. "That is amazing. You're a good egg, Ruth, the way you've been organizing all of this. Your father would be so proud."

"Thanks, Bev. Oh, before I forget, did the Johnsons ever confirm whether they wanted t-shirts or not? They haven't signed up yet," I say, holding up a list of Wixley Chiropractic patients who've joined the team and want t-shirts as well.

Her eyes grow wide as she holds up a finger. "They did. And so did Herbert Lee. I have their t-shirt sizes on a Post-it on my desk. Be right back."

We closed five minutes ago, so I'm surprised to hear the chime of the door sensor. I turn, ready to remind whoever it is that we're closed.

"Excuse me, is there any chance an adjustment could improve the effects of having two left feet?" Henry asks.

"No, sir. But we might be able to help with permanently removing that phone from your hand outside of work hours."

"Touché," he says, laughing and shoving said phone into his back pocket.

I'm about to ask what he's doing here when Beverly returns.

"Okay, here you go, Ruth," she says. As she hands me the Post-it, her eyes fall on Henry and her face lights up. "Well, well, well. You must be Henry!" She brushes past me and gives him a hug. He raises his eyebrows at me over her shoulder. Releasing him, she says, "I've been telling Ruth to invite you in for an adjustment. A healthy spine is the key to total wellness, you know."

"It's nice to meet you, Mrs. Wixley. I've heard a lot about you."

"Please, call me Beverly or Bev," she says giving his upper arm a squeeze, then turning back to me. "Jackson is waiting for me to look over some X-rays with him. See you bright and early." She glances at Henry, and when she sees he's preoccupied with an informational pamphlet on the benefits of receiving regular adjustments, she leans in and mouths, "WOW."

"Bright and early," I say cheerfully. When she's on her way down the hall, I turn back to Henry. "So what brings you here? I thought we had plans to see each other on Thursday evening."

"Oh, right," he says, moving closer. "I just stopped by to make sure you read the email I sent this afternoon about the mediation hearing scheduled for Thursday, June fifteenth, in Madison."

My face falls. "Are you serious?"

"Ruth, this means an acceptable resolution to the case could be reached very soon. We've been assigned a highly experienced magistrate judge."

I roll my eyes at the fact that Henry drove all the way over here to talk shop, and I give him a look I've probably never given him before. It says something I would never say to him out loud: Are you fucking kidding me?

"I'm totally kidding, Ruth. I mean, all the things I said are true, but that's not why I came here."

I gasp and slug him in the shoulder. "Henry! What are you doing here then?"

"I was just wondering if I could take you home and cook dinner for you."

"You want to cook dinner for me at my place?"

He nods. "Everything is already in a cooler in my car, so please say yes."

"Okay, yes. I just need a moment to shut down a couple computers and straighten a few things for tomorrow."

"Not a problem," Henry says, propping his arms up on the counter that overlooks my workstation.

When I get to my desk, I set down the t-shirt design, signup form, and Post-it from Beverly next to my bag and then tidy things up.

"What's that?" Henry asks, pointing to the design.

"That's the design we're going to put on t-shirts for the Fourth Annual Parkinson's Walk/Run at the lakefront. My mom and I have a whole team of people to help raise money for research."

"That's wonderful. When's the event?"

"July thirty-first. Why? Do you want to join us? I haven't submitted our registration yet or placed the t-shirt order . . ." I pause, hoping he'll say yes, but I'm prepared for him to say no.

"Sure, I'd be honored to join your team."

~

By six-thirty, Henry is preparing our meal, and I've just finished changing. Before I join him back in the kitchen, I stop in the laundry room to toss my dirty clothes into a basket on top of the washer. When I turn to leave, I hear Henry's voice. At first, I think he's whispering to someone, but then I realize he's singing "Sweet Caroline" by Neil Diamond.

I tiptoe down the hall and pause right outside the entryway to the dining room, which is right next to the kitchen. A second later, the chorus begins and I can't help laughing out loud, not because of his voice but because of his gusto.

His singing ceases.

"Ruth?"

I stroll into the kitchen, grinning widely. "Please don't stop singing."

He laughs as he spoons melted butter over the steaks cooking in a cast-iron skillet. "I only sing when I'm alone."

"Why? You have an amazing voice."

He shrugs and mock brags, "Yeah, well, I *was* in choir in middle school."

"Sweet Caroline" ends and "A Team" by Ed Sheeran begins. "I love this song," I say, closing my eyes for a second. Then I belt out a few chords, and Henry gives me a look I've grown used to seeing when people hear me sing for the first time.

"I know, I know. I can't carry a tune to save my life, but that doesn't stop me."

He laughs, "I wasn't going to say anything."

"It's fine. My brother jokes that I'm tone deaf," I say. Then I resume singing.

At first, Henry just keeps glancing at me, but then he surprises me and joins in. His voice really is amazing, so I find myself singing more softly just so I can listen to him. When it ends, he's blushing a bit. I excuse myself to the dining room to turn down the volume a few notches, so that the music has become indiscernible background noise. When I return, I grab some bowls out of the cabinet and begin putting together our salads with the fresh vegetables that Henry brought. He turns the heat down on the steaks and all the way off on the small potatoes he's just sautéed with butter, garlic, and chives. Then he joins me at the center island.

I smile at him as I shred some carrots onto our salads and say, "So, you're a terrible dancer—no offense—but a great singer, and I can bust a move, but dogs howl when I sing."

"We make quite a pair," he says, plucking a cherry tomato out of a bowl and popping it into his mouth.

Over dinner we talk about all the unimportant things that become important when you decide you really want to get to know someone, such as which side of the bed you prefer; the pronunciation of words like bag, sherbet, gyro, and kibosh; dogs or cats; ocean or lake; and sunny-side-up or scrambled. Henry tells some corny lawyer jokes, and I laugh at every single one, not even necessarily because they're funny. He checks his phone twice while we're eating, and then again when we finish.

"You know, Henry, sometimes I picture you sitting on your couch on a day off and holding your phone, ready to work. I'm not trying to be rude, but do you ever go anywhere without your phone? I mean, do you take it to bed with you?"

"Of course . . ." He thinks for a moment. "Never mind. Now that I think about it, I guess the answer to your first question is no, I don't go anywhere without it. Even when I take a shower, it's in the bathroom with me."

"I have something for you." I remove the napkin from my lap and place it on the table. Then I slide my chair backward and disappear into my bedroom to retrieve a gift for Henry.

"Is it something I need to follow you into your bedroom for?" he calls, making me laugh.

"You wish! I'll be right out . . . Here," I say placing a small turquoise gift bag on the table next to him. Then I sit back down.

"Ruth, what is this?"

I shrug. "Open it."

He removes the matching turquoise notecard and reads the message on it. "*Never get so busy making a living that you forget to make a life.*" He reaches into the nest of white tissue paper and pulls out the mahogany Zen Egg I got from the farmers' market over a month ago. I had no idea when I bought two what I would do with the extra one, but then when Henry stayed at work until after nine one night last week, I decided he had to have it.

"Thank you, Ruth. This was very thoughtful of you." He analyzes the egg for a bit and then cups it in his palm, running his fingers over the smooth surface. "What is it for?"

"It's called a Zen Egg. I got it from the farmers' market weeks ago. It's a type of stress reliever that's supposed to help you achieve inner balance. Watch," I say reaching for the egg. When he hands it to me, I set it in the middle of the table and pull it all the way to one side so that it's lying sideways, then I let it go and it begins teetering back and forth, quickly at first. We watch in silence as it slows to a stop. "Maybe you could do that a few times a day when you're at work. You're supposed to just sit and focus on how you feel as you wait for it to stop. Or you could just clear your brain and reset."

"I love it. Thank you," he says, reaching for the egg and standing to walk around the table to sit next to me. He turns his chair so that he's facing me, and I follow his lead. "Did you make up the quote?"

I chuckle and say, "I'd love to take credit, but it was Dolly Parton. My grandma was a big fan of hers and had a wall plaque with the saying on it hanging above the table in her kitchen. You know, I must have seen that plaque hundreds of times throughout my childhood, but I never really understood the meaning until I got injured and was forced to look at the life Adam and I had built for ourselves."

"What do you mean?"

"Everything about us looked good from the outside. Business was good, and we were both living a dream come true entrepreneurs doing what we love. But after a while, it wasn't enough for Adam, so he started focusing on how to parlay what we had over and over. In the process, he forgot about all the other plans we had, like having kids, going on a honeymoon, and buying a dog.

When a faulty clip allowed sixty pounds worth of weights to fall on my ankle as I did a lunge, I had a lot of time on my hands to think as I recovered. Eventually, I became depressed, not necessarily because of my ankle, but because I realized how unhappy I was working tirelessly just to accumulate more and more success and material things. Adam didn't understand why I didn't want to expand the business to include the nutrition side of QuickForm, so we started to drift apart. By the time he had an affair, I was addicted to my pain pills. Again, not entirely because I was in physical pain, but it was more a way to cope with the emotional pain I was in. Asking Adam for a divorce was the best decision I ever made." I look up, suddenly realizing that I just spilled my guts to Henry. And I immediately feel bad for making the last several minutes about me when I was only trying to give Henry some perspective with the quote and the Zen Egg. "Sorry about that," I say, standing to clear the table.

"No, don't be sorry." He stands, too, reaching for my arms and turning me to him before I have a chance to pick up my plate. Then he gently places his hands on my face, and we kiss. And I don't know if it's the unexpected meal he just cooked for me, "Sweet Caroline", the Zen Egg, or the fact that I just told him all the things I carry with me but prefer not to talk about, but I want to give even more of myself to Henry now. So before I can talk my raging hormones out of it, I take him by the hand and lead him to my bedroom.

CHAPTER 43

Wednesday, June 15
Henry

"Henry, you've done an amazing job with this case. I think we're ready," Bob Whitmore says, slapping the table. We're in the concierge lounge at the Madison Marriott West preparing for the upcoming mediation with Bucky's attorneys.

"Thanks, Bob," I say, humbly accepting the compliment, "but I can't take all the credit. Without Ruth Bateman, we wouldn't be where we are now, and Constance did a fair share of the legwork from the start." I smile at her with gratitude, and she smiles back. Only her smile is accompanied with a friendly alcohol-induced glint in her eyes. To avoid a potential uncomfortable situation, I should probably hightail it to my room the moment this meeting is adjourned.

"I agree one hundred percent," Bob says nodding. "Constance, would you mind getting us another round?" He holds up a finger and looks at me, "Henry, are you sure you don't want a drink? The night is still young, and the mediation doesn't start until nine-thirty tomorrow . . ."

"No, thanks, I'm good with water."

"Okay but be ready for at least one celebratory cocktail tomorrow night."

I nod as Bob turns his attention back to Constance and confirms that he'd like another of the same for his second drink. When Constance is out of earshot, Bob says, "Henry, not to pry or anything, but I've noticed you and Constance haven't been spending as much time together around the office. You know, during breaks and such . . . And her mother recently mentioned to me that Constance has been a bit

"

down lately due to some personal issue. Are things between you two . . . copacetic?"

I try to hide my shock at Bob's inquiry into my personal life. "Yes, absolutely. As you've probably already figured out, we're no longer seeing each other on a personal level, but rest assured things between us are just fine. We're still good friends." At least this was true several weeks ago. The last few times Constance texted to see if I wanted to go for a run or join her as a guest at QuickForm, I already had plans with Ruth, so I had to decline. If she was upset, she didn't let on.

"Good, good, good," he nods and then drains the last sip of whiskey from his glass. "You know—just a bit of friendly advice from someone who's been around the block a few times—it's generally best not to mix work with personal matters, especially those involving the heart."

Thanks for the advice, Bob, but it's a day late and a dollar short. Not that his advice would have done me much good when I first met Ruth anyway. After all, I haven't been able to get her out of my head since the night I drove her home from Posh. And now, seven weeks later, I'm pretty sure my heart is in way too deep to separate anything even if I tried.

"Here you go," Constance says as she places Bob's fresh glass of whiskey in front of him and a full glass of water in front of me.

"Thank you, Constance."

She responds to her uncle with a nod and sips her clear cocktail.

I acknowledge the gesture with a smile as I remove the lemon from the rim of the glass and squeeze its juice into the water. Even though it's only a little after seven, I'd like to just go to my room, so I can call Ruth and then fall asleep to CNN. But I feel like it would be rude to bail on Bob and Constance this early. Hopefully, Bob calls it a night after he finishes his drink.

Two hours later, we're still here, and I've thought about making an exit at least half a dozen times. Bob has a knack for keeping conversation flowing without pause. At the moment, he and Constance are telling me waterskiing and tubing stories from summer days spent at Bob's waterfront property in Eagle River. Prior to this, Bob was detailing the renovations that are being done to his lake house.

"Well, I'm bushed," I say when Bob and Constance both pause to take drinks. "I think I'm going to call it a night." I stand and lift my chair slightly, moving it under the table. Constance looks disappointed, but Bob stands to shake my hand.

"You get a good night's sleep, Henry. See you in the lobby at seven fifteen sharp."

"Will do. Goodnight," I say, nodding at Bob and then at Constance. Then I head for the exit as fast as I can without looking too eager. As I step outside the lounge and into the hallway, I take my phone out of my pocket to call Ruth. If I've learned anything about her, it's that I need to call by nine if I hope to catch her before she goes to bed. It rings two times before she answers.

"Why, hello there, Mr. Mancuso," she purrs, making me laugh.

"Hi," I say, a smile plastered to my face.

"How are things going over in Madtown? And please, Henry, I'd like the CliffsNotes."

"Good, really good," I say as I walk toward the elevator. "We went over the electronic data relating to Bucky's outgoing text log files, which has exposed evidence of widespread transmission of unsolicited text messages to hundreds of thousands of numbers. It's by far the most invasive, and illegal, text marketing program I've ever encountered, so I'm quite confident about the meeting tomorrow."

"Wow. Passionate, confident, handsome. Even if things don't go well tomorrow, I'd say the case has turned out favorably for me."

I smile and lean against the wall next to the elevator, knowing there's a chance the call will disconnect if I get inside. "Yeah, me too . . . But I still want to win the case."

"Not surprising," Ruth says with a chuckle. "So, what exactly will happen tomorrow?"

"Well, normally both sides would present written position statements proposing a resolution. But since there's no question Bucky's has broken the law here, they've already agreed to enter into a consent judgement, which means they aren't disputing liability, only damages. So, we'll present evidence of the number of actual violations—which will include the screenshots and phone records you provided way back when, as well as the database for the Perks program—to determine a reasonable settlement number. The judge will then review the evidence as a third party neutral, not an arbiter of fact, and will consider our proposed settlement. Of course, in addition to a settlement fund to afford meaningful relief to the thousands of people who've been affected, we'll also request that Bucky's permanently stop engaging in these illegal marketing practices. If granted, you would need to sign off on any settlement reached on behalf of the class."

"So, you're saying I get to decide whether we accept the outcome of this mediation?"

"Pretty much. If you don't like whatever solution we agree upon, you can always say no, but that would mean prolonging the case further and going to trial. Oh, and I forgot to mention that you'll likely be recognized for your willingness to spearhead this case and your assistance with prosecuting the case."

"What do you mean? Recognized how?"

"With a monetary reward, Ruth."

"But I told you I didn't want any money, just for the texts to stop. Like I said, I'm already happy with the outcome."

"I know you are, but I can't really go in there tomorrow and say my lead plaintiff doesn't want to receive a reward. That's just not how it works." She remains quiet, so I continue. "So, I'll call you tomorrow—most likely in the afternoon—to let you know how things went. And just so you know, Bob will probably want to have a conference call between the three of us."

"Yeah, okay. I trust you. You're a good lawyer," she says with a yawn.

"Thank you," I say. "You sound tired. I should let you go."

She yawns again, adding a little moan this time. "Okay. Nighty-night, Henry."

"Nighty-night. Sleep tight."

No sooner do I click to end the call do I hear Constance's voice. "Sleep tight?" she asks, breezing past me to press the elevator button.

Crap.

"Um, yeah, that was—"

"Ruth Bateman, right? I heard you say you'll call her tomorrow afternoon to let her know how things went and that my uncle would want to have a conference call."

Crap. Crap. Crap.

I'm relieved when the elevator doors open because now I have time to regain my composure as we step inside. Constance presses the button for the eighth floor, and I press the button for the tenth.

"That's right, it was Ruth. I just wanted to keep her up to speed and assure her that we're more than ready for the mediation."

"Do you tell all your clients to sleep tight, Henry?"

"Give me a break, Constance," I say staring straight ahead at the doors, visualizing them opening and me getting the hell off the elevator. I can feel her eyes on me.

Just as the door opens, my phone pings.

"Better get that. It might be Ruth," Constance says as she exits.

~

Thursday, June 16
Henry

As expected, the mediation went well, and as Bob warned me, I've mentally prepared myself for the celebratory dinner we're about to enjoy. But if it was up to me, I'd be on my way home to celebrate with the star of the case.

"Henry!" Bob stands to greet me as the maître d' escorts me to our table in a small private room. Constance remains seated with her lips slightly pinched, unwilling to make direct eye contact with me. Her demeanor was like this all day, but Bob seems oblivious. Perhaps he's just too wrapped up in the excitement of the mediation results. "How about a little bubbly?"

His grip on my hand lingers until I nod and say, "Sure, sounds good."

As Bob flags down a nearby server and orders a bottle of champagne and three glasses, I pull out a chair and take a seat at the circular table.

"Hi, Constance," I say, doing my best to act normal. I figure she'll either get over her suspicion about Ruth and me, or she'll eventually drop the passive-aggressive attitude and come right out and ask if there's something going on between us. If it ends up being the latter, I'm not quite sure what I'll say, but I do know I'm fully prepared to say goodbye to my friendship with Constance if it comes down to that.

"So, what do you two say we make that call to Ruth Bateman right now before this celebration gets underway?"

I check my phone for the time. "Sounds good. I believe she gets off work at six, so now should be fine."

Constance expels a hard breath through her nose and shakes her head slightly.

"What was that, Constance?" Bob asks.

"Oh, nothing. I just have a little tickle," she says, squeezing the bridge of her nose.

Bob looks back at me and rubs his hands together. "Well, let's get Ruth on the line then, shall we?"

I dial her number and activate my speakerphone as soon as the call connects. Then I place my phone in the middle of the table, so we can all hear Ruth clearly and vice versa. Secretly, I'm praying she doesn't answer because the thought of talking to her with Constance right here makes me queasy. I'm also hoping she got my text about twenty minutes ago warning her that we'd probably be calling soon.

"Hello," she says, friendly pep in her voice.

"Hi, Ruth, this is Henry Mancuso." The addition of my last name is cautionary. Hopefully it will squash any suspicions Constance might still have.

"Hi, Henry. How are you?"

"Good. Great, actually. Say, I also have Bob and Constance Whitmore on the line with me.

"Hi Ruth," Bob says with gusto.

"Hello, Ruth," Constance mumbles.

"Oh, hello! Wow, all three of you at the same time. I sure am glad Bucky's is footing the bill for this call." I hold my breath, wondering how Ruth's joke will be received. When Bob laughs, I exhale.

"That's a good one, Ruth," he says, his laugh tapering off. "Anyhow, we just wanted to fill you in on the results of the mediation and see if you have any questions. How does that sound?"

"Great. I'm all ears."

"Wonderful," Bob says looking at me. "Henry?"

I open the manila file folder that I brought with me and locate the agreed upon terms of the settlement. Then I clear my voice before I begin.

"Okay, Ruth, here goes. The agreement we reached requires that Bucky's will pay 11.5 million to its victims to resolve the case. The company has also agreed to discontinue its text messaging activities as part of the settlement and will instead market to people via an app that a consumer must affirmatively download onto their phone—which is what they should have been doing all along. Bucky's will also be enjoined from sending out unsolicited text messages anymore and will be required to institute robust training and best practices in its marketing department. Furthermore, all parties have agreed that you will be granted a service award for your involvement with the case. Congratulations, Ruth, these are fabulous results."

The line remains quiet.

"Ruth? Are you still there?" Bob asks.

"Yeah, I'm still here. Thank you for that detailed results summary, Henry."

"Ruth?" Bob asks again. "Do you have any questions? Are you at all curious about the proposed amount of your incentive award?"

In our line of work, we aren't used to clients who aren't interested in compensation, so I understand Bob's and Constance's confused expressions.

"Nope," Ruth responds plainly. "I just wanted the texts to stop, and they have. So as far as I'm concerned, the case has been closed for weeks. But congratulations to all of you on a job well done."

"Well, thank you Ruth," Bob, says laughing, "How about if we tell you how much your compensation will be anyway?"

"Sure. Sounds good."

"Okay, then," Bob says, smiling down at my phone in the middle of the table. "Ruth, you will receive twenty thousand dollars as a reward for your assistance with this case. And as far as I'm concerned, you deserve every penny."

"Wow, that's . . . wow, I wasn't expecting it to be that much." I suspect Ruth thinks the amount is ridiculous, but Bob is right, she does deserve every penny. "Anyway, I'd like to say how much I appreciate all the time and energy Henry put into this case. I know from the date and time stamps on his emails that he worked nights and weekends. So, I sure do hope he's in line for a raise or some sort of extra compensation as well."

It takes every ounce of willpower in my body to hide my shock and discomfort over what Ruth has just said. Not that I don't appreciate the gesture, but I worry her words of appreciation might raise another red flag for Constance.

But Bob chuckles, and Constance sits expressionless, sipping the champagne she's just poured into her glass. "No worries, Ruth. We know how hard Henry works, and his efforts to bring this case together will certainly be recognized. However, you should know that we're not quite finished yet, because it will still be several weeks before the final settlement is filed for preliminary approval by the court. During that period of time, it's important to keep the settlement confidential; Bucky's insisted on that to minimize media attention. While Henry is busy dotting all his i's and crossing all his t's on the final settlement, a claims administrator will send emails and postcards to the 640,000 class members informing them of the settlement and the ways in which they can submit a claim. After all of that, we'll file a motion for final approval."

"Phew! That was a mouthful, huh?" Ruth responds, making me want to laugh. If I didn't know her better, I'd think she just listened to every word Bob just said, but I know she's probably knitting or working on a puzzle.

"Yes, yes it was," Bob laughs. "Listen, if you don't have any questions. I'll turn it back to Henry."

"Nope, no questions at this time. Thank you, though."

"Okay then, Ruth. Nice speaking with you, and again, congratulations. Here's Henry." Bob gives me a nod as he reaches for the glass of champagne Constance filled for him.

"Ruth?"

"Yes, Henry?"

I can't wait to show you just how excited I am over these results. "I'll be in touch with you tomorrow then, just to make sure you're clear on all the details of the settlement. And feel free to call me if you think of any questions."

"Yeah, okay, Henry, will do."

"Well, congrats again on these great results."

"Thank you, you too . . . Goodbye."

CHAPTER 44

Sunday, July 31
Ruth

"Should we race to the finish line?" I ask Henry.

"No, of course not," he says. Then he speeds up, the distance between us growing quickly.

"Unbelievable," I say under my breath as I sprint to catch up.

We end up crossing the line at the exact same time. As we walk around aimlessly trying to catch our breath, volunteers congratulate us and hand us bottles of water.

"You're such a cheater, Henry," I say, still taking rapid breaths.

"Hey, I needed that head start, just to tie you."

"Well, this tie is under protest."

"Fine, we'll have a redo next year. Then I'll have more time to train properly. I mean, come on, you knew about this months before I did."

"Good job, slow pokes! I've been waiting for you for so long, I'm already on my second banana." My brother Tyler shows up with a finisher medal around his neck, water bottle in one hand and a half-eaten banana in the other. He and his fiancée, Molli, decided last minute to drive up for the weekend just to cheer on our team, but then they decided they might as well participate. Molli has a bad case of plantar fasciitis, so she's walking with my mom, Walter, and Joan.

"I told you he'd gloat if he beat us," I whisper to Henry.

He gives me an inconspicuous wink and greets Tyler with a handshake. "Nice job, man."

The handshake seems odd to me because they've already met, once last night when we went to my mom's house for dinner, and again this morning before the event started. Sue and her family also stopped at my mom's house last night. They couldn't make it for dinner due to prior obligations, but they were able to show up for some strawberry shortcake. It was surreal having those who are closest to me meet Henry, almost like a dream.

"You too, Henry. What did you two finish in? Twenty-six something?"

"Twenty-six twelve," I say, snatching the rest of his banana from its peel and taking a bite. "Where are those bagels?" I ask.

After we pay a visit to the food tent and I use the bathroom, we head back to the finish line to wait for other members of our group. When everyone is done, we have plans to take a team photo. Cluster by cluster, our group crosses the finish line, our cheers growing louder and louder until the last members of our team, Dave Collinson (who's now in a wheelchair) and his wife Betty, along with their son and granddaughter, who designed our team t-shirt logo, cross the finish line.

Before we take the group photo, we need to get everyone together, which proves difficult with over forty people. Some have young grandchildren with them who need something to eat, others need to use the bathroom, and some just want to get a cup of coffee. So, I announce to whoever is near that we'll be taking the photo in ten minutes by the designated photo op area, and if someone isn't there, they'll have to be photoshopped in. Henry and I congregate with my family members near some picnic tables with a clear view of the photo op area.

"Ruth, Tyler tells me you and Henry finished in under twenty-seven minutes," my mom says. "That's impressive!"

"What about me, Mom?" Tyler asks. "I did it in less than twenty-four."

"Yes, honey, I'm proud of you too." My mom pats his head. "Although everyone here, except maybe Henry, knows you ran track in high school. So, not taking away from your victory or anything, but you do have an unfair advantage."

Tyler sighs dramatically and then laughs. Henry does too, and I'm relieved by how comfortable he already is around my family. After all, it isn't every day I introduce them to someone I think I'd like to procreate with. Goodness knows we've been getting plenty of practice . . .

"Did you know this coffee is from Bucky's Beans?" Joan arrives with

Walter, and they're both holding Bucky's cups. Walter hands one to my mom too.

Karl May overhears Joan's comment and joins us. "Speaking of Bucky's, how's that case going?" He directs the question to Henry, causing all eyes to turn to him.

"It's going well. All because of our star witness here." Henry affectionately grips my shoulders from behind.

I hear a few coos from the women, including my mother, and Tyler rolls his eyes. "Did you know she accused me of signing her up for those texts?"

"I did not," Henry says leaning over my shoulder and turning his head so that we're eye to eye.

"Henry?"

Everyone looks over at a woman standing in the distance. I shade my eyes from the sun, but still can't make out who it is until she's upon us. I smile, and Henry drops his hands from my shoulders and walks a few steps toward Constance. Everyone around us begins chatting among themselves.

"Hey, what are you doing here?" he asks.

"I did this run with a friend," she says without expression, but I swear her eyes narrow a tad at Henry. When her gaze migrates over to me, her lips purse into a disingenuous grin. "Hello, Ruth," she says with a curt nod.

"Hi, Constance. It's nice to see you."

Her grin widens a tad but she doesn't respond. Instead she turns her attention back to Henry. "May I speak with you privately?"

"Sure," he responds. Then he quickly addresses me before following Constance over to the tree she was standing by when she noticed Henry. "I'll be right back."

"Okay," I say, walking over to join some of the women in our group. I keep my back to Henry and Constance, not wanting to appear nosey, even though I am curious why she seems upset. Is it possible there was more to their relationship than Henry let on?

The moment I step foot into the semi-circle, all eyes turn to me and my mom nods in Henry and Constance's direction. "Who's that?"

"Oh, that's just one of Henry's coworkers," I say, looking around the circle of eyes and coming to rest on my mom's. "She probably just wants to talk to him about something work-related." Everyone nods, satisfied with my explanation of why Henry is walking off with such an attractive woman.

Betty Collinson is the first to change the subject, but not by much. "Wow, Ruth. That man of yours is just as dreamy in person as I remember him from his picture on that website your mom showed us."

My mom and Rita May nod in agreement, and my mom says, "He joined us for dinner last night and his manners are exquisite."

"Yeah, I like him, Ruth," Molli adds.

"He is pretty wonderful," I say grinning from ear to ear as I look around the group of women. When my gaze falls on Joan, she decides to chime in.

"Yeah, Henry seems all right. He isn't much of a dancer though."

Henry

My heart is beating a mile a minute as I follow Constance. Damn it. Just when I thought she'd forgotten about my phone conversation with Ruth the night of the mediation. In fact, things have been completely back to normal between Constance and me for about a week now. We even had lunch together the other day, and she revealed that she's seeing someone new, which was about as big of a load off as the fact that she never once mentioned the phone call she overheard between Ruth and me. And I had to go and ruin it by being seen at such a public event with Ruth today. It appears we're headed for the tree where she was standing when she spotted me. I assume it's so her friend doesn't wonder where she is when he or she returns. But who knows, maybe she just wants to get me as far away from Ruth as possible.

I'm a good five feet behind her, so my unease only grows as she watches me approach. I've never seen this expression on her face before. It's a mixture of disgust and self-righteousness.

As soon as I come to a stop about a foot away from her, she says, "Now are you going to tell me there's nothing going on between you and Ruth? I roll my eyes and begin to shake my head, but she stops me, her tone harsh. "Henry," she pauses for emphasis, "She's a client."

I sigh heavily, closing my eyes and raking my fingers across the top of my head a few times. Then I let my hands fall to my sides as I sneak a quick glance over my shoulder in Ruth's direction. Her back is to us, and no one else in the group appears to be watching either. "Look," I say, turning back to Constance, no longer trying to mask how nervous I am, "I didn't mean for this to happen. It just did." I sigh again and wait for her to respond, but her expression remains stone-cold and she says nothing. "Constance, we're most likely only weeks away from final approval. So my relationship with Ruth is not going to affect the settlement."

"Henry," she says through her teeth, "are you nuts? If counsel for Bucky's finds out about this, there's no question they'll move to disqualify our firm from representing Ruth in the case. Not only that, but Benson Tillman & Whitmore could be sanctioned. Do you really want to lose the case and possibly your job?"

"No one will find out, I swear. Ruth and I will just stay away from busy places and lay low until she signs the final settlement."

She shakes her head, her wide-eyed expression unreadable. And just when I relax a little thinking she's going to let this slide, she calmly says, "You cannot continue to represent Ruth Bateman if you're fucking her."

I stare at her, mouth ajar, unsure what bothers me more: the fact that she just acknowledged Ruth and I are "fucking" or the calm way she said it.

Without warning, a tall guy with an athletic build steps up next to Constance. "Here you go," he says, handing her a bottle of water. Smiling, he inquisitively looks over at me and then back at Constance who's twisting the top off of the bottle he just gave her. "Uh, I'm Dean." He extends a hand to me.

"Henry," I say, shaking his hand. "Constance and I work together."

"Okay, cool," Dean says, shaking his head and glancing at Constance again.

She offers him a smile accompanied by raised eyebrows. Obviously fake.

"Well," I point a thumb over my shoulder, "I need to get back to my group for a photo, so . . . I'll see you at the office tomorrow, Constance?"

She nods, the fake smile on her face faltering for a second as we make eye contact.

"Good to meet you, Dean," I say as I turn to leave.

When I get about ten feet away from them, I take several rapid breaths, attempting to calm my nerves. Part of me wants to turn around and ask Constance if we can come to some sort of resolution that involves her not saying anything to anyone about Ruth and me, but the other more composed part of me is telling me things will be fine. Constance may be freaked out right now, but she'll calm down eventually and realize the situation isn't as big of a deal as she thinks it is. Besides, she's my friend, so I have to believe she won't do anything to ruin my career.

～

Ruth

"I'm back, ladies. What did I miss?" Henry asks as he reenters the circle between my mom and Joan.

On one hand I find it odd that he wouldn't be standing next to me, but on the other, I love the way he blends right in with the group without needing to be by my side the entire time.

"Oh, Joan was just telling everyone what a great dancer you are. Right ladies?" Grinning, I raise my eyebrows.

Henry laughs. "You know you don't have to lie to save my feelings, Ruth. I know I'm a terrible dancer."

Everyone either smiles or chuckles right along with Henry, except Joan who says, "You come over to my house, the both of you, and I'll teach you some real dance moves. Henry, you'll need more work than

Ruth. Because if my memory serves me correctly, you have zero rhythm."

"I'd be honored if you taught me your moves, Joan." He looks at me and I can tell he's trying hard not to laugh. "Ruth? Will you coordinate your calendar with Joan's and set up this lesson for us?"

"I'd be happy to."

CHAPTER 45

From: Henry Mancuso
To: Ruth Bateman
CC: Robert Whitmore
Date: August 1, 2016 11:30 AM

Hi, Ruth. We hope this email finds you well.

Attached is the court's order in our case granting preliminary approval of our settlement agreement with Bucky's Beans. The last step will be final approval, which we hope the court will grant after the hearing scheduled on August 26. We've been busy implementing the class notice program, which has gone very well. So far, we've received 60,000 claim forms from class members who want to participate in the settlement.

We'll keep you updated. If you have any questions or need any information, don't hesitate to reach out. Have a great weekend.

Henry J. Mancuso
Attorney at Law
hmancuso@bensontillmanwhitmore.com
350 E. Wisconsin Avenue, Suite 600
Milwaukee, Wisconsin 53202
Phone (414) 555-4242
Fax (414) 555-4241

I reread my email to Ruth about the preliminary settlement agreement before sending it. Then I pick up my phone to respond to her text asking if I can help move some things from her mother's house over to Walter's next weekend.

Me: You got it! But only if there's a reward in it for me...

Ruth: We have a dance lesson scheduled with Joan on Sunday. Is that reward enough?

Me: Funny.

Ruth: I'm almost done with the Mount Rushmore puzzle you got for me. Do you want to stop over tonight and help me put the finishing touches on it?

Me: I can't. I have to work late, most likely won't get out of here until around eight. Save it for tomorrow?

As I click to send the text, there's a knock on my door. I look up, startled, still leery about getting caught sending non-work-related correspondence when I'm at the office.

"Henry, Bob would like to speak with you." Always on the move, Bob's assistant, Don, disappears before he even finishes his sentence.

I wonder why Bob would send Don to get me. Why wouldn't he just call?

My phone pings.

Ruth: Of course. :) What time can I expect you?

Me: Seven, possibly sooner.

〜

"Hey, Bob. You wanted to see me?"

"Henry, yes . . . Would you mind closing the door?"

A pit forms in my stomach as I oblige. When I turn back around, he motions for me to sit in one of the chairs in front of his desk.

"Henry, I'm just going to come right out and ask you this . . . What is the nature of your relationship with Ruth Bateman?"

Constance.

Suddenly a wave of emotions rushes over me, leaving behind a mass of defensiveness, vulnerability, anger, and fear in the pit of my stomach. Before I can stop myself, I say, "Are you even allowed to ask me that?" But I know better. I've known better all along. And when it comes to the legality of my actions as an attorney at this firm, Bob can ask me anything.

"Henry," he says, his features softening, "she's a client, and her signature—or refusal to provide one—could still make or break the Bucky's case. The *multi-million-dollar* case you've been working on for months. But even more importantly—and I shouldn't have to tell you this—carrying on a relationship with a client is a serious conflict of interest. So, I have to know . . . does your relationship with Ruth Bateman violate rules of professional conduct?"

I stare through him, mouth ajar, emotions crippling my ability to speak. It's like time is frozen and I'm watching myself from afar. I don't want to lose the Bucky's case, nor do I want to lose my job. But I also don't want to lose Ruth.

Placing his hands behind his head and raising his eyes to the ceiling, Bob leans back in his chair and sighs. Free from the weight of his disappointed gaze, I do my best to compose myself, but self-preservation kicks in.

"Look, Bob, this thing between Ruth and I . . . it's not what you think. We're just friends." I've never lied about anything this serious before, but I don't know what else to do.

"Henry," he says, jolting upright and crossing his arms on his desk. If his stern tone wasn't still laced with compassion, I'd expect him to fire me on the spot. "*Any* kind of personal relationship with her—even if you aren't having sexual relations—could result in disciplinary action by the Supreme Court. And if Bucky's counsel found out, they would most certainly move to disqualify us from representing Ruth in the case. Hell, they would probably ask for dismissal and sanctions. *We* would get nothing. *Ruth* would get nothing. We both know all of this." Eyes wide, he implores me to respond.

Nodding, I make one last feeble attempt to avoid the inevitable. "I can assure you we're not having sex." Another lie.

Bob shakes his head, crestfallen. "Okay, here's the deal. I won't say anything to Stanley or Joseph about this, but you need to cut all personal communications with Ms. Bateman, effective immediately. And you need to do it in a way that does not jeopardize the Bucky's case. If you don't think you can pull through for me on this, I'll have no choice but to replace you as lead counsel, Henry. Understood?"

I inhale deeply, clenching my fists so hard it hurts. As indignant as I feel right now, I know I don't have a choice in this matter other than turning in my resignation. "Understood."

"Okay then," Bob says, with a signature slap of his desk. "When the final settlement is filed, you can proceed to see whomever you like, including Ms. Bateman."

Without saying a word, I stand and turn to leave. I have my hand wrapped around the doorknob when Bob speaks up again.

"Oh, and Henry?"

I release the knob and turn to face him.

"Am I correct to assume we both know who told me about Ruth?"

"Yes," I say with a nod.

"The two of you will be able to get past this, correct?"

As angry as I am with Constance, I know my relationship with Ruth is unethical.

"Yes. We'll be fine," I say with a weak smile.

"Thank you, Henry. I knew I could count on you."

His words make me feel sick to my stomach, because Ruth probably thinks she can count on me too.

CHAPTER 46

Monday Evening, August 1
Ruth

I'm getting ready for bed when my phone begins vibrating and sliding around on my nightstand. I quickly finish rubbing lotion into my hands as I lunge for it, hopeful that it's Henry calling. But when I see who it is, I groan and contemplate not answering. What could my ex-husband possibly want?

"Well, this is quite a surprise."

"Hi, Ruth. It's Adam."

"Yeah, I know. That's why I said it's a surprise to hear from you," I say, rolling my eyes. "What's up?"

"Does something have to be up for me to call and see how you're doing?"

"Adam, the last time you called was a year ago on the anniversary of my father's death, except that wasn't even why you called because you didn't even remember the significance of the day."

"Come on, I apologized for that. I had a lot on my mind."

"Right, like locating the outfit your mother dressed you in for your christening, so your son could wear it to his? Your son who I didn't even know Shanna had given birth to?"

He sighs and then mumbles. "I don't know why I even followed Shanna's advice to see if you're okay . . ." His wife Shanna and I used to be close when she worked for Adam and me at QuickForm. But then she slept with my husband, and that kind of put a damper on our friendship.

"Why would she suggest that?"

"Why are you suing Bucky's Beans, Ruth?"

Caught off guard, I inhale sharply and remain silent for a few seconds as I curse myself for taking Adam's call. "Not that it's yours or Shanna's business, but they spammed my phone with unsolicited text messages for months. That's illegal, FYI."

He sighs heavily. "Are you certain the messages were unsolicited?"

"Yeah. I'm pretty sure I would remember filling out a Bucky's Perks enrollment form, which is what's required for them to send someone marketing texts."

"Ruth, there were a lot of things you thought you knew back when you were abusing your pain meds, and there was a lot you didn't remember. Your slip ups caused dozens of issues for my . . . for *our* business."

"Wait, are you saying you think I'm abusing pain meds again or something equally as ridiculous?"

"I don't know. Are you? Because the Ruth I know would never sue a family-owned, fair-trade company like Bucky's Beans. The Ruth I know would have ignored a few lousy texts because she had better things to do with her time than sue a reputable company."

"You don't know what you're talking about, Adam."

"Oh really? Do you even know what the public thinks about your case? Or have your scumbag lawyers been shielding you from public scorn? Have you Googled yourself lately, Ruth?"

"No . . . Why?"

"Because you might not know all the facts like you think you do. Either that, or—yeah, I'll just say it—either that or you've fallen back into old habits."

"Adam, you don't know anything about me or what's been going on in my life for the past two years. You were too busy with QuickForm and taking your affair to the next level to bother checking in. And that's fine, because I think we're both happier and exactly where we're meant to be now. Why the hell have you been Googling me anyway?"

He scoffs, contemptuously. "I didn't Google you. Well, I did, but only because Tom Schmidt from the Bucky's location next to QuickForm in Madison mentioned your lawsuit to Shanna when she was in there getting a coffee the other day. He can't believe you would sue them either. I mean, Tom used to be your friend too, Ruth."

"I haven't spoken to Tom in like five years, so—"

I'm not surprised when Adam cuts me off. "Anyway, he told Shanna about all sorts of negative comments he found online regarding the case."

"Adam," I say calmly, exhausted from the unnecessary drama, "again, you don't know what you're talking about. Do you honestly believe Tom Schmidt is going to be affected by this suit? I mean, he's a franchisee with two stores. This case is against Bucky's Corporate."

"Yeah, whatever you say, Ruth. But for as many negative online comments as there are about this case, there are probably ten times that many people who would rather jump on the bandwagon and get a piece of the pie you and your lawyers are serving up."

"Look, I don't want to fight with you, Adam. We'll just have to agree to disagree here. But something I bet we can both agree on is that it's probably best if we don't talk again."

He clears his throat. "Yeah, okay, but I sincerely hope everything is okay with you."

"Things are better than okay, Adam. And believe it or not, this Bucky's case has a lot to do with it."

"Really?" He says, scoffing. "You know, this is actually reminiscent of the way you railroaded me out of all that money in the divorce settlement. What? Hundreds of thousands of dollars isn't enough, Ruth? So now you're soliciting lawyers to help you sue family-owned businesses in the hopes of beefing up your bank account even more? I suppose that's one way to avoid getting a real job."

"Fuck you, Adam. You know the money was never important to me. But I worked my *ass* off to earn it, so that's why it was awarded to me."

He scoffs again, solidifying my plans to never speak to him again. "I seem to recall—"

"Goodbye, Adam. Please don't try to contact me again," I say, disconnecting before he has a chance to respond.

For the next twenty minutes, I sit and process the entire miserable conversation Adam and I just had. I don't care what he thinks of me or what he *thinks* he knows about my life. But for some reason, I can't stop wondering what people are saying about the case.

When I finally settle into bed, I go against better judgment and reach for my phone. Then I Google myself. What I find makes me feel much worse than Adam ever could.

~

"Ruthie, it's after ten. What are you still doing up?" My mom whispers into her phone.

"I can't sleep."

"Well what's wrong? Did you try drinking a glass of warm milk?"

"No, Mom, I don't drink milk."

"Oh, right. Well what's wrong?"

"Adam called me tonight and—"

"Why that bloody two-timing—"

"Please, Mom, don't." She sighs heavily but remains silent, so I can talk.

"He called because Shanna heard about the Bucky's case from a mutual friend of ours, who happens to own two Bucky's Beans locations."

"Yeah, so? It's not like you're suing your friend. Besides, why does Adam care anyway?"

It's my turn to sigh. "Because, he felt it was uncharacteristic of me and thought I might be abusing pain pills again."

"What in the world?!"

"Mom, Mom, Mom. I know. It's illogical. I think he was just embarrassed because our friend asked Shanna about it. You know how Adam is all about keeping up appearances."

"Yeah, well, he's an asshole underneath what everyone else sees. But, Ruthie, you know this. Why would any of this be keeping you awake?"

"Because Adam mentioned seeing a lot of negative things online about me and the case and Henry and his firm. Some of the stuff is so nasty and preposterous, Mom."

"Why would you even look?"

"I don't know. Good question."

"Well, what kinds of things are people saying?"

"That I'm a gold-digger or an idiot who signed up for the Perks program and forgot. That I'm probably illiterate . . ."

"Well," my mom snorts, "you're obviously not illiterate. You're a college graduate for Christ's sake. And you're not the other things either, of course. Have you talked to Henry? Couldn't these things they're saying be considered slander?"

"Slander? Maybe. But to be honest, I'm more concerned about the people who are saying the case is frivolous. Those comments have me wondering if the text messages were worth making Bucky's pay millions of dollars. I know they're a big company, but I'm beginning to feel bad, Mom."

"They were breaking the law Ruth, and you said they knew it. Did you call Henry? I'm sure he can make you feel better."

"I tried to call him, but he didn't answer. I know he had a long day at work, so I'll just wait to talk to him tomorrow. He's supposed to come over."

"Honey, I say don't worry about the opinions of those online trolls. Some people just like to get others riled up, even if there isn't cause. And some are just born naysayers and troublemakers. The people making these rude comments online obviously don't know there's evidence to prove Bucky's was breaking the law. This case is legit, you and I both know that, and that's all that matters. Hey, maybe you could go online and set them straight? Give them a hard dose of reality by sharing some of the facts?"

"No, I can't do that. There's a clause that states I'm not allowed to talk to anyone about details of the case until the final settlement is filed."

"Well, talk to Henry tomorrow, and try not to lose anymore sleep over it. Okay?"

"Yeah, okay," I say with a sigh. "Thanks, Mom."

"Goodnight, sweetie. Give me a call tomorrow and let me know what Henry thinks about all this."

"Will do, Mom. Goodnight."

When I hang up, the comment section of an article about the case reappears on my screen. I know I should look away, but then I get a glimpse of the words *baseless*, *desperate*, and worst of all, *money-hungry*.

Thirty minutes later, I finally close the browser, wishing I hadn't ventured back down the rabbit hole. The strain on my heart from seeing so many mean comments about me and Henry, and the case in general is even greater now. I cope by telling myself none of it matters, especially with Henry by my side. Even so, I know I'm in store for a night of fitful sleep.

CHAPTER 47

Tuesday, August 2
Henry

It's nearly five in the afternoon, and the buzz around the office is beginning to wind down for the day. I got very little sleep last night and have had a difficult time concentrating due to the conversation Bob and I had yesterday. I can't stop wondering things like *What if I don't stop seeing Ruth? How would he ever know?* or *What if Ruth and I simply don't go anywhere public until the case is settled?* or *What if Ruth and I just quit our jobs and move to an island in the South Pacific?* Then there are the unsettling thoughts I can't seem to shake. *What if Ruth is so hurt that I would even consider not seeing her until the case is settled, and she decides she never wants to see me again?* or *What if we do take a break from seeing each other and drift apart?* After all, I don't believe absence always makes the heart grow fonder.

I open our ongoing text conversation, and contemplate canceling on her for tonight, at least until I figure out how to break the news to her. I could say I'm sick or that I have to work late again.

No, Henry. Waiting won't make telling her any easier no matter what you say. Just get it over with.

ME: I SHOULD BE THERE SOON. DO YOU NEED ME TO PICK ANYTHING UP?

I pause before I click send, wondering if I should tell her I need to talk to her about something. But why would I do that? When people do that to me, the only thing on my mind is what they need to talk to me about. There's no sense in causing Ruth to worry.

I turn off my computer and begin tidying up my desk when Ruth's response comes through.

Ruth: Nope. All I need is you. :)

I stare at her words as I lean back in my chair. Then I lock my phone screen, and my eyes fall on the Zen Egg Ruth gave to me the night we slept together for the first time. I reach across my desk and tilt the egg all the way to the right just like Ruth showed me how to do it. But when I remove my hand and pull it back, I accidentally bump the egg with my pinky, causing it to topple off the front of my desk.

So much for inner balance.

~

"Hello?" I call out, opening Ruth's front door as I knock a few times. After I close the door behind me, I remove my shoes and make my way through the living room and dining room toward the kitchen where music is playing.

Ruth is standing at the stove stirring whatever is in the skillet on top of the burner. She senses my presence and looks over at me right away, grinning. "Hi, handsome."

"Hi," I say as I move in for a kiss. When our lips part, I notice bags under her eyes. "Are you feeling okay? You look tired." I lean against the counter next to her.

"I had trouble sleeping last night," she says giving the beef, broccoli, and peppers she's cooking a final stir before turning off the heat. Then she looks at me and says, "We have to talk."

As I follow her into the living room, so many thoughts circle my brain. Is it possible Constance called Ruth? Or maybe Bob? I know he wouldn't tell her he knows about us, but I wouldn't put it past him to question her about her satisfaction with my job performance and communication skills.

Ruth pats the spot next to her, inviting me to join her on the loveseat. Being so close to her and smelling her spa-like scent makes me want to envelop her in my arms and never let go.

"What's up?" I ask, innocently.

"I'll get right to the point in order to make this as brief as possible—no lawyer joke intended," she says with a lazy grin. "I got a call last night from Adam, my ex, because he heard about the Bucky's case and wanted to know why I was suing them."

"Why is that any of his business? Does he want money from you?"

"No," she says, shaking her head, "Adam has plenty of money. He just thought it was uncharacteristic of me. But he also mentioned everything that comes up when my name is Googled."

I sigh, not even trying to hide my disappointment. "Did you look?"

She nods and then pinches up her face in a way I've never seen before. "Wait, you knew about all these articles and discussions online about the case?"

"No . . . I mean yes, but not anything specifically about you or the Bucky's case. This is what typically happens with consumer-related class action suits. People always voice their opinions online. Some are good, and some are bad, whether a case is legitimate or not. There just isn't a case that's immune to misinformed online trolls."

"That's what my mom called them," Ruth says, staring at the floor.

"This isn't a big deal, Ruth. Nothing anyone says online will affect the case, so please don't worry about anything negative that you've seen." I reach over and rub her back in slow circles. But then I remember what I have to do tonight, so I stop and place my hand back in my lap.

"That's not what I care about. I mean, it sucks to be called illiterate or an idiot pawn, but I don't care much what other people think of me. What I care about is the millions of dollars that Bucky's is going to have to dish out because of some lousy text messages that I could have simply ignored. Why can't people just ignore their phones?" She stands and leaves the room, but I don't follow because her footsteps never stop. She's poking around on her phone when she returns, and the irony is not lost on me, but now is not a good time for jokes.

"Ruth, Bucky's ultimately doesn't care. They made way more money on this scheme of theirs than they have to pay. It's more the principle of the matter, that when all is said and done, companies like Bucky's won't be able to ignore TCPA regulations."

As if she hasn't heard a word I've said, she shoves her phone in front of my face. "Henry, read this comment. It's on the settlement site where people can file claims."

I'm sad to see so many vultures here. Are you all really that desperate for $200 even if it costs a local employer $11.5 million? I just got the notice and my immediate reaction was disgust; with the suit and the attorneys. This is ridiculous! According to the legal notice I received, the attorneys will rake in approximately $4 million. I wonder if Benson, Tillman & Whitmore is dedicated to beating the bushes for class actions, and they finally found a star representative in Ruth Bateman. Bucky's is NOT a giant like Starbucks. This suit will hurt them. In fact, I can't help but wonder if Starbucks is in cahoots with this firm. DISGUSTING!

I hand back her phone and shake my head at the preposterousness of what I just read.

"Ruth, I can understand how someone as non-materialistic as you would feel bad for Bucky's over the amount of the settlement, but keep in mind that approximately 640,000 different telephone numbers received a total of approximately 50 million text messages from Bucky's over the past four years, without Bucky's having anyone's consent. And several thousands of those numbers were Imperial subscribers like you who couldn't make the messages stop. Numerous people, including some Imperial subscribers, filed complaints with the FCC and the Better Business Bureau even before your case was filed, but it persisted."

She sits back down and turns to face me. "Henry, I'm sorry, but I don't know if I can sign the final settlement agreement."

"What?" I hiss, not intending for it to come out so harshly. Ruth is equally as surprised by the sound of my voice, and it makes her stiffen and lean back from me a little. "I'm sorry. I didn't mean for it to come out like that. It's just . . . we've been working on this case for months, and it would be devastating if you refused to sign." Suddenly I realize Bob was right when he said I need to be careful about how I broach the topic of putting our relationship on hold. If Ruth refuses to sign, the case and my job are toast. But right now, I'm so ashamed of the way I just spoke to her that I can't even look at her let alone tell her we need to stop seeing each other for a while.

She sighs and falls back against the couch. "Me not signing could really hurt your career, couldn't it?" She glances over at me, her expression sullen. I nod but remain silent, fearing that anything I say might make this bad situation even worse. "And Bucky's would get off scot-free?" I nod again, finally looking over at her. But now she looks away, shaking her head and bringing her hands to her face. She rubs her eyes and groans. When she lowers her hands, she mumbles, "And no one in the class would get any sort of compensation for all those pain-in-the-ass texts." Suddenly, she stands and looks over at me with a shrug. "Well, let's eat."

"Ruth," I say, jolting off the couch as she turns to leave the living room.

"Yeah?" She asks. I'm relieved that she allows me to hold her hands as we stand facing each other.

"I don't want you to do anything you don't feel comfortable with." Ruth not signing the settlement would be a hard pill to swallow, but I don't know if I'd be able to live with myself if I tried to talk her into it at this point. It was a much different story before I fell for her. "Maybe take a day or two to—"

"Henry," she interrupts, "I'm going to sign."

"Are you sure?"

"Yeah," she says, leaning into me for a hug. "It wouldn't be fair to you or any of the other class members if I didn't."

"Okay," I say, giving her a squeeze, "but only if you're sure."

"I'm sure," she says, looking up at me. "Seeing all those nasty comments online just made me panic, you know? I should have known better than to answer Adam's call. I'll just have to avoid the Internet until the final paperwork is filed. I certainly don't want to fall down that rabbit hole again," she says, with a soft chuckle. "I'm hungry. Let's eat."

I follow Ruth into the kitchen where we spoon stir-fry onto our plates. Then we head into the dining room and eat in comfortable silence long enough for me to clear half my plate.

"Henry?"

"Hmm?" is the best I can muster with a mouthful of broccoli.

"Did we just have our first fight?"

"Yeah, I guess you could say that," I say smiling, but the smile fades quickly because I know our relationship is in for more than just a first fight tonight. And I'm being a complete asshole by not getting it over with sooner than later.

Ruth's face mimics mine with a frown. "What's wrong?" she asks.

I push my plate away and cross my arms on the table. But the distance between us is too great for the conversation we're about to have, so I stand and walk around the table. She watches curiously as I take a seat, turning it sideways so that I'm facing her. "There's something else we need to talk about."

"Okay," she says, adjusting her body so that our knees are touching, and she doesn't have to turn her neck to look at me.

"Bob Whitmore called me into his office today to ask about the nature of our relationship."

"Why would he ask you that?"

"Because Constance knows about us."

"And she told Bob?"

"Yeah," I say.

"But why does it matter to her? And why would she tell your boss? Wait, is that what she wanted to talk to you about on Sunday after the race?" I nod, as Ruth tilts and scratches her head. "Okay, I guess I'm not understanding something here. I mean, I assumed we should keep things involving the case separate from our personal lives, but I didn't know our relationship was supposed to be some big secret. Is it a problem that we're dating each other? Are you in trouble?"

"At this point, no," I say, sighing, "but I could be."

"How so?"

I close my eyes for a few seconds, delaying the unavoidable. "Ruth, Bob insists that we stop seeing each other until the final settlement is signed and filed."

"What?" She asks, pulling her head back in surprise. "Why?"

"Because our relationship is technically forbidden."

"Technically?"

"Ruth," I say, sighing and leaning forward with my elbows on my knees, "I've broken several codes of conduct with you, so there could be ramifications if we keep seeing each other."

"Like what?" she asks, her tone defiant.

"Like, my firm could be fined, and Bucky's Bean's counsel could file a motion to dismiss the case. Or I could be fined myself and even disbarred."

Ruth's shoulders slump as her chest deflates, and when she takes her next breath, her shoulders don't quite rebound. She stares at my chest, and I sense the wheels are turning in her head.

"Look, Ruth, all this means is that we need to take a break from each other for a little while, probably only until shortly after the final settlement hearing on August 26. And this doesn't mean we can't talk or text."

"I can't believe this," she says as she stands, grabbing our plates and heading into the kitchen.

I remain seated, waiting for her to return, but she doesn't. So, I go to her and find her leaning over the island with her head down on her forearms.

"Ruth?"

"Please don't look at me right now, Henry," she says through sniffles.

I rush to her side and rub her back, and I think about saying *screw it* and telling her to forget about everything I just said. But she stands suddenly and uses a dish towel to wipe her tear stained cheeks.

"Ruth, I don't want to put our relationship on hold any more than you do, but Bob made it clear that it's what I have to do. And I don't think it would be wise for me to test him."

"I get it, Henry," she says, nodding, "and I think you should go. Not because I'm angry, but because the longer you stay, the harder it will be for me to stomach this."

I think about protesting or pulling her in for a hug, but that would only make our goodbye tonight harder. So I simply say, "Okay."

She walks me to the door, and we stand there, Ruth just inside the threshold and me just outside of it.

"You know what's funny, Henry?" Ruth asks.

"I can't think of anything funny at this moment," I say, shaking my head.

"The fact that Bucky's Beans brought us together and now, in a way, it's tearing us apart."

CHAPTER 48

From: Henry Mancuso
To: Ruth Bateman
CC: Robert Whitmore
Date: August 26, 2016 at 4:30 PM

Good afternoon, Ruth. I hope all is well with you.

I have some important updates!

Today the final hearing in your case against Bucky's was held at the federal courthouse in Madison. The judge granted final approval of the settlement and will issue a written order in the next week or so, at which time you will be asked to sign the final settlement. The judge granted our request for a $20,000 service award to you. Each class member (i.e., everyone like you who received a text from Bucky's without consent) who filed a valid claim (approximately 100,000 claims in total were filed) will receive somewhere in the range of $75-95. So, it is a great result for a lot of people, which would not have been achieved had you not spearheaded this case.

So, again, THANK YOU, Ruth.

Once the final approval order is entered by the court, we need to wait another week to see if anyone objects. If no appeal is filed, then the class members will get their checks and you will get your check within two weeks from that time. If an appeal is filed, things could take a bit longer until we are able to get the appeal either stricken or withdrawn or until we win the appeal.

I will keep you posted on the timing of the process.

Henry J. Mancuso
Attorney at Law
hmancuso@bensontillmanwhitmore.com
350 E. Wisconsin Avenue, Suite 600
Milwaukee, Wisconsin 53202
Phone (414) 555-4242
Fax (414) 555-4241

I smile to myself as I fire off the email to Ruth. To say I'm missing her is an understatement. But as soon as the final approval order is entered, and she signs the final settlement, things can go back to normal between us. Hopefully. She hasn't communicated with me for the past two weeks because it was too emotionally difficult for her to only be able to talk to me or text me. She says talking to me only made her want to see me, so she suggested we just go cold turkey until the settlement is signed.

I open our ongoing text thread. My last three messages to her remain unanswered.

ME: GOOD MORNING, SUNSHINE!

ME: I DON'T THINK MY ZEN EGG WORKS VERY WELL WHEN I DON'T GET TO SEE YOU...

ME: I BOUGHT SOME KOHLRABI. NOW TO COOK IT...

I send another one nevertheless.

ME: I JUST EMAILED YOU SOME GOOD NEWS...

While I understand her silence, it still makes me nervous. What if she's changed her mind about me and decided I'm too stuffy or too neat or too worried about things at work all the time? I'm trying to fix that, but it was easier to shove litigation and pressing deadlines to the far corners of my mind when I had Ruth to look forward too.

A knock on the door pulls me from my thoughts. "Henry?"

"Oh, hey, Don. What's up?"

"Bob is wondering if you can meet him in the lounge in ten."

"Yep, sure can. Thanks."

I have a feeling I know what this lounge meeting is about, so I take care of a few tasks that need attention by the end of the workday and prioritize the paperwork into a neat pile on my desk. Hopefully I have enough time to attend to a few more items today still, but if not, I want them front and center when I get here Monday morning.

The area outside the lounge is quiet and the door is closed, which pretty much confirms my suspicion about this impromptu meeting. Whenever big cases are settled, my bosses like to show their gratitude to lead counsel and others who helped make it happen. Too bad Ruth can't be here for this. She still has no idea how important her role was in bringing this case to settlement, nor does she seem to understand how many people she's given piece of mind to in today's day and age of a phone-in-hand-24/7 work ethic. Studies have shown that text and email spam hinder productivity.

The moment I step foot in the lounge, uproarious applause and cheers fill my ears. This is followed by pats on the back, and a few small tokens of appreciation, such as balloons, a Bucky's Beans coffee mug and a bag of Bucky's specialty blend coffee. Bob gives a short speech recognizing all the time and effort I put into the case, and he also acknowledges Constance's contributions to the initial research. When he's done, people enjoy cake and beverages and slowly begin tapering out of the room, ready to start their weekends. But since I'm the guest of honor, I feel obligated to stay and chat until the very last person leaves. When Don, a paralegal named Becky, and two others leave at the same time, I'm left with Constance, who I haven't had a personal conversation with since Bob called me into his office to discuss my relationship with Ruth.

I make a beeline for the door and mutter, "Have a good weekend."

But she stops me.

"Henry, can we talk for a second?" Constance's voice wavers a bit.

"Sure. What's up?" I turn and face her, my hand clutching the doorframe.

"I just wanted to get a few things off my chest. You know, clear the air between us."

"Constance, you don't have to—"

"Oh, but I do. I know what I did by telling my uncle about you and Ruth was a cheap shot, and I'm not proud of myself for it. I mean, at first, I felt disgustingly satisfied, because I knew he would talk to you." She leans in closer to me and whispers, "You wouldn't believe some of the things that have gone on between people who work here and clients in the past. I've heard stories." She pauses and raises her eyebrows for a beat, then she continues. "Anyway, I did it because I was disappointed by the fact that our relationship had taken a sharp turn toward Friendsville. But then I started to reflect on how honest you were with me every step of the way, and at the same time I was noticing changes in you, like the way you no longer join anyone after work to shoot the breeze and how you barely ever smile anymore. And you probably don't even realize it, but sometimes when you're at your desk, you get this faraway look in your eyes while you're staring at your computer or at that weird wooden egg."

I wrinkle my nose, wondering why Constance has been watching me.

"Oh, don't go getting the wrong idea, Henry. I'm not stalking you. I'm just observant. Anyway, I realize what I did was bitchy, and it certainly makes me a shitty friend. But I'm truly sorry, and I hope you can forgive me?"

I'm shocked yet pleasantly surprised at the same time because I don't think I've ever heard Constance say anything this sincerely. "Um, yeah, of course. I appreciate the apology."

She opens her arms for a hug and I hesitate.

"Oh, come on, Henry. Just give me a damn hug."

As we leave the lounge and make our way toward our offices, Constance whispers, "So, are you still seeing Ruth?"

I huff through my nose once and glance at her sideways. "No, of course not. Bob asked me to cut things off with her until the case was settled."

"Oh," she says, her shoulders slumping a bit. "But the Bucky's case is just about settled, so you should be able to start seeing her again soon." She smiles over at me.

"Yeah, well, who knows how long it will actually take for the final settlement to be ready for Ruth to sign? And then—and I'm trying to not even think about this one too much—there could be an appeal," I say, pausing outside my office.

Constance checks the hallway around us before she nudges me into my office and closes the door. "Henry, go back to the way things were before I opened my big mouth. I won't say anything. I promise."

"I don't even know if that's going to be possible," I say, crossing my arms and shaking my head. "She hasn't responded to any of the Bucky's related updates I've sent over the last few weeks, nor has she responded to my last several texts."

"What the heck, Henry? You finally found something that makes you happier than work, and you sound like you're ready to just let it go? Sorry to butt in, especially when I caused this problem to begin with, but I think that would be a huge mistake."

"Yeah, well, I wish it was up to me. And for the record, this wasn't all your fault, Constance. I should never have allowed things with Ruth to progress as far and as fast as they did. I should have been less impulsive and waited. Then Ruth and I wouldn't be in this predicament."

"Henry, I'm pretty sure most of the greatest love stories are the result of people acting with impulsive hearts," she says with a laugh. Then she points to my desk. "Call her. Don't stop calling until she picks up. And if she never picks up, then go talk to her in person." She gives me one firm pat on my upper arm, then she opens my office door and leaves.

As soon as she's gone, I rush to my desk and dial Ruth's number. No answer. I hang up without leaving a message. Then I redial her. Again, no answer, as expected, but I leave a message this time. I want to say something heartfelt, and maybe something to make her laugh, but that's not what ends up in the message.

"Hey, Ruth. It's me . . . Henry. Just wanted to follow up on the email I sent earlier . . . about the final settlement? Because I don't believe I included information about the timing of your disbursement. Anyway, if all goes as planned, we expect to receive payment from Bucky's and have your check mailed to you on or shortly after September ninth, so if you could just call or message me to confirm your address . . ." *You idiot. You already have her address.* "Additionally, please be on the lookout early next week for a W-9 form in your inbox, because we'll need to issue you an IRS Form 1099 for the payment. Also, do you even want the check mailed directly to you? Because I could always drop it off too. Just let me know . . . Okay, well, that's it. Give me a call. Bye."

CHAPTER 49

Monday, August 29
Ruth

"Hi everyone. I'm happy so many of you made it to our meeting tonight. Before we adjourn, we have two special guests." Cady Reynolds, our group facilitator, gestures to her left, calling attention to a woman in a plain gray wrap dress and a man in a suit. They're standing about six feet from her. "Please welcome, Jenna Swanson, the facility board president of the network of nursing homes and rehabilitative care facilities that White Pines belongs to, and Keith Triviani, a representative from the local Wisconsin chapter of the Parkinson's Association. Jenna and Keith are here tonight to help us acknowledge the extraordinary philanthropic efforts of one of our long-standing group members."

When I realize Cady is smiling at me, I panic and glance at my mom to find her smiling at me too. I'll dance or make a fool of myself singing at the top of my lungs in public. But being acknowledged for doing something everyone should do if they have the means? That makes me uncomfortable. So, when Cady calls me up to the front of the room, beads of sweat instantly form in my armpits and on my back. My head is spinning as I make my way to where she's standing with our well-dressed guests.

"Ruth, I'm sorry to put you on the spot, but we all just want to thank you for the money you donated to this facility and to the Parkinson's Association in honor of your father. Many of us remember him fondly." She gives me a hug, and then I shake hands with the guests before each of them says a few words about how much my donations will help and what the funds will go toward.

After the brief and unexpected to-do, our group proceeds with the usual goodies, refreshments and chitchat that closes out every meeting. I don't feel much like socializing, so I ask my mom if she's okay with us leaving right away. She agrees, but if I know her as well as I think I do, it'll be at least fifteen minutes before she's done saying her goodbyes instead of the five she promised.

While I wait for my mom in the nursing home lobby, I scroll through the text thread between Henry and me for what must be the billionth time since we stopped seeing each other. The only person who knows I've been compulsively reliving the evolution of our relationship is Sue. Of course, she keeps reminding me that the Bucky's case will be over soon, at which point Henry and I can pick up where we left off. But I'm not so sure anymore if that will happen because I just don't know if Henry will ever be able to make the sacrifices that accompany a serious relationship when he's so passionate about his job and achieving professional success. Not that professional success is a bad thing, but there's something to be said for moderation and balance.

"I'm ready, Ruthie," my mom says as she emerges from the meeting area. She links an elbow around one of mine as we exit the building. "I'm so proud of you honey, and I know your dad is, too. You're such a good person."

"Thank you, Mom. I learned by example." I give her arm a squeeze before we separate and get into my car.

"So, honey, everyone inside wanted to know why you seem so out of sorts today. Does it have anything to do with Henry? I know you haven't seen much of him lately."

All I told my mom is that Henry has been extremely busy at work, and the sad thing is, if we were still actively dating, this could be exactly what it's like once we settle into a routine with our relationship. I guess spending time away from him has given me the perspective I needed to see beyond my longing for him. Now my brain and heart either need to come to an agreement, or one will win out.

"Actually, I wasn't completely honest with you when I told you he had some big cases added to his plate at work. Or, maybe he has, but I wouldn't know, because his boss asked him to stop seeing me on a personal level until after the Bucky's case was settled."

"Whaaaat? What kind of meddling control freak does he have for a boss, anyway? And why on earth would you and Henry agree to do that?"

"I don't know, Mom," I say with a sigh, even though I do. But I don't feel like I can adequately explain the situation to her without making Henry sound like a jerk. "Henry just wants to be the best lawyer he can, and I want him to attain his professional goal if that's what makes him happy. I certainly wouldn't want him to get in trouble for fraternizing with a client."

"Yeah, well, I think it's ridiculous. When will the case be over, anyway?"

"The final settlement has been approved, so now it's just a matter of getting all the paperwork completed, I guess."

"Oh, so does Bucky's have to pay any money, or did they just get a slap on the wrist?"

"The final settlement was for eleven point five million dollars, and I'll be receiving twenty thousand for helping with the case." When she doesn't say anything, I glance over at her to find her eyes wider than I've ever seen them.

"Ruthie, did you just say eleven point five *million?*"

"Yeah," I say with a nod, keeping my eyes on the road.

"Holy buckets!"

"Yeah, I know."

"So, what do you plan to do with the money? I know you like to put just about every spare penny you have in the bank, but maybe you should think about doing something special for yourself. Take a trip. Buy a new car. Goodness knows yours is libel to break down again any day now."

"I already spent it."

"What do you mean? You haven't received it yet?"

"The money I donated to the nursing home and the association?"

"Ruthie, you donated all twenty thousand?"

"Yep, and I matched it."

"What do you mean?"

"I donated twenty to the nursing home and twenty to the

association. So, once I get the check from the settlement, I'll only have spent twenty of my own money."

"Ruthie," my mom reaches out and squeezes my shoulder, "you never cease to amaze me."

"Well, I figure the settlement is sort of a windfall anyway, and I could never spend all the money I got from my half of QuickForm in the divorce settlement. It's not like I have kids to spend it on."

"Not yet, anyway," my mom responds in a singsong tone of voice. "Tell you what. As soon as you get home, you give Henry a call. Then you'll be one step closer to having those kids."

If only I knew for certain that were true . . .

CHAPTER 50

Saturday, September 3
Henry

I'm supposed to meet Anthony at Posh at seven, but I'm a bit early because it's been drizzling, and I was beginning to go stir crazy from being inside all day. There is one good thing that resulted from the rain today, though; Ruth is going stir crazy too, so she finally called me back. However, I say it's a good thing in the loosest sense of the term because the call didn't go as planned.

I started the conversation by informing her of an appeal that's been filed, which could prolong the case for months. Then I proceeded to spill my guts telling her how much I miss her and what a mistake it was for me to appease Bob Whitmore in the first place. After that, I asked if she'd be willing to start seeing me again, despite the appeal. But, like an idiot, I added that we would just have to avoid public places to which she scoffed and said it's probably best if we just wait until the case is fully resolved, reasoning that both of us probably need more time to figure out what we want anyway. And then she had to let me go to take a call from her friend Sue.

So now my hiatus from Ruth will continue for who knows how long, putting me in the biggest funk I've ever been. And that's why I decided to call the only person I know who's up for going out anytime, just to get out of my condo and out of my head for a little while.

The club isn't too busy yet, so most of the seats at the bar are open. I take the first available stool. Marty sees me and waves, but he doesn't come over to say hi right away because he's talking to a few staff members.

By the time Anthony arrives—five minutes late—I already have a bottle of beer waiting for him.

"Heyyyyy, brother," he says, giving me a pat on the back as he takes a seat onto the stool next to me. "Is this mine?" He points to the beer, and then takes a sip when I confirm.

"Thanks for coming out," I say.

"Eh," he shrugs, "I don't have anything going on tonight anyway since I'm trying to cut back on looking for honeys in bars. Mom thinks it's what's preventing me from meeting a nice girl." He laughs and takes another drink. "So what's the occasion?"

"I don't know," I say, shrugging. "I guess we could celebrate the fact that the Bucky's settlement has been approved . . . although some asshole appealed, but that most likely won't change the outcome."

"Well, cheers to that," he says, nodding and raising his bottle. I do the same, and we clink the necks of our beers together.

"Henry! Wow." Marty rolls his eyes to the ceiling, deep in thought. "Two times in four months! To what do I owe this surprise?"

"Henry just wrapped up a huge case for his firm," Anthony says.

"Nice work, counselor!" Marty raises his fist and I follow through with the celebratory bump.

"Thanks. This is my youngest brother, Anthony. Anthony, Marty and I were frat brothers back in the day. He owns this place."

"Good to meet you, Anthony."

As they shake hands, Anthony says, "Nice place. I stopped in here back in April and it was packed."

"Yeah, it'll start filling up within the next few hours, and it'll be standing room only by ten. How about some shots?"

"Yeah, sure. What the heck," I say.

"Sounds good to me," Anthony nods. "I'll take ten."

Marty laughs and gets to work preparing a few car bombs. "So, how much does Bucky's have to dish out?"

"Eleven point five mil. And they also have to pay Ruth twenty K."

Marty whistles and Anthony says, "Dayum! Your plaintiff made out like a bandit. Maybe I should take up suing companies for a living."

"Are there really people who do that, Henry? Spend their time looking for reasons to start up class action suits and solicit lawyers for help?" Marty asks.

"Yeah, I suppose, but that definitely wasn't the case here. Ruth is the least money hungry person I know," I respond, feeling a strong desire to defend Ruth, even though Anthony's comment wasn't an implication about her.

"Ain't that the truth," Marty adds, placing a shot of Irish cream and whiskey and a pint of stout in front of each of us. "Can you believe what she did?"

"What are you talking about?" I ask.

"What, you don't know? I thought you and Ruth were . . . you know?" He glances at Anthony who nods knowingly, even though he knows nothing about Ruth and me.

"Atta boy, brother," Anthony says, slapping me on the back.

I shake my head and turn my full attention back to Marty. "I haven't talked to her for a couple weeks. I mean, we talked briefly today, but it was mostly about the settlement . . . What did she do?"

"Hang on, let's do these shots first." We all grab a shot glass. "Congrats, Henry . . . Three, two, one . . ." When Marty says one, we drop them into pints of beer, and down the car bombs.

Eager to hear more about whatever Ruth did, I motion with a circular movement of the hand for Marty to continue.

"Hang on," he says, removing his phone from his pocket and poking around for a few seconds before handing it to me. It's an article from the Communities section of the *Milwaukee Journal Sentinel* with the heading *Former Co-owner of QuickForm Fitness/Nutrition Franchise Donates $40,000.* I stare, mouth ajar, at the picture of Ruth with the director of the White Pines Nursing Home and a representative from the local chapter of the Parkinson's Foundation.

"Ruth is awesome," Marty says. I look up from the article and watch as he wipes down the bar around us and polishes the tappers.

Anthony suddenly appears confused and says to Marty, "Wait a second. You know his plaintiff?"

I go back to reading the article.

"Yeah, I've known her since middle school. Henry didn't tell you she used to work here?"

"Nope," Anthony says, leaning into me to get a look at Marty's phone. "Hang on, I think I know her. Yep, she was here back in April, when I was here for a bachelor party." I tense, unsure whether or not Anthony will make some asshole comment, the way he always seems to when we talk about women, but all he says is, "She was really nice. Pretty cute, too, brother."

I stare at him for a second, shocked by benign remarks. "Thanks."

We order a couple more bottles of beer from Marty before he heads off to help with the steady flow of customers that are beginning to enter. "Later, fellas."

We both nod and sip our beers.

"So, does Mom know about Ruth?"

"Sort of," I shrug. "It doesn't matter anymore, though, because I fucked things up. So now I'm not even sure we'll be seeing each other anymore."

"Whoa," he pulls on his ears, "I think I'm hearing things. Did my goody-goody big brother just drop the f-bomb?" He chuckles at himself. "Seriously, though, what'd you do, man? Maybe I can help."

I crease my brow at him. "Yeah, right."

"Come on." He waves his fingers toward himself. "What's going on?"

"Fine, but I'm confiding in you under protest."

"Yeah, whatever." He holds up a finger, takes a long guzzle of his beer, and burps. "Go ahead."

"So, you met Constance . . ."

"Oh no, please tell me you didn't hide your relationship with Constance from Ruth."

"No, I didn't have to because there was no relationship, not by the time I met Ruth face to face anyway."

"Then what did you do wrong?"

"When Constance found out I was seeing Ruth, she flipped her lid and—"

"Hold up. I thought you said, you weren't a thing."

"It—just, it wasn't like that, Anthony. Are you going to let me finish, or what?"

He grabs his beer with one hand and motions for me to proceed with the other.

"So right after Constance found out—"

"Excuse me, but how did she find out?"

I roll my eyes, but it's a legitimate question, so I tell him about how she ran into us at the Parkinson's event down at the lakefront. Without a word, he nods for me to proceed.

"So anyway, Constance told her uncle who happens to be my boss—"

"No way."

"Yeah," I say with a nod.

"And then her uncle called me into his office basically to tell me I had to stop seeing Ruth until after the case is settled."

"Or what?"

"What do you mean? Or I would be removed from the case or maybe even fired."

"Oh," he says with a shrug. "So what happened when you talked to Ruth about it?"

"Well, she understood, but over the last few weeks . . . I don't know. I guess she's had plenty of time to think."

"Yeah, about what a douchebag you are."

"Thanks. That's helpful."

"I think you should just go to her place right now," Anthony says.

"Nah, I talked to her a couple hours ago. She wants to stick with not seeing each other until after the case is settled, and like I said, now that there's an appeal . . ." My voice trails off as I shake my head. "You know, it's almost like karma is sticking it to me for not having more of a backbone."

"Well, brother, you're the biggest nerd I know, so I'm confident you'll figure this out."

"I thought you were full of good advice."

"Nah," he says shaking his head, "Not when it comes to real deal shit like this. Now, if you had been dating both Ruth and Constance at the same time, no heartstrings involved, I'm confident I could have helped you with that situation. But not when you're practically in love and you fuck up. I'm going to have to learn from you on this one."

"What are you talking about? I never said I was in love."

"Practically." He sips his beer.

"What makes you think that?"

"First of all, Henry, when have you ever invited me out for a drink before? I'll tell you. Never. Second, you could have dated Constance if you wanted to. Don't think I didn't notice that shoe rack full of her shoes in your apartment that one night. But you didn't want to, which tells me you were looking for something she couldn't offer. Now, I have no idea what that thing could possibly be because hello! I mean, look at the woman. Third, and this is the most important piece of evidence, Ruth."

"And? I think your case just fell apart. What about Ruth?"

"That woman is a keeper. I hit on her myself back when I met her here in April, but she wasn't interested." He smirks when I roll my eyes. Then he continues. "You know, despite all the hassle I've given you ever since I learned how to talk, you're a good guy, Henry. Maybe a little neurotic sometimes, but a straight shooter nonetheless. And I think you might still be able to fix things with her. You just can't give up . . . which shouldn't be hard for you because you're the most compulsive person I know." He rolls his eyes, finishes his beer, and then holds it up so Marty knows he's ready for another. Then he turns his attention back to me and says, "Hey, any chance I can get Constance's number?"

CHAPTER 51

Sunday, September 4
Ruth

As I leave the farmers' market, I press my nose into the bouquet of magenta peonies I just purchased. The scent is exhilarating, so I continue taking whiffs until I get to my bike. I place my bag and the bouquet in my basket and catch sight of a woman with a sleek black ponytail. She's wearing workout clothes, and she's sitting across the street at a table outside Bucky's Beans with a dark-haired man. I pause, wracking my brain to figure out where I know her from. Then it hits me, and my breath hitches, because it's Henry's coworker Constance.

I can't let her see me, because if she does, the odds I'll tell her off are quite high. If it weren't for her, I like to think Henry and I would still be together.

Oh crap. Too late.

I quickly look away and get to work unlocking my bike. I hop on and am about to pedal off when Henry emerges from Bucky's. His head snaps to the right, and I follow his gaze over to the table where Constance is pointing in my direction. The mystery man calls out to Henry, "Hurry up, bro. Go now." Then he turns and looks at me, and I recognize him from a family photo on the Mancuso Construction website. It's one of Henry's brothers.

I watch in awe as Henry jogs across the street. When he's finally standing in front of me, I say the first thing that comes to my mind. "I'm surprised Bucky's Beans let you in."

He smiles, and my insides melt. Of course. "I was just using the bathroom."

"So, the three of you, Constance and . . ." I nod toward Constance and his brother across the street, but I never mentioned to Henry that I was stalking him on social media before we started seeing each other, so I let him fill in the blank.

"That's my brother, Anthony."

I nod. "You and Constance are okay then?"

"Yeah, we talked last week, and she gave me a sincere apology. In fact, she said she'd really like the opportunity to apologize to you, as well."

"Oh, well . . . I barely know her, so if you're over it, then so am I. So, the three of you are just hanging out in front of Bucky's Beans on a Sunday morning?"

"Well, they're sort of on a date. Constance just doesn't know it yet."

I raise an inquisitive eyebrow.

"The main reason we're here is because they agreed to help me with something."

"Oh yeah? What are they helping you with?"

"Making sure I didn't miss you."

He pauses, waiting for a response, probing me with his pleading eyes. "Not that I haven't been missing you for these past four weeks." He shifts uncomfortably from one foot to the other. "Look, I know I messed up . . . and I want to fix this so badly," he flails his arms as he talks, "but, I don't want to wait until you sign the final settlement because I don't want you to think I'm only trying at that point because the case is over." He shakes his head and raises his arms slightly, as if he's about to reach for my hands, but then he lets them fall to his sides. "Ruth, I'm sorry. I should never have let my fear of being removed from the case, or even fired, come between us." He shakes his head. "I'm an idiot."

"You are," I say, nodding and cracking a grin. "And a terrible dancer, too."

He visibly relaxes a bit, and we both glance across the street when two dogs start barking at each other. Constance is doing a good job of looking like she isn't watching, even though I know she is, and Henry's brother gives us a thumbs-up, causing us both to laugh.

"Well, it was nice seeing you, Henry," I say, torn over what should happen next. I've been contemplating his suggestion for us to just pick up where we left off but carrying on a relationship while in hiding doesn't seem like much of a relationship at all. And I'm afraid there's a chance he might choose work over us again in the future. "So, I assume you'll be in touch about developments with the appeal?"

His mouth opens and closes then opens again. Finally, he stammers, "Yeah . . . I, uh . . . sure."

"Okay, well . . . bye, Henry," I say, hopping on my bike. I only get a few pedals in before I hear his voice again.

"Ruth, wait!"

I apply my brakes until my bike comes to a full stop about eight feet away from Henry. Then I look back over my left shoulder at him.

"I'll withdraw from the case."

"What?" I ask, convinced I must not have heard him right. Then I turn my bike around to face him.

"I said I'll withdraw from the case. And if Bob wants to fire me, so be it. But I don't want to wait anymore to be with you."

"Henry, come on," I say, wheeling my bike forward. "I don't want you to give up something you've worked so hard for. And you love your job, so potentially losing it just so we can—"

"I love you more than my job, Ruth," he sputters.

Now I'm the one opening and closing my mouth, my brain struggling to send the words my heart wants me to say.

Henry closes the last few feet between us, and I finally realize how haggard he looks with his eyes bloodshot, his face unshaven, and his hair a mess. "Can we go for a run? Or a walk? Or maybe I could even go down the street and buy a bike . . ."

"You'd buy a bike right now?" I ask, my tone laced with sarcasm.

"Well, no, probably not . . . but I'd toss my phone in that trash can right now if we could go for a walk."

"Okay, Henry, that would be—" But I don't get to tell him how ridiculous that would be, and I don't get any other words in edgewise either, because he continues without pause.

"Or, if you're busy, it could be tomorrow or next week. Hell, if you don't feel like walking," he points in the direction of the Summit Stairway. "I'll even jog up and down those death traps with you one hundred times if you want me to."

Despite appearing emotionless on the outside, my heart is about to beat right out of my chest, so I do what I realize I should have done the moment Henry said he loved me. I put the kick stand down on my bike and move in so close to him that his breath causes wisps of my hair to tickle my face.

"I'll even settle for standing right here in front of your ex-husband's business and Bucky's Beans . . ." he says, raising his hands to my arms, causing goosebumps to crop up all over my body. Then he takes a deep breath and continues in a hushed tone. "I'll go anywhere and do anything you want, Ruth, if it means I get to be with—"

Before he can utter another word, I launch myself at him and wrap my arms around his neck. I'm only vaguely aware of the whistles from across the street and his arms enveloping me before we kiss.

EPILOGUE

Sunday, April 30
Ruth

Henry and I pull our bikes onto the rack and lock them up. Then we walk across the street to the farmers' market. We'll probably get the usual—coffee, veggies, and flowers. It's become our Sunday morning ritual, which sometimes includes the stairs too.

"Do you want to get coffee right away?" I ask.

"How about if we wait until we're done here? Then maybe we can take a walk along the path. We haven't done that for a while."

"Sounds good to me." He reaches for my hand, and I gladly give it to him. "So, what do you feel like having for lunch? Maybe we could get a bunch of these root vegetables, and make a salad?"

Henry picks up a parsnip and examines it. "What exactly makes this not a carrot?"

I roll my eyes and laugh. "You mean besides the fact that it's not orange?"

He grins with a shrug and grabs a few more while I choose a couple of beets, sweet potatoes, and a bunch of parsley. After we pay for our spoils, we head over to the flower stand. On the way, we stop to try some specialty cooking oils and end up buying some avocado and hazelnut.

When we arrive at the flower stand, Henry whispers in my ear, "I need to use a bathroom. It's an emergency."

"Gross," I whisper back.

"Meet you at the Coffee Cave stand?"

I nod and give him a quick peck on the cheek before he scurries off.

"I don't know how long I'll be, so you might not want to get the coffees until I get back," he hollers as he jogs backward.

I wave a peony in acknowledgement.

By the time Henry returns, I've added flowers and rhubarb to my bag, tried some gourmet mustard samples, and watched a cooking demonstration. Now I know how to make the perfect hollandaise sauce. He has something in each hand, but I don't realize what the items are until he holds them up.

"Henry, why did you buy coffee from Bucky's Beans?" I say, bewildered.

"I know, I know. But I *had* to go, and their bathroom didn't have a line." He shrugs. "I felt guilty not buying something."

I shake my head at him, feigning disappointment.

"Oh, come on, it's not going to hurt you to drink *one* cup of Bucky's coffee, is it?"

"Fine," I say, laughing. "So, are we going to take that walk?"

"I have a better idea . . . Follow me."

"Okay."

Henry weaves us through the farmers' market displays, so that we exit the square right by the trail entrance.

"I thought you had a better idea than a walk."

"We have to get to my idea somehow."

"Can I at least have my coffee?"

"Patience, young Padawan."

I snort laugh and keep walking. Henry loves Star Wars so much that he keeps a complete set of vintage figurines in a safe deposit box, but I've never heard him drop a quote before.

Without a word, he enters the trail and we walk until we get to the cut-through that leads to the top of the running stairs.

"Henry, I don't have the right shoes on for running. I mean, I could make these work, but not on the stairs."

"We're not running the stairs, Ruth." He glances back at me and grins.

We walk in silence until we get to the bench at the top of the stairs. I can't even count the number of times I've stretched at this bench or sat reading a book or watching the sunset.

"Okay, we're here." Henry takes a seat on the bench.

I remain standing. "That's what we're doing? Sitting on the bench?"

"Yeah, why?"

"Nothing," I say, sitting down next to him. "I like the bench."

I remove my sling bag and set it down gingerly, careful not to crush anything inside.

"Your coffee, madam." Henry hands one of the Bucky's Beans cups to me.

When I take hold of it, something doesn't feel right. "Henry, I don't think this cup has anything in it," I say gripping the lid and prying it off. When I look inside I know right away what I'm looking at, but it still feels like hours have passed by the time I'm done processing all the thoughts running through my brain.

"Ruth?"

I raise my eyes from the shiny object inside the Bucky's Beans cup and find Henry in front of me on one knee.

"May I?" he asks, his hand hovering over the cup.

I muster a weak nod. Then he reaches into the cup and pulls out the ring.

"Ruth Ellen Bateman, will you be my wife?"

"Yes," I say, nodding and watching as Henry slips the ring on my finger. "A thousand times, yes."

ACKNOWLEDGEMENTS

First and foremost, I want to thank *you*, the reader, for the time you devoted to my characters. I hope you enjoyed reading Ruth and Henry's story as much as I enjoyed writing it.

A HUGE thank you to my beta readers: Alica Flechner, Bria Starr, Jamie Biggins, Jenny Hanson, Marnie Ide, Polly Barreto, and Sarah Fluegel. Your feedback and suggestions were invaluable. I hope you all know how much I appreciate your support!

Russ Karnes – Thank you for setting me straight on all the legal aspects of this book. I may have allowed a few ethical no-nos to slide, but I won't tell if you don't. Henry had to get the girl somehow!

Shout out to Farnham's Faithfuls! I'm so thankful for each and every one of you, and I hope you all continue to be part of my journey.

Thank you to all the individuals who helped piece this book together: Amy Queau (cover and promo materials), Barbara Malmberg (copy editing), Beth Cranford of Panda & Boodle (promotion and ARC management), Carol Ann Eastman (blurb), Leah Campbell (developmental editing), and Karan & Co. Author Solutions (formatting).

Dante, Noah, Cole, and Addison – I love you guys! Your continued love, support, and understanding mean the world to me.

MORE BOOKS BY K. J.

Click Date Repeat

Click Date Repeat Again

Don't Call Me Kit Kat

Visit kjfarnham.com for more information.

ABOUT THE AUTHOR

K. J. Farnham was born and raised in a suburb of Milwaukee. She graduated from UW-Milwaukee in 1999 with a bachelor's degree in elementary education and went on to earn a master's degree in curriculum and instruction from Carroll University in Waukesha. She then had the privilege of helping hundreds of children learn to read and write over the course of twelve years. Farnham now lives in western Wisconsin with her husband and three children.

Connect with K. J. at kjfarnham.com